PRAISE FOR NA

"The camaraderie of a small town is captured in all its glory in this story of rediscovered love, lies and deceit. Trust comes in small doses and is lost just as easily as the clever plot unfolds, especially when unusual characters provide surprises." - *RT Book Reviews on Sweet Tea and Secrets*

"Fabulous, fabulous read! Be sure to have a tissue with you as you read this sweet book. [*Life After Perfect*] is full of emotion and heartfelt struggles of love and life." *Tabitha Jones - A Closet Full of Books*

Every Yesterday

ALSO BY NANCY NAIGLE

Always On My Mind : Pick Your Passion Novella 1

Come A Little Closer : Pick Your Passion Novella 2

THE BOOT CREEK NOVELS

Life After Perfect

Every Yesterday

NANCY NAIGLE

Montlake
Romance

Text copyright © 2016 Nancy Naigle

Published by Montlake Romance, Seattle

www.apub.com

Amazon, the Amazon logo, and Montlake Romance are trademarks of Amazon.com, Inc., or its affiliates.

ISBN-13: 9781503938908
ISBN-10: 1503938905

Cover design by LEADesign

Printed in the United States of America

To my daddy, for all the neat car memories from my childhood. Even if he did wreck the Porsche right before my sixteenth birthday, and bought me a Vega instead. Yes, it still stings, but I treasure those memories of him driving with the top down wearing that blue-and-white Porsche Club jacket. Coolest dad ever.

Chapter One

The oppressive heat took a toll on folks this time of year in Boot Creek. The humidity hung on Megan's skin and permeated her hair, now three times its normal size. As she sorted through her mail, the envelopes clung to each other, damp and lacking that crisp sound of paper she'd normally expect as she opened them.

August. It was always hot in North Carolina in August, but for some reason this summer seemed heavy—like winter and spring had gorged on too many baked goods. Megan missed the normal hustle-bustle of neighbors out on Main Street grabbing lunch and finishing up errands, but it was so stifling that people were staying inside. The mayor had even suspended the road-crew work until this heat wave passed.

Megan dropped the junk mail in a trash can next to the light post on the corner of Main Street, then ran her freshly painted nail under the seal on an envelope from the town of Boot Creek. They hadn't wasted a moment billing her for Daddy's prized possession. She'd only had the 1958 DeSoto Adventurer convertible for a few weeks.

Apparently since the old car had antique tags, she got a flat rate regardless of the value. She wasn't sure how much the car was worth, but word had traveled fast that it was hers now and the offers she'd already received were impressive.

Johnny Morris had offered to put in a whole new air-conditioning system with dual zones at Balanced Buzz, her candle business, in exchange for Daddy's car, but there was no way she could part with that car. Daddy was a lot of things, including an embarrassment at times, but she was a daddy's girl and that car meant the world to him, so it meant the world to her.

That car wasn't going anywhere, even if Balanced Buzz could really use that air-conditioning upgrade. This time of year it just didn't pay to make candles in the hot part of the day. The air-conditioning in her old building worked hard enough without her adding heat from melting beeswax to the equation. So Megan adjusted her hours to keep the expenses down and profit margin wide. And that was fine with her, because she always had been a night owl.

To her, the value of Daddy's car lay in the memories they'd shared riding around in it. Enough memories to fill that car, and that was really saying something. That model had to be one of the longest two-door cars ever built. Darn thing just barely fit in her garage bay.

And seeing's how she lived in what used to be a gas station with commercial-sized mechanics bays . . . that was saying something. It wouldn't surprise her to learn that this car wouldn't fit in the garage of a modern-day home.

Lucky for her, daddy had hooked her up with the gas-station-turned-house and workshop when she graduated from college. Maybe that was the reason he'd left the car to her and not his way-too-young-for-Dad, go-go-dancin' bride, Tiffany.

The thought of that girl made Megan bristle. To be fair, Tiffany wasn't a dancer anymore, but it was no secret that Daddy had *discovered* her at Headlights Bar off the interstate a few exits down. Not one of his finest days.

Tiffany had no clue how special the car was. She'd begged Daddy to sell it and buy a new sports car. Something flashy and red. No surprise that Tiffany had gone right out and bought herself a bright red Corvette as soon as that life insurance check cleared the bank. Thank goodness Daddy had updated his will. Tiffany never would have let Megan have the car otherwise. Even though everyone knew that was Daddy's intention. Tiffany was a gold digger from the word *go*.

Standing there on the corner of Water Loop Way, Megan felt her heart squeeze. A rush of heat soared through her body. *Don't let this be a heart attack.* This wasn't the first time she'd had that sinking feeling and pain in her heart right down to her gut since Daddy died. Now the DeSoto was hers, and that was all she had left. This bill made him being gone feel that much more final. Was that enough to give a gal her age a heart attack?

She pressed her hand against her heart and took in a breath. *Relax.* Sweeping a hand under her nose to chase that tickle that came right before tears fell, she straightened and inhaled deeply.

Tucking the rest of the mail into her purse, she shifted on her feet. *How long had she been standing there?* The pavement was scorching. She wished she'd worn her tennis shoes instead of these strappy heels. When she'd put them on, she'd thought it would be a good short walk to break in the shoes she'd be wearing in Angie's wedding, so her feet wouldn't be killing her all night at the reception next weekend. Bad idea. She crossed over Cabot Street and tugged on the door to Mom's shop, Bootsie's Bouquets.

Brightly colored summer blooms filled tall hand-painted cones that Megan had painted for Bootsie, her mother, years ago. They'd held up well. Next to the flowers, racks of beautiful ribbon that Mom made special buying trips to pick out looked like a kaleidoscope of texture and color. Across the room, an antique breakfront painted whimsical lavender and distressed with turquoise accents held a hefty inventory of

Balanced Buzz candles. Mom was Megan's biggest fan. She hand sold a fair share of candles each year, but most of Megan's sales came from her storefront on the Internet.

"Good morning, Mom." She forced an easy smile, hoping that Mom wouldn't notice the panic she'd been feeling just moments before.

Bootsie raised a hand in the air from behind the counter where she was ringing up a customer.

Megan headed straight for the glass-front refrigerator where the fresh flower arrangements were stored. She opened the doors, holding her arms out to the side. Her skin drank in the cool air, and thankfully her heart rate began to slow. It was only three lousy blocks from her house to Sew 'n Sew Formal where she was meeting Angie and the others for the final dress fitting. And after only one block, she was sticky with sweat. Crazy. How gross to go to a dress fitting feeling like you just finished a hot yoga session? She watched her mom walk her customer to the door. The man carried a long white box with a generous lipstick-red ribbon tied around it. Roses, no doubt.

"There a movie playing in there?" Bootsie asked.

"Real funny." Megan smirked, but the truth was that phrase gave her pause. Not because it was something Mom had always said. No, it reminded her of Dad. And Mom knew it. Her parents may have been divorced for going on eight years, but no one knew Daddy better. He'd made that comment a million times when Megan was growing up—and that memory tugged at her. But not like most dads would have said it, because he wasn't complaining. He knew looking in the fridge for a sweet treat was a waste of time. She got her sweet tooth from her Dad, but Mom had been such a health nut there'd never been anything besides fruit and yogurt. Luckily, he'd rescue her from the waste of time standing there wishing for a cupcake or soda, suggesting they go out and hunt down a snack together. Living one block off of Main Street had made life very convenient for that, and it was probably all the extra time they'd spent together dodging Mom's health-nut kicks that had made her closer to him.

"It's hotter than h—"

"Don't even say it." Bootsie narrowed her gaze.

"Heck. Hotter than heck out there." Megan let the door slam, thankful for that last rush of cool air that pushed against her. Even now, close to thirty, Mom ruled.

"You trying to make some sort of new fashion statement?"

Megan looked down at her soft pink blouse, opened over a bright pink tank top and faded blue jeans. "What's wrong with this?"

Her mom homed in on her feet.

"The shoes?"

"Yes. I can't say that high heels and blue jeans is exactly a good look. Although it is nice to finally see you wearing something a little ladylike."

Mom was always hounding her about being a lady. It was old when she was thirteen, and now closer to thirty . . . it was still not welcome advice.

Bootsie's lips bunched. "You know you can't wear open-toed shoes without your toenails painted. Totally taboo."

Megan wasn't sure what made her mother think she was the fashion police, but still, there she was, ready to make an excuse. "I'm just wearing them to the fitting, and we have pedicures set up for Thursday. I promise I won't let anyone see me. Besides, I thought I'd break them in, but there's not much to these things for as much as they cost. About burned my toes off out there."

"Fine. Well, since you're here, Angie's ribbon finally came in. I've got it over by the register." Bootsie turned and hurried to get the ribbon. She made up for being short by walking two or three steps to the one of any average person, which had always made Megan think of the Energizer Bunny, the way she scampered. Bootsie lifted two large spools of ribbon for Megan to see. "Sure hope it matches this time." She bounced the two big spools in separate hands, looking a bit like a scale of justice. "I got this roll of white with pearlescent seed beads along the edge, just in case we have to go to plan B. Take them with you, so Angie can decide what she wants to go with."

"You always think of everything." Megan walked over and took the two spools of ribbon and tucked them into the top of her oversized leather handbag. "Thanks, Mom," she said, leaning over the counter to kiss her on the cheek. "Love you."

"You're welcome, darling." As Megan headed for the door, she called out, "Send me a picture of you in your gown. I'm dying to see you in it."

"Come with me. You know Angie won't mind. It'll be fun."

"I can't," Bootsie said. "This weekend is the first high school football game of the season. I've got orders for thirty-eight corsages to make for that, plus putting together all of the bouquets and arrangements for Angie's wedding. I can't get away. Text me, though."

"Yes, ma'am." Megan knew what the unspoken words that followed would have been. *High time you walked down that aisle too, Megan.*

∽

Since Daddy's unexpected passing, even Mom had been gentler. Megan's heart ached for her dad. He drove her half-crazy most of the time; Mom had always said that was because Megan was so much like her daddy, but knowing he'd never be back made it darn near impossible to breathe sometimes.

Megan crossed over at the second block to Sew 'n Sew Formal and Tailoring. When she walked inside, soft music filled the store. Funny she hadn't noticed it the last time they'd all met there to pick out the dresses, but darned if it didn't sound a lot like the funeral home. She shook off that thought. *Maybe everything felt like a funeral lately.*

Last night she'd decided that she needed to be honest with Angie about the DeSoto. It wasn't going to be an easy discussion, but ever since the car had been delivered to her, she'd been a nervous wreck about it.

Daddy had agreed to let Angie and Jackson use his prized convertible as the getaway ride for their wedding. It had really surprised Megan, because Daddy never let anyone drive that car. It had been a generous gesture on his part. But then Angie had been like a second daughter; she and Megan had spent so much time together.

Yet now that Megan had the car tucked safely in her garage, she wasn't sure she could risk taking a chance on it getting damaged. The Adventurer had never even seen a raindrop. What if something happened? What if it rained? Dad leaving her that car came with an unwritten agreement that she'd love it just like he had.

Written or implied, she took it seriously.

So, after a lot of thought, she'd decided to rent a limo for Angie and Jackson's big day. She'd even sprung for the champagne package. Five hundred dollars for the fanciest car they had was a small price to pay for protecting her last connection to Daddy.

"There you are," Carla, the owner of Sew 'n Sew Formal, said, sounding a bit stressed.

"Fashionably late," Angie said with a laugh. "Carla was worried to death. I wasn't."

But Megan knew better. Angie had been just waiting for something to go wrong and ruin her perfect happily ever after. She was so darned certain that if she'd only paid attention to the warning flags when she married Rodney, her good-for-nothin' first husband, she could have spared herself a lot of heartache. So now, Angie was hyperaware.

Carla waved her hands in the air, clearly frustrated to be off schedule. "Come on over here, Megan. Everyone else is already in the back waiting. You're the maid of honor, dear, you're supposed to be the first one here."

None of them lived more than a couple miles away. What was the big deal? Okay, so she'd dawdled the whole way over. And she'd intended to be on time today. For a change. Maybe she wasn't quite as ready to have that conversation with Angie about the car as she'd thought.

"I stopped and got the ribbon Mom reordered."

Angie held up her hand and crossed her fingers. "I'm praying it matches."

"Me too." Megan held up the ribbon that was supposed to match and the white, pearl-edged ribbon. "We've got options. It'll work out."

"Brilliant!" Angie heaved a sigh of relief. "You always have a backup plan."

Carla led Angie and Megan to the fitting room area.

Katy sat on the love seat next to Flynn, who owned the B&B in town.

"Megan! Finally!" Flynn, the teetotaler of the group, spun around in such delight that if Megan didn't know better, she'd think she'd been sipping champagne, but that was highly unlikely for any of them in this bridal shop, since Carla was the preacher's wife.

Carla moved through the room as if she were on roller skates. "Now that we're *finally* all here, we can begin."

"Sorry." Megan was pretty sure Carla still hadn't forgiven her for the time Megan had accidentally ridden her bicycle through the woman's treasured rose garden. It had been no picnic for her either. Dr. Hansen had had to dig stickers out of half of Megan's right side that day. The woman had been snippy with her for the next fifteen years. Talk about holding a grudge.

Megan lowered herself into an old velveteen Queen Anne chair. The hodgepodge of fine antiques and practical things, like the tall plastic oscillating fan, held its own kind of charm. The air-conditioning was no competition for the heat in this old drafty building. Wispy fabrics fluttered every time the fan made a thankful pass from left to right.

"Here we go." Angie followed Carla into the bride's dressing room. The heavy door clicked closed behind them. The elegant etched glass that adorned the back of the door had to have been from the early nineteen hundreds—the glass wavy and scratched.

Megan's nerves fluttered as they waited for Angie. Katy and Flynn chattered about potato salad recipes, but Megan only half listened. Her mind was on Angie and the wedding. Jackson was so good for her best friend, but her own anxieties about relationships and weddings wouldn't quit nagging at her. Why couldn't she just be happy for Angie and not worry so much?

A moment later the mirrored door opened and Angie stepped out onto the raised, carpeted platform.

A collective hush fell across the room.

Angie's smile was wide, but a nervous twitch played at her lips. She held her arms out and turned slowly, the ivory chiffon gently sweeping the floor. "What do you think?"

A simple sleeveless A-line, with subtle beading at the waist, looked as elegant as her dark hair, which Carla had swept up into a loose chignon.

"Oh, Angie." Megan blinked. *Why am I so emotional today?* "You look beautiful. Jackson is going to fall in love with you all over again when he sees you in that dress."

Carla walked around her, tugging and smoothing Angie's gown. "Looks perfect. How does it feel?"

"Perfect," Angie whispered.

"It sure is," Flynn said, then reached over from the love seat to where Megan was seated and grabbed Megan's hand. "I hope I'll be as beautiful when I'm a bride."

"You will be." Megan hoped Flynn would find a suitor soon. Bless her heart, the girl was dying to be married. Why was it the girls who wanted to get married never attracted the settling kind, and yet it seemed like every guy Megan went out with wanted a committed relationship? And she was never going down that road again. She'd found her soul mate, and Kevin had not only broken her heart, but wrecked her soul. A loss she still carried around like it happened yesterday.

Angie pointed toward Katy. "I have a feeling Katy might be your next customer, Carla."

Katy blushed. "We haven't gotten that far yet." Katy, the newest resident of Boot Creek, had made fast friends with Angie the first week Katy happened into town. And even though Katy had only meant to stop for gas in Boot Creek, she'd come on the day of the Blackberry Festival and met Derek Hansen. It had been the day she was running away from heartbreak, and what she'd found in Boot Creek was a second chance at love and a whole new career.

"You will," Angie said. "I know Derek. And yeah, he was broken when Laney died, but he is whole again with you."

"He completes me too," Katy said. "We're not rushing things, but when the time's right, all of you will be there at my side too. Right?"

"Of course," they all agreed.

Megan lifted her hands in the air. "Angie, I think it looks like I can check off final wedding dress alterations from the list." Her goal was to complete every single thing on this project plan on time with zero problems. Yes, everyone kept saying that was an impossible goal, but she took her goals seriously and was determined to make that happen.

Angie pressed her hands together and raised her fingertips to her lips. "It's all coming together. Thank goodness. I'd already told myself that if there were any hiccups, I'd heed the signs and throw this all in reverse."

Megan certainly wasn't going to be the one to start that. That limo would just have to be cancelled. "It's going to all go according to plan, Angie. I promise."

"And I put together all the paperwork and itineraries for the honeymoon," Katy said. "I brought the packet with me. I'm jealous that y'all are going to Alaska for two whole weeks. That is so on my bucket list now."

"We could never have planned a two-week honeymoon if you and Derek hadn't offered to keep Billy. I'm still so anxious about leaving him so long," Angie said. "I know he'll be fine with y'all. He's so excited. But . . ."

"And he'll be fine. He loves Derek, and you know how I feel about him. The practice sleepovers have gone fine."

"I know I'm a worrywart when it comes to him. I can't help myself—he's a handful. All boy. I don't think you know what you've got yourself into."

"Are you kidding me? I'm excited," Katy said. "Derek and I are going to have a blast playing house. It's good practice for us. And I've always wanted to go school shopping. Now I have Billy as an excuse. Usually I pretend I'm stocking up for children that I don't have so I can take advantage of all the amazing deals. I mean really. Who doesn't go gaga over school supplies?"

"True," Angie said, her brows knitting together. "Maybe I could squeeze in taking him school shopping this week."

"Don't you dare steal my fun, Angie! You can do school prep with Billy for the next ten years. And you'll be home in plenty of time for his first day of school."

"I would have never been able to plan this wedding without y'all. I have the best bridesmaids ever." Angie's eyes glistened, and as much of a pain as Megan could imagine her own mother would be in planning a wedding with her, she couldn't imagine not having her mom around to do it.

A tear spilled down Angie's cheek. "I love y'all. You're the best friends any girl could ask for."

"As maid of honor, I forbid any sappy crying jags. Even though we are pretty awesome." Megan stepped onto the platform and handed Angie a tissue. "Don't be getting weepy on us, you'll stain your dress."

Angie dabbed at her eyes. "We might need some wine on Saturday. Do you think they allow wine in the brides dressing area? I'm suddenly very nervous."

"Not like back out nervous. Right?" Megan asked.

"No. Not like that. Maybe nervous isn't the right word. Excited. Anxious. Insanely lucky. Too-good-to-be-true lucky."

"No such thing," Megan reassured her.

Carla walked over to the door at the far side of the room, then clapped her tiny hands together. "Okay, ladies. Let's get your dresses on and check them one last time for fit."

"Y'all's turn," Angie said. "I'll be waiting right here."

Carla rushed the girls along.

Megan, Katy, and Flynn followed Carla into the large dressing room. Their blue gowns, the color of summer skies in Carolina, hung on shiny silver hangers from hooks, one next to the other, along the wall. In the center of the room, a tall pedestal table gave the girls a little bit of privacy as they changed.

As soon as Carla left the room, Flynn said, "I hope my dress fits this time. Carla took it in the first time and out the second. I swear she got the measurements mixed up with one of y'all's. I hadn't gained or lost a pound."

"Wouldn't doubt it." Megan laughed. "Old lady Carla has to be pushing her late seventies. She did the alterations on my mom's wedding gown and that was over thirty years ago."

As a little girl, Megan used to stare at the bridal portrait of her momma that hung in the hallway of their home. She'd looked so beautiful. And Megan dreamed of wearing that pretty white dress with the layers of chiffon. That was a long time ago. And all of those fairy-tale dreams had been shattered that summer night seven years ago.

Megan was the last one to step into her dress. Katy zipped her up just as Carla came back in carrying a box of silk flower bouquets that had seen better days. Years-old dust caked the green silk leaves in the stand-in bouquets. Megan's mouth twitched in amusement as she rolled ick off of one of the petals. Flynn's shoulders rocked as she got a fit of the giggles over it too.

Katy and Flynn lined up at the door, and Megan fell in behind them. Megan wasn't the cry-at-a-Hallmark-movie kind of girl, but she had to admit this was pretty exciting. And realizing how very different Angie's life was going to be now filled her with joy.

The door swung open and the girls filed out of the dressing room.

Angie gasped, a wide smile spreading across her face. "Y'all look beautiful." She swept at a tear with the balled-up tissue she held in her hand.

"You're crying," Flynn asked.

"Again?" Megan said.

"She's fine," Katy said.

"Happy tears, right, Angie?" Megan forced a smile. This was going to be one long week.

"Totally happy tears. It's overwhelming. Everything is so perfect. After being married to Rodney, and the hell he put me through to get that divorce, I never thought I'd be happy again. And now, not only do I have a son who brings joy to me every single day, but also I have the best friends. Y'all are so special to me. And I have Jackson. He loves me. He gets me, and I love him. The perfect guy. Perfect family. Perfect wedding venue, caterer, flowers, photographer, and even the perfect car to drive off in after the wedding. Could it possibly be any better?"

Megan swallowed hard. *Probably not the perfect time to mention not letting Angie use the car.*

"Not one red flag," Angie continued. "I mean, it's got to be some kind of sign when everything falls into place like it has. I know you remember, Megan. There was problem after problem planning that wedding. Right up to the day of. Why didn't I see those snapping red flags?"

"Because you were in love with the idea of being in love, and the man you wanted Rodney to be," Megan said. "Let it go. But I do remember you crying when the justice of the peace croaked on you the morning of the wedding, and you had to scramble for a new one. And that the cake was chocolate instead of almond, which I still say Rodney had something to do with."

Angie's lips curled. "Had to have been him. After all, it was his aunt who made the cake. You don't just mix something like that up."

"And why we're not using her for your cake this time," Flynn piped in. "You don't have to worry about that nincompoop anymore."

"Unfortunately, I still have to deal with him because of Billy, but my boy is worth every aggravation that man ever caused me. This time there aren't any warning flags. Not one last-minute hitch." She reached her hand for Megan's. "And that reassures me that things are going to be different this time. I really *am* this lucky."

Megan's heart shrank. *How can I let Angie down? She'd been so excited to use Daddy's car for her wedding. What kind of maid of honor am I?* "I won't let anything ruin your day." Megan hugged Angie. "And I know Jackson is right for you. Don't you worry."

"Let me get a picture," Carla said, waving her hand to get them to scoot in. "Smile, and say happy."

"Happy," they said in harmony.

Carla waved her arm toward the group, then clicked off a couple pictures. "Okay, you girls all go get changed. Angie and the rest of y'all, do you want me to have the dresses delivered over to the bridal area at First Baptist Saturday morning?"

"Yes, ma'am," Angie said. "That'll be a big help, Carla."

Katy was the first to get changed and leave. Megan hung back, hoping to get a minute alone with Angie where she could discuss the car with her, but between Flynn talking about the arrangements for all of the out-of-town guests that would be arriving the next day to stay at her bed and breakfast and Carla running down a punch list of things with Angie, Megan finally begged off.

Probably a sign.

Megan still had to finish several special orders including the guest gift votives that Angie had asked her to make for everyone coming to the wedding, and that meant she was going to need to pick up an extra order of beeswax from the local apiary to fill the orders she'd get this week. With a couple quick hugs, and promises to catch up later, Megan stepped outside. At least a slight breeze was kicking up now. In the last hour and a half, it had at least turned bearable out here. The breeze blew through her hair, cooling against the hot sun. It was during these dog days of summer like today that Daddy would have taken her for a ride in the Adventurer. There'd be no ride today, though. She hadn't even had the heart to start the thing since the tow truck had delivered it and maneuvered it into the tight quarters of her garage bay.

Daddy, I wish I knew for sure what it was you wanted me to do with this car now that you're gone, because riding in it will never be the same without you.

Chapter Two

Seated, as usual, in the first class section of the Boeing 757 in 2F, right side window, Noah Black would be off this plane and on the road before the last passengers disembarked.

The young girl next to him, who'd slept the whole coast-to-coast flight, stood and fumbled with the overhead compartment.

"I'll get that for you." Noah got up and opened it for her, handing her a bright pink leather tote bag and a matching rolling suitcase that easily weighed more than fifty pounds.

"Thanks," she said.

"You're welcome." His black leather duffel bag felt like a pillow compared to her bag.

The flight had left California late, but made up time along the way, arriving early at the Raleigh-Durham Airport.

Noah traveled often, and it was usually his luck that when his plane arrived early, they'd get stuck sitting on the tarmac waiting on a gate. Not so today.

Their gate was open and they'd pulled right in. Ahead of schedule. Hopefully, Jackson would already be here. Noah would have preferred to rent his own car, but Jackson had been adamant about picking him up. And since Jackson was the whole reason Noah was in North Carolina, he'd saved the argument. Besides, Ford was supposed to be coming in today too. If he knew Jackson, they were in for a good time tonight.

It had been a while since he, Jackson, and Ford had all been together in one place at the same time. Nearly two years actually. They were long overdue for a good night of beer, brown liquor, and basking in stories of the glory days back in Nashville. Even if what brought them together was a wedding. Bad enough he was getting married after knowing the girl less than a year, but here? In a town with a population so small that every one of the townsfolk could fit in the Grand Ole Opry at one time?

Seriously, in a town that small how was a guy supposed to have any privacy? He snickered at the thought of dating in a town like Boot Creek. He loved women, but he also loved his freedom, and from what he found online about the town, it wasn't big enough to keep a secret in. And with a dating pool that small, someone was sure to drown. And it would probably be him when he ticked some girl off. No, the last thing he wanted was a serious relationship. Been there, done that—twice—and he had no intention of starting a line of those T-shirts.

What the hell had Jackson been thinking? Maybe it was something in the water.

Note to self: Don't drink the water. Probably tastes like old sweaty boots anyway.

He'd take Los Angeles and its quirks any day over a small town. Heck, he'd go back to Nashville, or his hometown of Franklin, before settling in a little town, and he hadn't even left Nashville on good terms.

The airline attendant finally opened the door and cleared them to exit.

The couple and two businessmen from the first row filed out, and then Noah followed the girl with the pink luggage up the ramp toward the airport terminal. The air on the jet bridge held the pungent aroma of sweat and fuel. Holding his breath, he swept around the girl and then the old couple who were dawdling in the suffocating space, arguing about how to dial their granddaughter to come pick them up from their new smartphone. Text or call?

At least the air in the terminal was cooler. He wove between haggard travelers to make a pit stop in the men's room. By the time he came out, darned if that same old couple from his flight weren't just making their way through the terminal.

"I don't know," the woman said.

The old man's head bobbled. He grumbled, but it sure wasn't under his breath. "I told you to ask, Suz."

"Didn't need to. I read the booklet in the seat pocket like they told us too. It looked easy. There should be signs."

"Well, clearly there aren't, else we'd know which way to go." The old man shoved his hands in his pockets. People nearly plowed into the old guy as they hurried past to make their next connection.

Noah could picture his grandparents trying to navigate the airport. Probably would have looked like this couple, although Granddad never would've flown. He loved to drive. Noah stepped in front of the couple. "Is there something I can help you with?"

The old man spun around, then slowly raised his head from his slumped stature all the way to meet Noah's grin nearly a foot above him. "Why, yes. I think you can. Where is the baggage claim?"

"Easy," Noah said. "Follow this long hallway all the way to the center. Then turn left."

The old man glared at his wife.

Noah stifled a grin, about to even the score. "There are signs. It's well marked."

A smile spread across the old woman's face. "You wouldn't happen to know how to text, would ya?"

"Actually, I'm an expert at it." Noah held out his hand and the old woman passed him her phone. "Who are we texting?"

"Flynn. My granddaughter"

"Interesting name." Noah hit the contacts list and swept through the very sparse entries to one labeled Flynn Crane. He tapped the screen, which displayed a picture of a blonde woman who appeared to be about his age and not half bad looking, then typed in the message: *Plane is early. See you at baggage level carousel in Terminal 1.*

A loud swoosh sounded as the text went out.

The old woman clapped her hands. "Thank you. She sent me this phone and I'm still figuring it out."

"No worries." Noah leaned down between the couple. "To send her another message, click here and type in the message, then hit this button. Got it?"

The man who'd been peering over the top of his glasses, pushed them back up on his nose. "Thanks, son."

"You're welcome." Turning, he hitched his duffel bag up over his shoulder, making a beeline for the baggage claim area where he was supposed to be meeting Jackson and the guys.

Noah's phone went off in a trio of alerts. He pulled it from his shirt pocket and thumbed through the messages.

> Jackson: Yo CA Dreamer. Plane landed ten minutes ago. Where are you?

> Noah: On my way.

> Jackson: You schmoozing the stewardess or the girl seated next to you? Twenty dollar bet riding on you.

Then Jackson texted a picture of himself and Ford mugging for the camera waving twenty dollar bills.

Noah laughed. Boy, they'd be disappointed to hear the real reason he wasn't down there yet. Stopping to take a leak and helping an old couple sounded more boy scout than he cared to admit.

The last time Noah and the guys had been together was in Vegas for the Barrett-Jackson car show. He had schmoozed the airline attendant and taken her out that night. So, the bet wasn't a bad one.

That had been less than two years ago. There'd been plenty of schmoozing hot women on that trip, and although his life hadn't changed since then, a lot had changed for his friends.

Back then, they'd all vowed their bachelorhood was the most important thing to maintain, aside from their friendship. And while they used to run four strong, one had gotten married to a girl he'd met on that Sin City trip, and since they were expecting their first child any day now, there'd only be three this time.

That was one of his biggest beefs with the whole marriage thing. People changed. At least he'd been lucky enough to realize that before he walked down the aisle and ended up losing half his stuff. He liked things just the way they were. Not a thing wrong with being single.

Noah and Ford had agreed to come in early for the wedding and stay an extra day to help get Angie moved in to Jackson's house. Noah would bet a hundred bucks that place would look a lot different in just six months. Ruffles here. Girly colors there. Probably all of Jackson's most prized possessions quarantined in what women liked to call the "man cave," which was really a place to hide from the world all the good stuff men love.

The way Noah imagined the man cave, there'd be a turnstile instead of a door. The price of entry? Your man card. Never to be seen again.

Noah's teeth ached. He opened his mouth, relieving the pressure on his jaw. Grinding his teeth had become a habit with all the recent talk of weddings. He'd never let a woman come between him and his stuff. She'd probably want to use the precious square footage of his garage as a guest room addition. No, ma'am. Not in this lifetime.

And now Jackson Washburn, who he'd thought would be the last one of their tightly knit group to marry besides himself, was getting married to a girl from this tiny North Carolina town.

Noah felt even more tied to his bachelorhood. He had a week to talk his best friend out of this crazy delusional state. Or at least slow him down. What was the hurry anyway? Jackson and Angie hadn't even been together a year.

He stepped on the escalator down to the baggage claim area. From here he could see Ford holding a cardboard sign that read: **MR. NUDE AMERICA CONTESTANTS.**

And Jackson stood next to him with a fake movie poster with Noah's face photoshopped onto some guy's body, running from three women through a city street. One holding a gun, one with a wedding ring, and one carrying a baby. The movie: *The Bachelor.*

"Funny." Noah gave them a chin nod. Just like old times. There was hope. He stepped off the escalator and walked over to his friends. "How've y'all been?" Noah and Ford shook hands, and then Noah turned to Jackson. "I know how you've been. Brainwashed. What the hell?"

Jackson grasped Noah's hand and slapped him on the shoulder. "Hey, don't knock it until you try it. Not half bad having someone to cook, clean, and tell you you're the best thing breathing every day."

"You drank the Kool-Aid?" Noah fixed his gaze on Jackson. "You have time to come to your senses, ya know."

"Shut the hell up, man." Jackson laughed. "Thanks for being my best man."

"Yeah, what was that all about? How did he get to be the best man?" Ford hitched his duffle bag up onto his shoulder.

"I picked Noah as the best man because I wasn't sure if you'd even be able to make it all the way from Alaska. Besides, I figured it might be Noah's only chance to get that close to actually doing the deed."

"You've got a point," Noah said. "Can't argue with you there. But it also better mean I get to escort the hottest lady down the aisle. That *is* the only reason I'm here."

Jackson shook his head. "Why would I waste her on you? Not like you'd make an honest woman out of her."

"No. But she just might thank me for trying."

Ford elbowed Noah. "Don't be so sure."

"Whatever. One of these days you'll find the right woman, Noah, and all that smack-talking is going to have been a waste." Jackson said.

"One thing that won't be a waste is the extra days we came in to help you get settled. Or to talk some sense into you," Noah said.

"Don't waste your breath on that," Jackson said. "I'm marrying Angie, and there's nothing that would change my mind. As far as I'm concerned, I'm damn lucky to be marrying her. And her son, Billy, is the coolest kid you've ever met."

Noah's heart wrenched just a little too tight. Jackson really did seem happy. Not exactly what he'd expected to see and hear two minutes into the trip. He'd figured it would take Jackson all week to bring the hard sell. "You really are happy. I can see it in your face." Noah extended his hand. "Put her there, man. I'm happy for you."

Jackson relaxed into a grin, and his stride took on a more confident casual pace as they headed for the baggage claim.

"So where is this Podunk town where you found a girl who's so danged special she's got you jumping through hoops?"

"She's not just any girl, she's perfect. Damn near a goddess."

"You're a lost cause." Noah groaned. "Let's get the hell out of here before her father Zeus strikes us with lightning or something."

"Let's get." Jackson led the way outside and across to the parking garage to his four-door GMC pickup truck. Jackson tossed his bag and Ford's luggage into the back seat and then climbed behind the wheel.

"Nice truck," Noah said.

"That's a compliment coming from you." Jackson navigated the parking garage and headed for the interstate. "What's your latest project car? I saw the '42 Ford coupe. That car was sweet. Angie found a YouTube video of it and showed it to me just last week."

"We've done six or more cars since that one." It surprised Noah that Jackson's gal had been interested enough to look up a car video, though. "Since we're doing restorations for other people, I don't get as connected to them as I used to with my own. I sold that Ford coupe for a nice profit, though."

"I'm not surprised. It was impressive."

"Those videos really pay for themselves," Noah said. "Just hired the guy that does the videos and social media. He's working on the video for the latest project—a full-body-off restoration on a 1931 Bugatti Royale Kellner Coupe."

"You have a Bugatti?" Jackson said. "Damn, you are doing good."

"It's not mine. It'll take us a year to complete. Can't say I'll mind having that parked in the shop for a while. It'll be a beauty. This guy has more money than he could spend in four lifetimes and is sparing no expense in getting that car perfect."

"A Bugatti," Ford said. "Not sure I've ever seen one. Sounds impressive."

"Oh, it is. And this is the nicest one I've ever seen." Noah pulled out his phone and thumbed through some pictures. "Here. Look at this. I'm telling you this car has some sweet lines. Look at the way that front fender curves. And a throaty engine that'll make your heart race."

"Sounds like you're dating her." Ford looked at the picture on the phone, then handed it over to Jackson. "I think you need to start thinking about women instead of cars," Ford said. "You're worrying me, man."

Noah took the phone back and looked at the picture with a smile. Lately the cars did top his list of favorite things to do. "Hey, I find a girl with curves like that, who can make my heart race . . . then we'll talk."

"You'd probably just ask her to marry you and break it off again." Ford said, and Jackson nodded right along with him.

"That's enough out of you two. Especially you, Jackson. You're the one jumping in the deep end. Don't come whining to me if you figure it out too late." Finding out late would have just put everything he worked so hard for at risk. He'd considered his two broken engagements mistakes of the best kind.

"Just pointing out that you keep giving us hell about getting married when in reality you were the first to even think about it."

"I woke up, though. Didn't I?" He lounged against the window. The last thing he wanted was to be reminded of those mistakes.

"To put it in car terms," Jackson said. "If you have one car that breaks down on you all the time, it doesn't mean you then just walk everywhere the rest of your life. You test-drive a new model."

"I find a model like this," Noah said raising the phone in the air. "She'll damn sure already be taken. Seriously sexy. Seductive. Elegant. And the leather seats so supple that when you run your hand across them, you don't want to ever stop."

"You've been sucking to many exhaust fumes, man," Ford shook his head. "And you're in California. Practically a Costco of women. Not like you're up in Alaska with me. And even I get out more than you, it sounds like. You talk about that car like she's a woman. The perfect woman."

Noah sucked in a breath. It was true, and if a woman ever aroused him like cars did, that would be one fine day. "If I ever meet a woman that fits that description—makes me feel like that car does. I will marry her. On the spot."

Jackson glanced at Noah. "Guess your bachelorhood is safe."

"Completely," Noah said. "But cars and women are similar in some ways. Cars can be moody, but they can also make us feel cool. They are sexy as hell. Can even make us look sexy. They can be fast and loud, dangerous and so empowering you don't even care if the man stops you and writes you a ticket. In fact, if he does, it's more proof of what she can do."

"Okay, that's just weird," Ford said. "Maybe you're a candidate for one of those android girlfriends they were talking about online a few weeks ago."

"I heard about that. No emotion. No negative feedback. No bitching if I'm late or spend too much money on another car. Yeah, I'd give it a try," Noah said.

"I think I'm glad I'm getting married," Jackson said. "Not sure I want a bride who can short-circuit."

"Trust me. Women short-circuit too. Been there. Done that," Noah said with a laugh as he leaned forward between the seats. "How long a ride is it?"

"Hour and a half northwest. Anyone need to grab something to eat before we get there?"

"No, I'm good," Noah said.

"Me too."

"Cool. One of the bridesmaids owns a bed and breakfast. That's where y'all will be staying. She said she'd have some snacks for you when you arrive. For a small town we have lots of great places to eat. We get some good foot traffic at the interstate end of town."

"As long as there's a burger within driving distance, I'm good to go." Noah watched the sun-drenched landscape zoom by as they sped down the highway.

"You're set then, because the Blue Skies Café has about the best burger you'll ever have. Anywhere. Beefalo. Angie worked there and her boss is throwing us a party. Guy knows how to cook. And those beefalo burgers rock."

"Cross between beef and buffalo?" Noah asked.

Jackson glanced into the rearview mirror, making eye contact with Noah. "Yeah. It's awesome. The farm I worked for supplies all the meat to the restaurant. I swear that'll ruin you for any other burger."

"Kind of like Boot Creek ruined you for any other town?"

"Yeah. It's a good place to be. I wandered in and I guess I never left. But I'm not the only one. I swear the place has a one-way door . . . people come and never leave."

Noah turned and looked out the window at the light traffic and wide open spaces. *Well, this was one guy who'd be leaving Boot Creek at the end of the week with no regrets.*

Chapter Three

At the corner of Water Loop Way and Crump Farm Road, lights shone through the glass block windows of what used to be the only gas station in Boot Creek back in the sixties. Of course, that was when Water Loop Way was the main road through town. That hadn't been the case for a long, long time.

Now the old Mobil station was Megan Howard's residence and the home of Balanced Buzz, the beeswax aromatherapy candle company. It was a perk that she was located straight across the street from the post office too. What she couldn't deliver locally, she shipped out from there.

Megan pulled her red Karmann Ghia under the cover of what was once the canopy over the gas pump island. Now it was just a convenient carport, especially on nights like tonight when she hadn't expected rain and didn't have an umbrella handy. She hated to curse the rain. She knew the farmers had been really hurt by the long dry spell. Maybe the rain would save the crops and finally cool things down a little bit.

She unlocked the building and headed straight back to the work area she used for Balanced Buzz. One hundred mason jar shot glasses filled the cooling racks. She'd wicked and poured them late last night. Plucking six jars from different places on the rack, she lined them up under the light to check them. The wax was setting right, and the color was consistent. She held the swatch of fabric from her bridesmaid dress next to the candles.

A perfect match. Just like the bride and groom.

She went back out to her car and got the bags of craft supplies she'd picked up in town and carried them inside, leaving the front door unlocked for the girls who would arrive shortly. A trip to the craft store was never a cheap one for her. All the things on her list would have fit in a single bag, but those impulse purchases had filled two more. She couldn't deny herself all the cool stuff she found when she made the trip into the city.

It felt like the *Pretty Woman* moment as she walked back inside with all the bags dangling at her sides by their handles.

Sorting through all of the goodies, she spread out what they'd need tonight on the long worktable in the back of the workshop, and then she tucked the rest of the treasures in the storage closet to go through later.

She was just arranging all the ribbon, glue, and beads on the table when the old bell that had been a part of the Mobil station sounded. Someone had pulled in front of the building. Not an electronic sensor, but one of those old hoses that kicked the bell when a car crossed over it.

She poked her head out around the partition as Katy and Flynn walked inside. "We're here," Flynn called out.

"Hey y'all. I was just getting set up." She and the girls would be working on decorating the candle jars for Angie and Jackson's wedding this Saturday.

"I love the feeling of this place. It's like the history of the old service station still hangs in the air," Katy said. "It has such a great old vibe to it. I could totally live here."

Megan wrinkled her nose, "Right. Because Lonesome Pines is such a shack?" Everyone knew Lonesome Pines was the nicest place in town.

Probably in the five neighboring towns too. And now Derek and Katy were working on reopening the creek-side estate as a retreat, breathing new life and purpose into the place.

Everyone in town was so excited—having highly compensated physicians at the new retreat was sure to boost their quiet little town's economy.

"That's like comparing apples and oranges. And this place is like . . ." Katy seemed to be searching for the word. "A pomegranate. Extra special and unexpected."

"I think I like being a pomegranate. Come on back," Megan said. "I've got everything we need."

Katy followed Flynn and Megan to the back of the workshop toward a long table. Beyond the large windows that lined the wall to what used to be one of the bays in the original garage, night-lights sparkled like little stars against the shiny paint of the big black and gold car parked there. "Is that your dad's car? The one Angie and Jackson are using for the wedding? I heard it was a classic car. Not sure what I expected, but it wasn't that. It's huge," Katy said.

"It sure is," Megan said. "Kind of like Daddy's personality."

"How are you doing?" Katy asked. "Angie told me how close you and your dad were."

"I miss him like crazy. I still can't believe he's gone."

"Understandable."

"He drove me crazy when he was alive. We were so close, until he remarried. I'm sure the last thing I said to him was something snarky. I can't even remember for sure what it was."

"I'm sure he knew you loved him."

"I do love him. Did. Whatever. I wish that stupid wife of his had called me as soon as they'd taken him to the hospital. I might have been able to at least talk to him before he died."

"Don't torture yourself with those thoughts."

"I do. I can't help it. But at least she finally gave in and had the car delivered. She didn't want to, but the lawyer made it pretty clear she didn't have a leg to stand on."

"It's a whale," Katy said. "What kind is it?"

"DeSoto Adventurer." And even though Daddy had been the one to offer it to Jackson and Angie to drive away in, it was killing Megan inside. She wanted to protect it. It was the only thing she really had of his. She refused to let herself get caught up in that right now. She pasted a smile on her face. "It's a cool car, from what I understand there aren't many of this model out there anymore."

"You could probably make two cars out of the metal used to make that one," Katy said.

Megan hadn't considered that, but Katy had a point. "It looks bigger in here than it does outside."

"It's big no matter how you slice it," Flynn said with a laugh. "We needed that car when we were in college. Instead we were stuffing ourselves in your Karmann Ghia. Good thing I was a gymnast."

"I had to have very limber friends," Megan said with a laugh. "I don't know what I'm going to do when Mom and I need storage space for the holidays. I had to have the guys push all of my shelving against the walls to make room for the car. I guess I'll have to stack stuff in the work area and in my apartment."

Flynn jumped up. "I know. You could just fill up the car!"

"True. Why didn't I think of that?" She swept her hands against each other. "Another problem solved. Is there anything we girls can't do together?"

"Or you could get your space back by selling the car. It's really pretty. I've heard some old cars can be worth a ton of money, and that one looks very well kept," Flynn said. "And more practical than using it as a storage bin."

"It's pristine. Daddy always bragged that the Desoto has never seen a raindrop, but I can't sell it."

"Maybe someday." Flynn's expression softened. She'd lost her dad a few years back, so she knew what Megan was going through.

"Never." The words had come out like a bite. She caught herself immediately. "I'm sorry. I didn't mean to snap at you. I'm still a little emotional about it all, and it's the only connection to him I still have."

"Don't apologize. You know you don't have to do anything you're not ready to. Plus, who else has the room to store a car this size?"

"True," Megan agreed.

"I brought some extra stuff I had that I thought we might be able to use too." Flynn owned the only B&B in the town, if one didn't count Lonesome Pines Inn, which wasn't officially an inn anymore since Naomi Laumann had turned it over to Katy and Derek to use for Derek's doctor's retreat business. The timing couldn't have been better for the tall, reedlike blonde to take over the business from her grandparents.

"Thanks," Megan said.

Flynn started pulling craft supplies out of what seemed to be a never-ending bag. "Stuff I'd gotten on sale that's been sitting in my hope chest for way too long."

"Anyone hear from the guys today?" Megan asked.

"Not me," Katy said.

"All of the guys are staying with me at the B&B. Jackson stopped by on the way to the airport to pick up Noah and Ford."

"Is Ford the one from Alaska?" Katy asked.

"I can't keep them straight either." Megan pulled out a chair.

"Yes. Ford is from Alaska." Flynn leaned forward with a sparkle in her eyes. "I'm dying to meet these guys. Those pictures Jackson had were from like seven years ago, but they were all hot. Why is it good-lookin' guys always seemed to travel in tribes?"

"I don't think I've noticed that," Megan said.

"The only one I could find online was Noah," Flynn said.

"Okay, now you just sound like a stalker," Megan said.

"I am not stalking. I'm curious. I hope Ford isn't like five feet tall or something since that's who I have to walk down the aisle with. That would suck."

Megan had never had to deal with the problem of being too tall for someone. Of course, as pretty as Flynn was, Megan wasn't sure any guy would have a problem with her height. "Don't sweat it." Megan nodded for Flynn to follow her. "We don't have to marry them, and no one will be looking at us as we walk out of the church with those guys. All eyes will be on Angie. So, who cares?"

"Easy for y'all to say. Katy has Derek and you don't want a relationship. I do." Flynn pouted like she always did when they got on the subject of men, but then living in a small town could feel like slim pickings sometimes. "It'd be kind of nice if this guy was at least a potential candidate. We don't get that many new guys in Boot Creek."

Katy winced behind Flynn's back. This was an old subject that got rehashed often.

"You can have mine if yours is a dud. Now quit moping. Come help me get the candles." Megan hoped Flynn would quit her pouting if they got down to work.

"While y'all do that, do you mind if I take a look at your apartment. Angie's told me about it, but I've never seen it."

"Sure. Make yourself at home."

Katy went to the right toward the apartment and Flynn followed Megan to the left where Megan's workshop was filled with all the equipment she needed to keep Balanced Buzz going. Against the back wall the cooling racks wrapped around two walls, but only five feet high. No sense having anything taller than she could reach.

"What can I do?" Flynn picked up one of the shot-glass-sized mason jars. "These are too precious."

"They're cool, aren't they? Can you grab those two boxes from the top shelf labeled 'Lids'? We'll need those. You can put them on the bottom shelf of the cart." Megan wheeled the plastic, two-shelf utility cart across the room and started loading the candles onto the cart.

Flynn carefully placed the lid boxes underneath. "I'll help you get those."

The small glass jars fit easily onto the cart. "That's all of them."

Flynn pushed the cart like a gurney across the glossy black-and-white tiled floor through the workshop and around the corner to the table in the next room. Megan usually used this space for projects. At one time she'd even used it as an art studio, but that had been years ago.

Flynn parked the cart up against the end of the table. "You have to admit it would be nice to have someone new in town." She unloaded the two boxes of lids onto the table.

"Someone new as in someone of the male persuasion, I take it," Megan said.

"Well . . . anyone, but yes, men. And if they show up for a wedding, doesn't that have to bring some kind of good fortune? I mean, what's more romantic?"

"We're back on that again," Megan mumbled.

"The Blackberry Festival," Katy said as she walked in. "That's what got me to stop in Boot Creek. You can just troll the gas station on festival day. Worked for Derek."

"I hate to break it to you, Flynn, but we think weddings are romantic. Men, not so much. In fact, I think weddings make most guys nervous. Nearly gun-shy."

"I can never catch a break," she said.

"It's going to be fine." Megan patted Flynn on the arm and headed back to the table. "If you quit trying so hard, you'll find someone."

"We better at least have some fun."

"Quit being such a downer," Megan said. "Of course, we're going to have fun. It's Angie's big day. She's our best friend. And I'm sure those guys are going to be great. Jackson is. We'll be all dressed up and the reception is at Derek and Katy's. What could go wrong?"

Flynn shrugged. "You never know."

Katy took a seat at the table. "Megan's right. When you quit look-ing so hard you're going to find a great guy. Right now your biological clock is almost scaring me!"

Even Flynn laughed at that.

"I think you're trying too hard." Katy patted Flynn's arm.

Megan was pretty sure she didn't have a biological clock, because the last thing on her mind was kids, much less a husband.

No, thank you. Not with her family or her history with men.

Megan had to really bite her tongue from starting in on Flynn about her obsession with finding a man. It was like she'd rather pick the wrong man than be without one, and it was hard to watch the train wreck.

She nodded, settling in at the table. "Okay, we'd better get started here."

Katy took one of the jars off the cart. "So, what exactly are we doing to all of these?"

"The stickers that normally go on the front will fit right on the bottom. That way if anyone wants to reorder they can, but we'll be decorating these custom for the wedding guests. Angie gave me creative license, so here's what I'm thinking. I have this ribbon in soft yellow that should match the rosebuds and other flowers really nicely, plus it will look summery fresh against the blue beeswax candles. I had some charms made. See?" She held out a stacked set of silver-stamped charms. The bottom one was round with THANK YOU around the bottom edge. A shiny silver heart sat on top of that..

"Those are adorable."

"Aww."

Each tiny charm had ANGIE AND JACKSON and the wedding date on it.

"If you don't think it's too much work, I have these pearls we could string on each side of the charm to kind of hold it tight. I think that would look nice."

"It's for Angie. Nothing's too much work."

"We'll have to decide if we want to decorate the glass jar or the metal top. I'm thinking the edge of the mason jar top. Honestly beeswax burns pretty hot. In the small jar, I'd be kind of afraid the glue wouldn't hold. We don't want them to fall apart. At least on the lid they should stay looking nice."

"Agreed." Katy picked up a pair of scissors. "I can cut ribbons to the right length, and we can kind of do an assembly line."

"Works for me." Flynn pulled the box of beads and charms in front of her.

Megan slid boxes of permanent glue dots toward each of the two girls like a drink in an old western bar scene, then pulled one in front of herself. "These glue dots were the next best invention since sticky notes." She picked up a jar and placed the brand label on the bottom.

Katy took a lid from the box and pulled a ribbon around the top. "Think we need a little extra to make room for the charms?"

"Yes," Megan said. "And probably overlapping just a little will give us a smoother look."

Katy clipped two identical lengths, then handed one to Flynn to assemble as a prototype.

Flynn quickly threaded the beads and charms in the center of the ribbon, then placed glue dots along each end. Three on each side of the charms. She carefully wrapped it around the edge of the lid. "It's cute."

"It is." Megan reached for the lid and placed it on top of the jar she'd already labeled. "What do y'all think?"

"Really nice guest gift. I think it's great," Katy said.

"Me too."

"All right. We should be able to knock these out pretty quickly."

It didn't take more than the first ten for them to find a perfect rhythm that kept the production rolling with no wasted time. That was Katy's specialty. She could organize anyone and anything. That's why she'd been the perfect candidate to fill that festival and tourism coordinator job for the town. Boot Creek was going to be sorry they'd made it a one-year contract, because Katy would be stepping down in just one more month and they'd have to find someone to fill her shoes. That was not going to be easy. This year's Blackberry Festival had exceeded any other year prior, and she'd even launched two successful watershed projects.

"I'm totally stealing this idea if I ever get married again." Katy tightened the soft yellow ribbon around the spool and used a glue dot to secure the end.

"Think you'll ever do that?"

"Get married again?" She twisted the cardboard spool between her fingers. "At first I thought no way, but I love Derek, and just because my ex was a jerk, doesn't mean that Derek will ever be. Why wouldn't I?"

"Just wondered."

"I loved being married most of the time. Being able to be yourself. Being with someone who can make you laugh when things get tough, because you're never going through any of it alone. There's always someone in your corner."

"Until they're not," Megan said.

"True. And even good marriages turn bad. But even as bad as mine ended, I had some amazing years. I'm going to continue to honor those good times, and the bad ones . . . well, they led me to Derek. Can't really complain about that."

"Sure can't. He adores you. And none of us ever thought we'd see Derek happy again, much less serious. You gave him his life back," Megan said.

"He kind of gave me mine back too. It's really good." Katy shivered. "Sorry, I just got a chill. Is it chilly in here or is it just me?"

"It's all that talk about men cheating and bad relationships," Flynn said. "It's bad mojo to talk ill of true love."

Katy and Megan both threw pads of glue dots at Flynn, who ducked just in the nick of time.

"That is not why," Megan defended herself. "Keeping the building temperature steady is nonnegotiable in my line of work. My candles are sensitive to heat and humidity changes. I could either waste hours and hours adjusting pouring temperatures and drying times and reheating jars to compensate, or just keep the building consistent year round so I don't risk ruining product. And I hate waste. The problem is this stupid air-conditioning system is about on its last leg."

"I know a guy. Want me to connect you with him?" Flynn asked.

"No. I'm trying to get one last summer out of it. If sales this Christmas are as strong as they were last year, I'll be able to finally afford to replace it. Just a couple more weeks and hopefully fall will be here."

"I think we are done," Flynn said. "One hundred candles in adorable little shot glass mason jars decorated with tops screwed in place. Ready to go."

"That was fast. They look beautiful," Katy said.

"I think Angie will be happy with them. I'll bring them over to Lonesome Pines tomorrow if you have room to store them, Katy."

"Sure, that'll be fine. I've got one whole room of stuff for Saturday."

"How are we going to transport all of these little suckers?" Flynn asked.

"I've got the boxes the jars came in. I don't know why I didn't think to have us put them back in the box as we finished them. I'll do that tomorrow. They'll be easier to take over to the inn that way."

"I don't mind sticking around and helping you pack them up," Katy said. "I can take them with me."

"No. That's fine. I can do it in the morning. Besides, that way I can double-check that the glue dots have held overnight. I'll drive them over tomorrow, Katy. No sense messing with them tonight."

Flynn said, "If we could only build relationships as easily as putting those gifts together, then we'd be on to something."

"If you think about it," Megan said, "We kind of have all the parts of a relationship represented here in one of these little candles."

Flynn looked confused.

"Sometimes relationships make you drink. The shot glass." Megan picked one up and pretended to toss it back.

Katy jumped in. "Glue dots. Getting through sticky situations with someone you love is always easier."

"And ribbon. Sometimes they tie up all of your time." Megan smiled, and paused.

"I get it," Flynn said. "Candles. Things can get heated up."

"Totally!" Megan laughed. "That is the best part. And the charms, a man will charm you . . ." She picked up a jar from the table and unscrewed the top. "And want to screw you." She screwed the top back on.

"Make love," Katy corrected her. "Relationships aren't as bad as you think, Megan Howard. One of these days you're going to meet your match."

"That'll screw up all of my plans," she said.

"Famous last words." Katy got up. "You ready, Flynn? I'll drop you back off at the B&B."

"Yeah. Gran and my grandfather got into town this afternoon. I'm sure they'll be sitting up waiting for me to get home. They still think I'm, like, twelve or something."

"You do have a full house this week. I can't wait to see them," Megan said, walking the girls outside to where Katy had parked under the awning. "Thanks for y'all's help tonight. Even if you are trying to jinx me with all that relationship talk."

Chapter Four

Noah saw Jackson pull up in front of the Crane Creek B&B from the upstairs window. As he turned to put his wallet in his pocket, he heard the screen door downstairs slapping closed behind someone with an enthusiastic "Good Morning, Jax" behind it.

They're a friendly bunch out here.

It was hard to imagine living in a small town like this as an adult. Everyone knowing each other and all of your business. Growing up in Tennessee, it was the neighbors that usually ratted you out. Everyone knew everything. That could be a real problem when it came to dating, especially since all of the women he'd seen so far had been attractive. Even by California standards.

Noah took the stairs two at a time, then turned at the landing. As he reached for the edge of the door that was wide open, he bumped smack-dab into a tall woman. She hiccupped a gulp of air and froze in his arms, her cheeks flushing.

"Sorry." He'd grabbed her arm in the confusion. He released her and stepped out of her space.

"It's okay," she said, sweeping her hair behind her ear. "I should've been looking. Jackson's here for y'all." She stuck out her hand. "I'm Flynn."

"Yeah. Hi. You're in the wedding party too. Thanks for letting us stay here."

"My gift to the bride and groom," she said. "You'd better hurry or Jackson will start honking his horn and wake up the neighbors."

"Right." He headed for the door, then stopped and turned around. "Flynn? You said your name is Flynn, didn't you?"

"Yep. I know. It's kind of a weird name."

"No. Actually, I was talking to an older couple yesterday. They had a granddaughter named Flynn. I helped them text her."

She tilted her head slightly. "At the airport?"

"Yeah. They were on my flight." Small world. Small town. Maybe the odds were better than they seemed.

"You're the guy who helped my grandparents?"

He smiled at the recollection. "Nice folks. Reminded me of my grandparents, actually."

"Yes. They own this place, though they're living in a retirement community now. They'll be at the wedding. That was so nice of you to stop and help them. They haven't stopped talking about you."

"How about that?"

"Small world." Her eyes twinkled.

Too small, sometimes. "Well it's a really nice place you've got here."

She smiled as her blue eyes wandered the foyer. "Thanks. I like it too. Maybe tomorrow morning you'll get up early enough to partake in the breakfast. I'm a terrific cook."

"Something to look forward to," he said. That girl's biological clock was ticking; he could feel it from her first blush. Better steer clear of her. He had no need for that kind of drama. "We're going to be pretty busy this week helping Jackson and Angie. Guess we'll play it by ear." Polite. Noncommittal.

Her smile waned a bit. "Right. Y'all have a good day."

Jackson honked the horn as he stepped outside.

"You're going to wake up the neighborhood," Noah called out, to which Jackson responded with another blast of the horn.

Noah climbed into the front seat.

Jackson tapped the steering wheel. "Up for something fun today?"

"And that would be?"

"Fishing. I've got the best little honey of a hole over off the creek."

"Works for me." He hadn't been fishing in years, and that was one thing he'd always enjoyed.

Jackson pulled out of the driveway and out onto the road. "Angie made us lunch."

"Got beer?" Noah asked.

Jackson turned toward him and stared. "Seriously? Can't fish without beer. Everyone knows that."

"Atta boy. Hope you're still talking like that in a few months. Or a year," Noah said.

"Nothing's going to change just because I'm getting married," Jackson said.

"Uh-huh."

"Not unless I want it to. Angie's great. I still can't believe she agreed to marry me."

"Can I get you to repeat that so I can record it?" Noah thrust his phone at him. "I'm going to need proof."

"You gonna die on that bachelor sword? None of us is getting any younger." Jackson leveled a gaze at Noah.

"What? Something wrong with that? You don't see Ford running down the aisle either."

"Well, that's because he lives in freaking Alaska! I have a feeling there's not much up there to choose from. So that might not be entirely by choice."

Jackson gunned the accelerator of his truck. "For the record, my commitment-phobic friend, a guy doesn't need an assortment. Just one right one."

"She play that on a recorder under your pillow?" Because the problem with the assortment analogy was that, in his experience, nuts had always been hiding under creamy, sweet caramel. And those weren't always easy to avoid until it was too late. No, he'd just stick to the friend zone.

"Funny." Jackson managed a choked laugh.

"Speaking of types. Ford might like Flynn. She seems like his kind of girl—blonde and leggy. If he's ready to settle down, that girl is too. She's got that vibe going as loud as a tuba in a marching band."

Jackson grinned. "Why do you think I have him escorting her down the aisle?"

"And you found yours in Boot Creek. Hook Ford up with Flynn and you'll have another buddy to hang around with. Guess there's worse places to live."

"Sure is, but Angie's the perfect partner for me no matter where I live."

"You think she'd ever leave this little town? I always thought you'd end up back in Tennessee."

Jackson paused. "Well, I didn't really ask, but I'm sure she would. She loves me. We're a good team. We'd figure it out together."

"Famous last words," Noah muttered, but he was glad Jackson hadn't heard him over the loud roar of the tires on his truck. Because it even sounded snarky in his own head.

About thirty minutes later, Jackson turned onto a gravel road and, after kicking up dust for about a mile, they finally pulled up in front of a small boat ramp and dock that had three small boats tied up along it.

"One of these boats yours?"

"Yep," Jackson said.

"Hope it's not that little metal johnboat. I'm not up for bailing water," Noah teased.

Jackson hopped out of the truck and grabbed a bait bucket and tackle box from the back of the truck.

"I've got the cooler," Noah said.

Jackson led the way. The dock looked a lot ricketier as they got closer to the first boat.

Noah pressed his lips together as Jackson stepped into the little, seen-better-days aluminum johnboat.

Noah wondered if the boat would even hold the weight of the cooler and the two of them. He'd never been one to really like the water.

Jackson got up and stepped back on the dock. "I'm joking. Come on."

"Good. I swear I was getting a little seasick just then," Noah said, following Jackson toward the blue sparkly boat at the end of the dock. "This is way more like it. Nice paint."

"Thanks." Jackson opened the live well and then put the cooler between the two back seats. He took out a plastic container from the top of it and put it in a separate storage hopper on the back of the boat. "This is our lunch. Angie is the best cook I've ever met. Girl can cook anything. She made all of my favorites for us. Fried chicken that'll smack your lips for you, and her famous fried mac-n-cheese bites. Let me just remind you. She's mine."

"You won't see me fighting for her, even if she's the next Paula Deen." Noah pulled one of the fishing poles out and started fixing the line. "Been a while since I've done this."

Jackson grabbed one of the others. "Thought as busy as you are, this would be a good thing to do."

"We eating what we catch or releasing?" Noah asked as he twisted a knot on the tackle.

"We've got the barbecue tonight, but we can filet them and fry them up tomorrow night."

"Works for me." Noah pulled the tackle box closer with his foot, and popped open the top. He pulled out a knife and some weights. "Any wagers on biggest fish?"

Jackson snickered. "Some things never change."

"By that I guess you mean that I always win." Noah grinned.

"That remains to be seen, but you have always wanted to bet on everything."

Noah slapped Jackson on the back. "All in fun, my man. No money, whoever catches the biggest fish doesn't have to do any of the filleting."

"I'm in. Don't be whining that I've got an advantage because it's my boat. Fair's fair."

"You're on."

Jackson fired up the boat and sped through the murky water of the wide creek. Looked more like a river to Noah, but he didn't know much about boats or water so he kept his mouth shut. Only reason he ever went fishing at all back in Tennessee was because it was a great way to sleep off a hangover.

"We have to dress up for this thing tonight?" Noah asked. Leave it to women to plan a party—they always go all crazy on the unnecessary details. Just give him a cold beer and some good conversation and he'd call it a success.

Jackson slowed the boat to a stop near the shore where a fallen tree laid sprawled half in the water. "Nope. It's casual. Should be a good time."

Noah cast his line and dropped his hook right into what looked like a sweet spot near the deep end of the tree.

Jackson dropped his line on the other side of the tree, and darned if he didn't get a nibble almost as soon as his bait hit the water. He played the fish for a few seconds, letting out the line and then reeling it in a little at a time until it got tugged beneath the surface. He whipped the line quickly to set the hook and reeled the fish in. "Grab the net, man."

Noah moved to the edge of the boat with the net and scooped up the fish.

"Got the first one," Jackson beamed.

Noah shrugged. "The bet's for the biggest. Not the first." He recast and tried again.

After four hours the sun was beginning to get too darn hot, and on full stomachs they'd had just about enough. "You ready to call it a day?" Jackson tugged on the bill of his hat.

Noah said. "How about we do fifteen more minutes. I'll give you one last chance to beat me."

"I have another spot on the way back. We'll stop there for fifteen." Jackson started the engine and puttered down the waterway.

Even after they'd stopped, and Noah hit a lucky run of four fish in a row, none of them were larger than the largemouth bass Jackson had landed.

Jackson slowed the motor as they got closer to the dock, and pulled it right up alongside. "Can you grab that line?"

Noah took the rope that they'd coiled off the front of the boat and tossed the top over the pylon. "Got it." The high-pitched squeal of a wood duck made Noah nearly jump off the boat. "What the—"

"Ducks." Jackson laughed. "They nest over there. I think they're celebrating my victory."

Noah stepped off the boat, reaching for the gear as Noah passed it over. "You nervous at all, Jackson?"

"I'm really not. I know I love her." He put the fishing rods back down in the center storage unit. "The whole standing up in front of people and saying stuff kind of makes me anxious, but it's important to her. I know you don't really get it, Noah, but I swear I hope you find someone like Angie someday. It's a different kind of happy. I can't explain it."

Noah hated to rain on Jackson's parade, but that was the last thing he wanted anyone wishing for him.

"I see your face," Jackson said. "I'm telling you. For real. Man to man. Friend to friend. I never knew what I was missing."

"I'm happy for you. Glad you're happy, even."

"You are not," Jackson said with a laugh.

"No. I am. Doesn't mean I'm joining the ranks of the married. But I'm glad for y'all, even if weddings aren't my thing."

"Well, when you see what we're riding off in, you might feel differently."

Noah raised his hand. "If it's a horse-drawn carriage, I'm not scooping poop. Just saying that right up front."

"No. Angie's maid of honor, Megan, you'll meet her tonight, her dad has a pristine show piece of a ride. Well, Megan has it now. Her dad recently passed away, but he'd offered to let us use it for the wedding before he died."

Finally. Something Noah was interested in talking about. "Really. What is it?"

"A 1958 DeSoto Adventurer."

Noah spun around. Did he just hear that right? The words played back in his head almost as if he were translating a foreign language. "Did you say a '58 DeSoto Adventurer? Why the heck didn't you tell me about this?"

"I told you we were driving a classic car."

"There's classic and there's collectible. And didn't you remember that that was the kind of car my granddad had?"

"I guess I didn't realize it was the same car. Just old. That thing is sweet, though. I think it's got, like, a total of twenty-eight thousand original miles or something crazy like that. Convertible too. Incredible."

He was sure a broad dorky-ass grin was spreading across his face. "Incredible is right. More than incredible. I've been on the hunt for one of those for the last ten years." Could this seriously be happening?

"That DeSoto is a tank of a car. I thought you liked those sporty-looking hot rods. All ZZ Top–ish." Jackson did the comical hand gesture from the old videos, which had been Noah's favorite song for the chicks and the cars.

"That was a '33 Ford Coupe and I do, but my granddad taught me all about cars with his Adventurer."

"Can't you have any kind of car you want now that you're in that business?"

"I wish it was that simple. There were only a few of those Adventurers built in 1958. Even fewer that were convertibles."

"So it's extra special."

"Exactly. Limited edition, and the ones you do find have been neglected or ruined by someone trying to turn it into something it was never meant to be." Excitement built inside of him. It was the chase. Just like with women. The hunt was as much of the satisfaction, and if he'd actually finally stumbled upon the car of his dreams in this little town, Boot Creek may become a special little map dot to him too.

Chapter Five

So many cars lined Main Street in front of the Blue Skies Café, it almost felt like Blackberry Festival time. Megan strolled down the walkway, not surprised by the turnout. Angie was well liked by the people who knew her, and her customers loved her too. Angie was one of those people that had no barriers. Even though she'd been through plenty of situations in her life that had given her cause to shut down . . . she'd risen above them all. She was the first one to volunteer or show up to offer a hand when someone needed it. Megan wished she were more like that sometimes. It just wasn't her way. She was more of a dove, while Angie was like a cockatiel. Social, friendly, and whatever she said sounded like pretty music.

Even before Megan opened the door to Blue Skies Café, the aroma of good food surrounded her. She walked inside.

Standing room only.

When ol' man Johnson had said he wanted to host a pre-wedding/going-away party for Angie, his number one waitress, Megan had no idea that he'd meant that he was going to invite darn near the whole town. Folks in these parts loved his food, so no one was about to miss this spread. But on top of that, anyone who had ever met Angie loved her. All of her best customers seemed to have turned out.

Megan spotted Angie leaning against one of the booths. If she didn't know better, she'd have thought Angie was ready to take the person's order. But tonight was in honor of the hardworking girl, and ol' man Johnson had brought in a group of young folks from the 4H to wait the tables.

The bright green shirts of the 4Hers moved through the crowd like Olympic speed skaters.

Inching her way through the crowd, Megan finally made it over to Angie. "What a turnout."

Angie spun around and hugged Megan. "Is this nuts?"

"A lot of these people won't be at the wedding, right?"

"Exactly. Customers mostly." Angie's eyes were misty, her smile genuine. "I mean who wouldn't show up for free food? But it was really sweet that they'd come. And did you see Johnson put up a tip box for me? He dropped in a one-hundred-dollar bill to get things started. It was so thoughtful. I'm going to miss working here."

"No you won't. You worked your butt off here."

Angie looked around. "True, but it's been a good living. Billy and I've done fine with my income from this job, and ol' man Johnson has been so patient with me through the divorce, the harassment from Rodney, my car problems, and Billy getting sick when he started school. I swear I couldn't have asked for much more."

"Well, you've got much more now," Megan said. "You've got a great husband who is going to soak up half that burden from now on. And the job with Derek and Katy at Lonesome Pines is going to be so much better for you. Besides, if Billy gets sick, you can stick him in one of those rooms at the inn, or better yet, work from home."

"I can't believe my life has changed so much in the past year. I never even dreamed my life could be like this."

"You know what they say, when you least expect it . . . you'll find love. And you deserve it."

"That sure was the case with Jackson. The only reason I even went out to Criss Cross Farm was to show Katy around that day. Then I saw Jackson."

"Someone say my name?" Jackson wrapped his arms around Angie's waist from behind.

"That was me. Hey, sweetheart." She leaned back and turned her face toward him for a kiss. "Love you."

"And more," he said. "I wanted to introduce your girls to my guys."

"Great." Angie tiptoed and waved Flynn and Katy over. "I'm sure they've met Flynn already."

Megan stepped back as Katy and Flynn gathered. Suddenly it was as if they were being lined up for some kind of hoedown. *Swing your partner.*

"We'll get some time together to talk, but I wanted to get y'all introduced," Jackson said. "The dark-haired guy with the California suntan is Noah. My best man."

"I think we're going to need name tags," Katy said with a laugh.

Megan wondered just how much work Noah did to maintain a tan that dark. Then again, Angie *had* said Noah was kind of the playboy of the group. He looked the part too. Hotter than hot, with a little salt in his pepper hair and eyes as dark as chocolate ganache. His full lips were shadowed by a day or two's growth, and although it hadn't ever been one of her favorite looks, it looked particularly good on him. Even a little dark and dangerous in a sexy sort of way.

His lips parted, as if he knew what she was thinking. A dimple forming at the lower right of his cheek. "I'm Megan," she said, mostly to save herself from his stare. "Guess I'm your other half. The maid of honor."

A faint line appeared between Noah's brows as he studied her. Other half? "That's an interesting way to describe it."

Jackson tugged the tall guy with the shaggy long brown hair by the arm. "And this one who looks jet-lagged is Ford. All the way from Alaska."

Ford smiled and held his beer up. "By way of one long layover in Colorado, but I'm here. I promise to rest up and be proper fun the rest of the week."

"I can promise you good rest and hearty Southern breakfasts," Flynn sidled up to him. "I'm Flynn. You and I haven't met yet, but I own the inn where y'all are staying."

Ford's face lit. "Oh you had me wondering for a minute there how I was getting so lucky. Nice to meet you, Flynn. And thank you. I'm about thirteen hours past needing rest at this point."

"You just let me know if you want to get on out of here early. I can give you a lift," Flynn flashed him a sweet smile.

Megan turned her back to Flynn and Ford. "Am I the only one feeling that vibe all the way over here?" she mouthed the words.

Katy pressed her lips together and shook her head.

Angie broke the buzz that was pulsing between Ford and Flynn. "And Katy here was the magic that put me in the path of Jackson to begin with. She's the newest of us to Boot Creek, but she's one of the gang already. Her better half is the one walking me down the aisle and giving me away—Derek."

Megan caught the hiccup in Angie's voice. If it were Megan getting married and Dad had missed it, she'd have felt the same way. Angie's dad had died when she was just a little girl.

Jackson clapped his hands and rubbed them together. "Great. Now everyone knows someone. Have fun tonight. I have a feeling this week is going to fly by."

Megan watched Flynn cast her best flirting in Ford's direction again. Did that Alaskan know what he was in for? If nothing else, there'd probably be some hot and heavy fun between the two. Then Flynn would be in love and Megan, Katy, and Angie would be consoling her for two weeks after Ford fled back to Fairbanks, or wherever the heck he lived in Alaska. It would take that long for Flynn to finally admit to herself that she didn't even know the guy, much less love him. And that he really wasn't so perfect after all.

"They are so cute together," Katy said.

"He doesn't seem the lawyer type."

"He's not," Katy said, leaning in. "He has his law degree, but he decided that wasn't how he wanted to spend his life. Now he's a craftsman."

A craftsman? Visions of taxidermy flashed in Megan's mind. Whalebone carving. Followed by a not-quite-so-elegant hat covered in hand-tied fishing lures in every highlighter color imagined.

Katy pushed those images away quickly with more details. "He's a glassblower. Apparently a pretty darned good one. He's going to meet up with a glassblowing company not far from here while he's in town. That's why he rented his own car."

"Glass? Really?" She looked back in his direction. She could picture him in a long lab coat and safety glasses working the hot molten glass. But right now he was working Flynn, and it was nice to see her with a genuine smile on her face. "I need another glass of wine. Want one?"

"I could use a refill," Katy said.

"Good. Because this maid of honor needs to probably do that whole toasting thing and I make much better toasts with a couple glasses of courage in the hopper."

"Better you than me. I can never come up with anything clever to say for those things."

They went over to the lunch counter that had been turned into a bar for the night and the bartender set them up.

Megan and Katy sipped their wine as the crowd continued to grow, and the noise level rose to nearly shouting level.

"Okay, here goes nothing. If I don't say something soon, it'll be too loud to get anyone's attention. Give me a hand up onto this chair."

Katy spotted Megan until she was steady, then kept one hand on the back of her leg for safe measure.

Megan tapped the side of her glass with a spoon. "Can I have your attention?"

Friends, neighbors, and family hushed and pulled in closer. "Welcome!" She raised her glass in the air. It was nice to see so many of the people they'd known all of their lives together having a good time. "I'm Megan. I know most of you, but for those I haven't yet met, I've known Angie since grade school. Thank y'all for joining us to celebrate Angie's retirement from Blue Skies."

Her customers hooted and whistled.

"And help me wish her well on her upcoming nuptials."

Megan watched Jackson tug Angie closer and kiss her on the temple. It made her ache just a little for that kind of love, but she knew she could never risk that kind of hurt again. You love too much, you hurt too much. That was a simple equation.

"Angie and I've been best friends since the day we met at Boot Creek Elementary School. If we could have gotten air miles for each minute we spent talking on the phone over the years, we could've traveled around the world a few times. We've laughed together, cried together, laughed until we cried, okay fine, or until I snorted, which always made her laugh even harder, but all the same it was good. We've been there for each other through the hardest times in our lives, and I couldn't be more delighted to see her happier than I've ever seen her . . . with you, Jackson."

Everyone clapped and Jackson kissed Angie as the onlookers *aaaawwwwwed* in response.

"How many of y'all believe in love at first sight? Show of hands." Megan raised a hand in the air.

A smattering of hands rose. Noah stood across the way with his hands folded across his chest, a beer in one hand. He had one of those, "Really?" looks on his face, which she promptly ignored.

"Yeah, I used to be a skeptic too," Megan said, making eye contact with Noah. "But these two are proof that it happens. The smile on Angie's face the first time she mentioned Jackson's name was the widest, brightest smile I'd ever seen. And when I met Jackson, I knew why. I love the way you love her, Jackson. You made this girl believe in love at first sight. Help me give our host tonight, ol' man Johnson, a round of applause to thank him for this fabulous night."

Derek stepped over and reached for Megan's hand to help her down. The volume in the room soared back to where it had been a few moments ago, and folks went back to mingling.

From across the room someone let out a loud whistle, the kind that usually requires a couple fingers in your mouth. All heads turned in that direction.

Noah didn't bother to stand on a chair. Didn't need to at over six feet tall, but he had everyone's attention.

Show off.

"I'm Noah Black. Jackson and I go way back to our days in Tennessee. I'm from California and Ford here traveled all the way from Alaska. Angie, when Jackson called and told me he was getting married, I couldn't believe it, but after meeting you I can see how and why he fell so deeply in love with you. I believe marriage is a wonderful thing for Jackson. It will teach him loyalty, self-restraint, and compromise. It'll even develop his sense of responsibility and so many other things he wouldn't have even needed if he'd stayed single."

The men laughed, the women groaned.

Megan grabbed a fresh glass of wine from the bar and took a long sip. Well, if that wasn't the most backhanded compliment she'd ever heard. Even if he did have a point.

"Seriously, everyone is here tonight to wish you two well, and I think I speak for everyone when I say we are so happy you included us in this very special occasion. This time next week you'll be honeymooning."

Noah leaned toward Jackson. "Not mooning. Those days are now in the past. May the countdown begin?"

Guys slapped Jackson on the back, but Megan heard the undertones, the unspoken in Noah's speech. She couldn't agree with him more. Being married changed a person. That was one heck of a price to snare a long-term roommate. At least he was straight up about what he felt, unlike the men that would tell you what they thought you wanted to hear.

Megan grabbed a plate off the buffet line and headed out back to grab a burger and to keep herself from chastising Noah. It wasn't her place, but really why had he seen the need to make a second announcement?

Several couples were eating out on the back lot. It was cooler out here without all the body heat of the packed restaurant. But the party was inside. With her plate politely full of a little bit of everything ol' man Johnson had cooked up, Megan went back in.

"Mind if I slip in here with y'all?" Megan asked Derek before she registered that Noah sat on the other side of the table.

Keep your enemies closer.

Derek slid over to make room. "Sure. Join us."

The atmosphere was casual and fun, but something about Noah set her on alert. She wasn't sure why. Derek was telling a couple she didn't know and Noah about his plans for the retreat.

"The retreat is for the doctors. A place where medical professionals can renew themselves. Regain balance."

The woman sitting across from Derek said, "I can't imagine dealing with end-stage cancer like you did. It has to tear you apart."

"It is hard. Wears on you emotionally. But the drive to heal, to find something that will work, keeps you going. I was burned out way before I realized it. Even before Laney had fallen ill."

Megan caught the subtle choke in Derek's words. "Keep them healthy so they can heal more people," she offered.

"That's the plan."

Megan ate while the others made small talk and drank. An older couple walked up to the table, Flynn in their wake.

"Hello, Derek. How have you been doing? Flynn tells me you are doing very well." Her eyes twinkled. "You deserve happiness again."

"Thank you, Mrs. Crane. I'll have to introduce you to Katy. I'd love for you to meet her."

"Then we will," the woman said.

"Rich." Derek shook the old man's hand.

"It *is* a small world," Noah said, reaching across the table to shake Rich's hand too.

"You know them?" Megan asked.

"He is the sweetest boy."

Somehow Megan doubted that. And the guy sitting across from her was far from a boy.

Rich Crane bobbed his head. "Nice young man. Johnny-on-the-spot to help us out at the airport. He didn't have to do that either. Just walked right up and offered. Appreciate that, son."

"It was my pleasure," Noah said. "I'm sure you'd have done the same."

Flynn wrapped her hands around her grandparents. She was inches taller than both of them. "What are the odds y'all would have been on the same plane, much less had a conversation, and then be sleeping under the same roof? It was like fate that we were all supposed to meet."

Megan tried not to roll her eyes, but she had a terrible poker face. She knew full well what was going through Flynn's head. First it was Ford. Now Noah. They were going to have to hide Flynn just to protect all the other single men from her relentless flirting. Bless her heart.

Suzy Crane beamed in Noah's direction, like she might be hoping pretty boy Noah was the right boy for Flynn too. "Flynn told us that you're the best man in Angie's wedding."

"Yes, ma'am. Jackson and I have been friends for years. Since high school days. Angie seems like a sweet girl. I'm honored to be a part of their big day."

Puh-lease. Megan wasn't buying that for a minute. She heard the subtext in his little toast earlier. He wasn't happy that his friend was getting married. He'd probably be the first one to give him a ride out of town.

"And sweet Megan. How's your momma doing? Is she here tonight?"

"She's doing great. You know how she is. Working nonstop. She and her flowers are inseparable. I'm sure if you walk down to the shop she's there whipping up corsages for the big football game Friday night. She had a ton of orders."

"Such a sweet woman. You look just like her."

"Thank you." When she glanced up Noah was staring at her. She pressed her hands down on the table and smiled, focusing her attention back on the Cranes.

"Angie tried to get Derek here to be the maid of honor. But he refused."

Noah almost choked on his beer.

Derek took a sip of his. "My reaction exactly." They tapped their beer bottles together across the table. "Some things are best left the way they were meant to be. And I personally think Megan makes a much prettier maid of honor than I would have."

"I'm sure of that," Noah said, giving her a little nod. Darn if his mouth didn't look good with the beer dampening his lips. He licked the droplet away.

With that, Megan excused herself from the table. "It was so good to see you," she said to the Cranes. "I'm sure we'll get to spend some more time together this week." She couldn't get away from that table and Noah's constant staring quick enough. She put her plate on one of the trays near the kitchen and then headed for the bathroom. She just needed a minute. She wasn't even sure why she was so bothered by that guy. He hadn't done or said a thing wrong. Maybe it was the heat in this joint. She'd never been one much for crowds anyway. She ran her hands under some cool water and took a breath. It was the heat, she told herself as she tried to relax, the heat hung mercilessly, there was no way the air-conditioning could keep up with everyone coming in and out of the place.

I'm fine.

I'm overreacting.

Definitely just the heat. And the wine. And the press of all of those people. She felt better already. She checked her makeup and reapplied her lipstick, a soft pink that made her skin look more tan.

Angie was standing outside of the door, probably trying to take a potty break, but no one would give her a moment's peace.

"Hey, gal," Megan said, giving Angie's shoulder a casual squeeze. "You doing okay?"

"Great."

The couple that had been talking to Angie excused themselves and she gave them a wiggly finger wave. "Drink this," Angie said. "I can't have another drink. I don't know how many I've even had."

"Well, it is a party. And you're the guest of honor."

"Who'd like to be able to walk out of here at the end of the night."

Megan snagged the glass of wine from Angie's hand. "My duty as maid of honor." She took a generous sip of the cool liquid.

"Thanks so much for that sweet toast earlier. You didn't have to do that."

"I know. But it seemed appropriate. And I knew ol' man Johnson would love the round of applause."

"Oh, he ate that up. Big ol' teddy bear. He'll never admit it, but I could tell."

"I thought you'd appreciate that."

"So much. One of my regular customers just walked in. I guess I'd better go say hello."

Megan raised the glass of wine in a silent toast as Angie hurried off. Most of the people in the room were coupled. She didn't want a husband, or even a boyfriend, but at times like these, being single in a sea of duos made her feel like the odd man out.

No one would notice if she disappeared for a little while. She slipped out the backdoor and hung close to the building, in the shadows. She could catch some night air and quiet before going back in.

The smell of the burgers on that big cooker reminded her of Daddy grilling when she was a kid. He was a master of the barbecue. It was a nice night, and the crowd of people that had been out here eating earlier had dissipated. Seemed most were enjoying the bar and desserts inside now.

"Hey. Too much going on in there for you?"

She stumbled over her own foot as she noticed Noah. "Hi. No. I was just getting some fresh air. You found my secret hiding spot."

"Not that good of a secret if the new guy in town can find it."

"True."

"Don't let me stop you. There's plenty of room."

Walking away would be rude, so she took a seat.

"I like your outfit. That color blue is really pretty on you."

Charmer. "Thank you," she answered politely, not really taking much from the compliment. He probably handed them out like handing out speeding tickets at the Indy 500. Pointless.

"I know what you mean about the fresh air. All that lovey-dovey stuff going on in there can get a little suffocating." He tugged at his shirt collar.

Okay. She liked him better. A little anyway. "True that."

"You ever been married?"

"Kind of personal for a first question, don't you think?"

"You don't want to answer it?" He folded his arms.

"Nope. You?"

"Nope. Never been married? Or nope, you don't want to answer, which means you have been . . . probably several times."

Touché. "I've never been married. A status I rather embrace." His quick wit tickled her.

"Looking?"

"You asking?" she challenged.

"Hell, no," he said, without even a nanosecond's hesitation.

"Thank God."

"I'm not your type?"

He almost sounded disappointed, and she wasn't quite sure why she found that a bit appealing. "I don't have a type," she said. "I like doing what I want, when I want. It works for me."

"I know what you mean. Me too." He leaned forward on the concrete table—the striation of his biceps noticeable even under the dim glow from the moon. He tapped her ring finger. "So why the ring?"

He noticed. She wiggled her fingers. "This? My dad gave it to me when I turned sixteen. It fits on this finger best. And it's not a bad way to keep guys at arm's length if they are the type on the prowl for a single gal to turn into their happy homemaking bride." She caught his gaze. "Or the kind that will be gone the next day anyway."

He leaned back. "Why are you looking at me like that?"

"You seem like the latter."

"Well, I'm definitely not the first one. Not looking for a bride. But I'll be here through at least next weekend, so I'm not the latter either." He held her gaze for a long moment. "So . . . the ring. Good idea. And way more subtle than the 'Stay Ten Feet Back' sign I usually hang around my neck. Maybe I need one of those."

She scrunched her nose. "I'm not so sure diamonds and sapphires would be a real good look on you. In fact, might send the wrong message altogether."

"Don't think I could carry off the gems, huh? Well, maybe just a band then." He gave her a wink, and she liked that he thought he could match her wits for wits. But she had her doubts that he could. "You always a smarty-pants?" he asked.

"I may have been accused of that a time or two . . . or twenty before."

"Cute as you are I guess you can get away with it."

Was he flirting? Or just a kindred spirit? "You think I'm cute?"

"I said it, didn't I?" He turned and watched his friends. Shaking his head. "I used to think I knew these guys as well as I know myself, but things are changing now that Jackson is getting married."

"Maybe you're next."

"No, ma'am." He took her hand in his and stroked the ring on her finger. "I like the idea of a woman independent enough not to want to be tied down."

"That sounds like a man who has had his heart broken."

"Don't need a broken heart to know you don't want one. I'm a solitary man. I like it that way."

Megan wasn't sure how to respond to his very serious tone. So she kept her mouth shut. Wasn't so far from her own beliefs anyway, so who was she to judge?

The tension in his jaw eased and a slight smile teased the corners of his mouth. "So, Megan-who-wears-a-ring, I get the feeling you don't like me so much."

"I don't even know you."

"My point exactly. So, do I remind you of someone? Did I say something wrong?"

His honesty caught her off guard. And the truth was she didn't even have an answer. Not a good one anyway. "No. I'm not even sure why, but you're right. My guard went up. I can't put my finger on it. You gonna tell me what it is I'm feeling?"

"Hell, no. The day I start pretending to know what's on a woman's mind, you may as well send me to the crazy house." He waved a finger back in forth in the direction of her head. "No telling what the heck is going on up in there."

She laughed. A real hearty laugh that ended in a little snort. "Sorry. I do that sometimes."

"It's kind of cute."

"That's twice you've called me cute. Stop that."

"Yes, ma'am."

"And all that ma'am stuff. What is that all about? We're the same age."

"I was brought up by a good old Tennessee gal who believed that 'yes and no, ma'am,' was the proper way to show respect, and I guess it just stuck."

"I was brought up that way too. But I'm not going to call you sir."

"Fair enough. I'm the best man. You're the maid of honor." He looked around at the empty lot around them. "You and I seem to be in the minority—those without dates. Think we could call some kind of truce and pal around this week—no strings, no expectations?"

"You serious?"

"Yeah. I like your sass. I damn sure don't want to have to dodge that ticking time bomb of a baby maker—"

"Flynn?"

"Oh yeah. That would be the one."

She couldn't blame him. Flynn would dog him all week. "Well, we do seem to be on the same page here."

"Yeah, and it seems the guys I thought were on my team are defecting."

"You're going to have to be a better quarterback then."

"I'll take that under advisement." He extended his hand. "My new partner in crime?"

"For the week." She shook his hand. A nice firm grip.

"Think we should go back in?"

She slumped forward. "In a minute?"

"You twisted my arm."

"Oh, we are going to get along fine," she said.

"Jackson said you make candles for a living."

"I do. Aromatherapy candles. All natural. I make them from beeswax that I get from a local beekeeper."

"So you hand pour them. Like one by one?"

"Just like that."

"That has to take a long time."

"I've got a pretty good system. I never intended for it to become huge. I'm very happy with the size of the business."

"How do you come up with the smells?"

"*Aromas.* Smell is what you do to test a carton of milk when the date has passed."

"Yeah, that's not good."

"Never is. Why is it we always want other people to smell stinky stuff? I think guys started that."

"We probably did." He stood up. "Come on. Let's go back in. I'll buy you a free drink to seal our deal."

"Okay." She followed him back into Blue Skies Café. The crowd had thinned out some. There was even a booth empty toward the front.

He went straight to the bar and got a beer. "You still drinking wine?"

She nodded.

"Wine for the lady."

"I'll grab that table," she said as he waited for the bartender to pour the wine. She slid into the booth. When she looked up, he was walking toward her. She wondered where he'd sit. Next to her or across from her.

Like a proper gentleman he gave her space, sitting across from her in the booth.

He handed her the wineglass, then held his beer in front of her. "To a week of no-bs fun and helping our friends start their new life together on the right foot."

She tipped her glass toward his bottle. A smile played on her lips, and suddenly he didn't seem nearly as bad as she'd made him out to be in her mind earlier. He was playful and fun. No problem.

"Jackson drove us around Boot Creek. It's not a very big town, so I guess it's safe to say you live nearby."

"That would be a good bet. Within walking distance." Great, now he'd think she was inviting him over. Not her intention at all.

"Lived here all of your life?"

"Yep."

"I grew up in a small town outside of Nashville. I spent most of my youth wishing for a bigger place to live."

"I've never felt the urge to move somewhere else, but then I pick up and go where I want to go whenever. So I've never felt stuck by living here. But it's nice when you know everyone in town. It's comfortable."

He listened intently. Never interrupting her as she spoke. Like he was really listening. Which seemed kind of odd.

"I hadn't thought of it that way. Makes sense."

"If I'd never been able to travel. I might feel very different. You live in California now. Big state. What part?"

"Near Los Angeles."

"Busy."

"Good for business. I don't live in the city, though."

"On the beach?" That would explain the tan.

"Yes. Great view, but the lots are so small I have to keep my cars in a separate garage near my business. My garage is bigger than most of the lots on the beach."

"How big is your garage?"

Was that some kind of metaphor? Noah pressed his lips together. "I own fourteen cars. But I have space for twenty."

"Four—" Megan put down her wineglass. "Fourteen? I have one car taking up a third of my whole house right now. I can't imagine that times fourteen. That's a car lot. And in California? That had to cost a fortune."

"In some towns, I guess fourteen cars could be a car lot." Her animated reaction made him smile. "So I love cars. There's worse things. And I guess most people have one car, but it's my business too."

"Well, technically I have two," Megan said. "The one I drive, and then the one that is now unexpectedly taking up residency in my house. But then I didn't seek that one out."

"How's that? Is there a car Santa I've been missing out on? Because I'd make the nice list for sure."

"No. My daddy recently passed away. He didn't leave me any of his money, but he did leave me his favorite car. To his young wife's chagrin."

"I can understand that."

"The young wife part, or the car?"

"The car. Definitely not the wife . . . young or otherwise. That he left you the car says a lot more than money about his love for you." That was the kind of man he understood.

"It's a 1958 DeSoto Adventurer and that thing takes up a lot of space. Even in my house. And I'm fairly certain I have one of the bigger garages around since my house used to be a gas station."

But he already knew that. And he knew exactly how much space that car took up. "Nearly two hundred twenty-one inches bumper-to-bumper you've got there." Had he just said that out loud?

"Impressive when you put it that way."

"Oh, there's a lot more than that impressive about that car."

"I'm surprised you've ever even heard of it."

"It's my business." He pulled his wallet out of his hip pocket and slid a card across the table. "I opened California Dreaming Restoration in a two bay garage. Now I have over twenty-five thousand square feet. We cater to the richest car enthusiasts in the world."

"Impressive." She ran her finger across the raised print on the card.

"I like the way your eyes dance when you talk about that car." Why was he wondering what her fingers would feel like against his skin? "Do you have any idea what you've got on your hands?"

"Absolutely." She raised her chin.

"1958?" Of course, he already knew that from Jackson. An I'd-like-to-thank-the-Academy speech bounced through his mind. She had no idea that she was going to want to sell him this car. But she would. They always did.

"Convertible."

His heart shifted into overdrive. His pulse cranking up to about 140, matching the top speed of that year and model. "Who'd believe a car like that would end up in a small town like this?"

"Believe it, sugar." She took a long sip of her wine. "My best memories with my dad were with that car. He loved that more than anything, except for me."

Warning flares signaled in Noah's mind. *A daddy's girl, and her daddy's car. This may not be as easy as I'd hoped.* "No way he'd have left that car to you otherwise. He loved you very much."

"Thank you." She lowered her eyes, then twisted the business card in her hand again.

He hoped she wasn't going to cry, because one thing he didn't do well was women and tears. "I'd love to see your car. Is it in good shape?"

She looked up. Those dark clouds lifting. "Pristine. Never seen a raindrop."

"As it should be." Her lips were full and pink. Probably from the wine. It wasn't going to be hard to spend his time with her this week. "You've got to take me over to see it."

"Sure," she said.

Noah's foot danced under the table.

Angie came over to their table. "Sorry to interrupt, but Megan, I need you to come with me. We're going to get more wedding party pictures taken for the album."

"Okay." Megan shimmied across the vinyl seat and stood next to the table. "We'll get together this week," she said to Noah.

He nodded. Man, *this* close to actually seeing the car. He sat there for a minute, but all he could think of was that car. Sitting there moping about it wasn't going to get him any closer to that deal. He got up and walked over to where Jackson and Ford were talking.

"That'd be great if you don't mind," Ford was saying. "I'm seriously a zombie right now."

"I'll take you back over to the inn. The girls are taking pictures. They'll be awhile."

"Can I catch a ride too?" Noah asked.

"Sure. Come on," Jackson said.

The three of them went out the front door and got into Jackson's truck.

As soon as Jackson got behind the wheel, Noah lunged forward between Jackson and Ford. "It really is a 1958 DeSoto Adventurer. I asked her."

"I told you it was," Jackson said. "You think I don't know what kind of car we're driving away in on our wedding day?"

"I'd almost convinced myself that I was going to have to give up the idea of getting my hands on one. You don't understand, man. This is a big deal to me."

Jackson straightened. "I don't think you'll get your hands on this one either."

"You never know. I'm a great negotiator. Come on. I've got to see it."

"You'll see it Saturday, because I'll be driving it."

"Let me drive y'all, man."

"No. I promised Mr. Howard I would be the only one to drive it, and we even discussed the route in detail. He was very particular about that car."

"Yeah, but Megan owns it now, right? I can get her to let me drive it."

"No. Don't screw this up."

"Drive me by her place. She really lives in a gas station?"

Jackson drove up the block and turned left. "Sure does."

"What the heck? I mean who does that?"

"Don't knock it. It's a cool place. She runs her business out of it too. Not a storefront, but a workshop for her candle company. Most all of that is online sales. She's doing really well for herself too. We have to make it quick. She lives here on this next corner."

"Is that her car?" Noah asked.

"Yeah. I'm sure she walked over. Most people walk where they can around here."

Jackson pulled under the awning past Megan's little orange Karmann Ghia.

"Elegant. Fast. Expensive."

"What?"

Noah hadn't even realized he'd uttered the catch phrase, but it applied. He could see Megan as being all of those. Elegant. Fast and expensive. "The Karmann Ghia. That's how that car was described back in the day. Cute cars."

"You can see the DeSoto through those windows," Jackson said.

Noah bailed out of the truck and ran to the window. Sure enough. Original black and gold. And it looked in excellent condition. He was dying to get in there and touch it, examine it, really see what was under the hood. He hadn't been this excited since he got to second base with Jenny Lou Sable in the sixth grade.

He turned and jogged back over to the truck. The passenger window was down, so he leaned inside. "I've got to have that car."

"Right."

"I'm serious. I don't even care what it costs."

"She'll never sell it. It was her father's and he passed away recently."

"I'm charming. I'll get it."

"Not gonna happen."

"What makes you so darn sure. Everyone has a price."

"You don't know Megan."

"I'm going to have that car. I'll put money on it that I'll have that car."

Ford put his hand up between the two guys. "Now, y'all slow down. You know how your bets always get out of hand."

"No. Not this time. I'll take that bet, Noah. Because you really are California dreaming if you think she's gonna sell. Hundred bucks."

"I bet she'll sell and I bet she'll do it by Sunday morning. Make it a thousand."

"You're a lunatic, Noah. Seriously. You're going to put a thousand dollars on the table that you'll get that car from her this week?"

"Yeah. Here's how sure I am." He took his phone out and dialed California.

"Who are you calling? It's like ten o'clock."

"Hey, Sonya. How're things going? Great. I just found the '58 DeSoto Adventurer. Nope. Not kidding. Set up a cross-country hauler. For next Sunday. Yep. Here's the address."

"You're not serious. You don't have anyone on the phone."

"Only seven o'clock on the West Coast. I do too. Here." He shoved his phone inside the cab of Jackson's truck and pressed speaker. "He doesn't believe I'm ordering transport before I have a deal on this car, Sonya."

"Hello?" Jackson looked skeptical.

"Hi. Who is this?"

"Jackson. Who is this?"

"Sonya at California Dreaming Restoration."

"You really work for Noah?"

"Sure do. And trust me, if he's found a 1958 DeSoto Adventurer that he likes . . . he'll get it. This is not the first time he's had me do this. Got that address for me?"

Jackson gave him a what-the-heck look. "The address is 12665 Water Loop Way."

Sonya's soft voice livened a bit. "That's gonna cost you, boss. About as far coast to coast as you could possibly get, huh?"

"It's worth it. Set it up." Noah hung up the phone and laughed. "This is great. Even worth sacrificing a brother of the bachelorhood to the old ball and chain of matrimony." He slapped the side of the truck.

"Go ahead. Talk your big game. You just get your money right. I'm going to do something extra special for Angie with your thousand bucks, so you better be ready to pay up. On Sunday. No IOUs."

"I'm ready, but I won't have to pay. Come on, let's get the hell out of here before she shows up."

Noah hopped into the backseat. Jackson pressed the gas pedal before Noah even had the door closed, which was probably a good thing, because if he'd had the chance he'd have walked back over and taken one more look. His heart raced. He'd been afraid to let himself even believe it could be true. The last one he'd found had been one long plane ride from California to Boston, and then a three-hour car ride, only to find that the car had been ridden hard and wrecked a few times. Poor thing was cockeyed on its frame, kind of crabbing along the road. What a disappointment that had been, but that one sitting in the old gas station bay sure looked like the real deal.

Granddad. I found the one, man. And she's not getting away.

Chapter Six

Noah sat at the kitchen table, sipping milk from a coffee cup. Unable to sleep, he'd come downstairs and made himself at home in the kitchen. He'd planned to rummage around to find some cookies, but Flynn was organized to a fault.

Everything that didn't move seemed to be labeled, right down to the pantry shelves. Her pantry looked like a grocery store. He'd had an inkling that if he looked hard enough, he'd find a cash register and he could probably swipe his debit card and make a purchase. But since he hadn't found one, he helped himself to an assortment of cookies. A couple from each of the boxes on the *C* section of the pantry. Right between the cake flour and crackers. Didn't seem logical to him. But alphabetical was about as good as any order once you got used to it.

He dipped an oatmeal chocolate chip cookie into his mug. How was he supposed to sleep knowing the car of his dreams was right here practically under his nose? Dying to see it up close, and hear it run, he was going to have to figure out a way to connect with Megan . . . and quick.

A noise came from the front of the house.

He stopped chewing, straining to listen.

Another rattle. At the front door, and not like someone coming home with a key, besides he was pretty sure everyone was here and accounted for because the lights in Flynn's part of the house had been dark when they got home.

He sat up straight, stretching to listen closer. There it was again. He sprang to his feet. Maybe crime was alive and well, even in this small town. It only took about six long-legged steps for him to get to the front door. Surprise would be on his side.

He waited off to the side as the handle jiggled once again.

Someone lunged their shoulder into the door, and it flew open. Something fell to the ground.

Noah didn't wait to see what it was. He spun and looped his strong forearm around the shoulder of the intruder, pulling them tight against his chest with his bicep around their neck.

Then something heavy landed right between his shoulder blades, knocking the breath out of him.

More than one? He didn't let go of the intruder, although he was off balance.

The lights came on and the shrill sound of a woman's voice thrummed through his mind. "Stop! No!"

"Damn." Noah rocked forward, loosening his grip. But when his eyes focused on the person who he had in the choke hold, and then up into Megan's wide-eyed expression, he knew that the element of surprise had worked. Only now he was the one surprised. "I'm sorry. I didn't—"

Flynn wriggled free from the choke hold. "What were you doing?" Flynn pushed his arm down and stepped away from him. "You scared the pure living daylights out of me."

"Out of us," Megan echoed, her purse dangling from its straps in her white-knuckled death grip.

"I thought you were an intruder."

"It's Boot Creek. Not Los Angeles."

"It's the middle of the night. And for the record, we don't have intruders where I live either, but it can happen anywhere."

"It's an old house. The door sticks. Jeez." Flynn rubbed her chest, which was tinged pink. "What are you even doing awake?"

He straightened, stretching the dull ache down the middle of his back.

"I'm sorry. Did I hurt you?" Megan asked.

A shadow of alarm touched her face. He leaned forward, with his hands on his knees. "Knocked the breath out of me." He blew out a few breaths and then stood back up. "I won't need to worry about your safety. That was a hell of a punch, but I'm fine."

She lifted her purse in the air, and shrugged. "I have this bad habit of collecting way too many coins in the bottom of my purse. It's heavy."

"I can vouch for that." He blew out another breath and stretched his back. "I'm pretty handy, Flynn. Why don't you let me take a look at the door while I'm here this week? To make up for the choke hold."

"That would be helpful. Thanks," Flynn said looking him up and down.

Noah suddenly felt very underdressed in a pair of shorts. They'd been drinking. He knew that glassy-eyed look girls got at closing time. But then again, closing time would have been an hour ago. "You girls been out on the town? It's, like, three in the morning."

"We know that. What are you doing up?"

"Couldn't sleep. Thought I'd have a snack when I heard someone coming in. I thought you were asleep."

"You have that much crime in California that you automatically attack when you hear a noise?"

Okay, he asked for that. He may have overreacted to the situation. "No. Not really."

Megan burst into a fit of giggles. "Can you imagine if he'd actually knocked you out, Flynn? That would have been the biggest news the

Boot Creek Bugle ever covered." She turned to Noah. "I bet you'd have made the front page."

"Which would have sucked because I'd have upstaged the bride. I'm sure that's the headline this week."

He pointed toward the kitchen. "I think I'll go back and finish my snack." *That was embarrassing. Thank goodness Ford hadn't woken up. He'd never hear the end of it.*

Flynn and Megan walked into a room off the back of the B&B. He heard the door click closed behind them but could still hear them talking. He shoved the cookie in his mouth, then washed out the mug and put it in the dishwasher.

What'll you do for an encore, idiot?

He walked to the front door, grabbing one of the house keys off of the bureau next to it. The last thing he needed tonight was for Flynn to lock him out by accident. He didn't have any idea if Megan was coming back out or not, and he wasn't about to go knocking on Flynn's room door to find out.

Get some air. Maybe they're so drunk they won't even remember.

He was more awake now than he'd been when he first came downstairs. Not too bad a thing, though. Maybe this would be enough of a body clock interruption to get him on East Coast time.

Outside, the night sky was dark. No interruptions from big city lights or the glow from neighboring towns. Just a dark, inky night sky and stars. A bird chirped out a warning from a nearby tree. Or maybe it was a hello. Frogs sounded like out-of-tune banjos twanging back and forth.

He hadn't heard these night sounds since he'd been back in Franklin, Tennessee, growing up. He'd spent as many nights as he could sleeping out in the tree fort he and his dad had built together. Even long after a tree fort should have been cool, into his teens, he'd taken refuge in that thing. He could have just as easily ended up like that tree house guy on the cable network, building swanky adult tree houses, had he followed the love for building that his dad had had rather than the love for cars that he and his granddad had shared.

A trio of chairs nestled up to a small round wicker glass-topped table on the far end of the porch. He plopped down in one of the oversized chairs and propped his feet up on the porch rail. It was one of those no temperature nights. Not too hot. Not too cool. Just enough breeze to keep the air moving.

He stared into the sky.

Being a Scorpio, he still remembered how to find that constellation from his days in the planetarium back in grade school. The stars and planets had always fascinated him. Maybe that's why fast cars interested him. Kind of like rocket ships, only on Earth where he had control.

The bright star Antares was easy to spot; he followed that to the outline of the scorpion. He wished on Antares as he often had as a kid. Of course, he couldn't remember if he'd ever had any of those wishes come true. But one more wish to get that car deal sealed soon or later couldn't hurt.

Then again, he was pretty sure he didn't need any help. He'd made those kinds of deals hundreds of times. This was in the bag.

Wishing on stars was a kid's game.

Megan walked out of the front door, pulling it closed quietly behind her.

"Hey," Noah said.

"What?" She turned and stomped her foot. "Do you have a goal of scaring a certain number of people each day?"

His smirk irked her. "What? You don't do anything without a goal?"

"Maybe. And what's so wrong with that?"

He shrugged. "Might miss something if you don't take the time to be spontaneous once in a while."

"I'll take my chances, thank you. Why are you always popping up out of nowhere? What are you doing out here?"

"Sitting. Enjoying the quiet. I couldn't sleep."

"Now I probably won't sleep—thanks for the middle of the night adrenaline shot." She started down the porch, and then turned to walk up the block.

Noah got to his feet and jogged out barefooted to catch up with her. "You walked?"

"I didn't fly."

"It's the middle of the night."

"It's not that far."

"I could walk you."

She turned and pulled her hands on her hips. "Oh, really. And then who is going to walk you back to be sure you don't get lost? You go back to the inn. I know my way home, thank you very much."

"I was just trying to be nice."

"Well, don't. I kind of prefer to take care of myself."

He raised his hands in the air. "Got it. Loud and clear." And he liked her more and more. She was feisty. And she had his car. He wouldn't let her get far for long.

"Thank you." She flipped her long hair over her shoulder and walked away, her long beach curls bouncing with each step.

Noah reluctantly let her be. Taking slow steps backward in the direction he'd come. He didn't turn his back on her. She was too good a sight to waste.

~

Noah could barely drag himself out of bed the next morning. Even the smell of bacon and Ford giving him a hard time for missing the home-cooked meal wasn't enough to help him shake the cobwebs.

That last gander at Megan walking down the street last night had been just as mind-consuming as the possibility of the car of his dreams being within arm's reach.

But he'd stalled as long as he could. They'd all come in town early to help Jackson get ready for the wedding. Getting his bachelor pad ready for his ready-made family, that is. Jackson had decided early on that he could use their collaborative brute force to make easier work of getting his stuff moved around, and then Angie's things packed up and moved in. But a few weeks ago that had become the secondary priority.

Jackson had challenged them to help turn a guest room into the best boy's room they could dream up for his stepson. Noah had had a race-car bed when they were kids, and Jackson had coveted that thing. Heck, all his friends had wished for one just like it. The bed Dad had built had been made out of MDF, and that wood-wanna-be weighed a ton, but Noah was going to do one better—and it was going to blow little Billy away.

He got out of bed and rounded up Ford to head over to Jackson's house.

~

And when they rolled up into the driveway, Jackson was standing in the middle, staring at the huge crate that had been dropped off.

"When you said delivery, I thought you meant like a box from UPS," Jackson said. "What the heck?"

They guys piled out of the rental car.

"This thing was delivered by a big rig with a Tommy lift. I don't think we're moving it." Jackson leaned his whole weight into the crate. It didn't budge.

Noah clapped his hands together, rubbing them together in excitement. "It's fine right where it is. The stuff inside is smaller."

"What exactly did you ship here? You're not human trafficking, are you? You could send a whole crew of workers in this thing. Hello, anyone in there?"

Noah walked over to Jackson's truck and helped himself. "You said you wanted to build some kind of car-themed bed for Billy. I told you I'd send some stuff." He pushed tools and boxes of screws from side to side. "Don't you have a hammer or a crowbar in here?"

Jackson walked over, and without so much as a glance, reached in and pulled out a hammer.

"Thanks." Noah went to work on the wooden crate. "Billy's bed is going to rock. This is going to be the room I'd have for my kid . . . if I were going to have any. Which I'm not."

Jackson said, "You could practically fit a whole Smart Car in that box."

"That wouldn't be saying much. And that would not be the car bed of a boy's dreams either."

The wood groaned as Noah pried, loosening the corners of the crate. He tossed the smaller pieces off to the side. "Kindling is free."

"Good. We'll need that in a few months," Jackson said.

"Derek and Ford are going to start painting the room while you and I work on the bed," Noah said.

"All right." Jackson shoved his hands in his pocket. "Looks like you've got a plan."

Noah tapped the side of his head. "Oh, yeah. Right up in here." He started pulling out pieces, some wrapped in brown paper, others rolled in bubble wrap. "Some old license plates. We can use them for lamp shades, or shelves for Billy's toys, or something. I thought they'd be fun."

"Cool."

The next wad of paper looked like a loaf of bread. Noah unrolled the paper, revealing a stack of car emblems. "Chevrolet. Dodge. Ford. GMC. Mercedes. Porsche. Even VW. An assortment of brands here. Don't want to influence the young mind."

"That box is huge. There's got to be something bigger than that stuff in there."

Noah smiled. "You bet there is. Help me lift this out, Ford."

Ford walked over and helped Noah hoist a long, thick rectangular box over the side of the crate. They laid it on the grass.

"Do the honors," Noah said to Jackson, who whipped out a pocketknife and slit the packing tape. He tugged one side of the box down, exposing a bright turquoise corner of steel. "Get the heck out of here, man."

"Nice. Right?"

Jackson used his knife to remove the rest of the box. "Billy is going to go ape. He may never get to sleep."

The turquoise blue Chevrolet truck tailgate had all the character of a truck used hard. "I thought Angie might like it better if we at least gave her a color she could live with."

"The blue is perfect. And the dents and scrapes make it even cooler. You thinking this will be the headboard?" Jackson looked like he'd just had his first kid and was going to hand out cigars. "Man, this is going to be great. Think my new bride would mind sleeping in a truck bed?"

"Uhh, yeah. She might not be a fan of that. And that will not be the headboard." Noah worked the other side of the box. "*This* will be the headboard."

Jackson leaned in to get a look. "What is it?"

The guys teamed around the crate each grabbing an edge. Only about six inches deep, it was every bit of four feet high when they pulled out the metal shell of the back of a '57 Chevy truck cab, back glass window and all.

Noah reveled in Jackson's delight.

"You've outdone yourself, man," Jackson said.

"I'm not the biggest fan of matrimony, but Jackson, I want you to be happy and I think it's really cool that you wanted to do this for your new son. You're going to be a great dad."

"Thanks, Noah. That means a lot. You're going to make me a hero in that kid's eyes."

"I'm betting you're already kind of a hero in his eyes, but I'll take the Best Man of the Year trophy anytime you're ready to hand it over." Noah slapped Jackson's hand in a high five. "There are a few other things in this crate I tossed in. We may or may not use. Some taillights. I don't know how long all of this is going to take, but you can always do some other projects later with this junk, or just toss it."

"Did you get the paint for the room?" Ford asked. "Because while y'all are going gaga over car parts, Derek and I need to get to work on priming and painting that room."

"Got the paint, and I've already taped off the woodwork," Jackson said. "I'd hoped I'd get that room at least primed before y'all arrived. Didn't happen, though. It's been crazy trying to keep it a secret from Angie."

"No problem. We can knock it out," Ford said. "I brought beer. We can do anything with enough beer."

"And pizza. We'll need copious amounts of pizza," Noah said. "You do have pizza delivery out here, don't you?"

Jackson shook his head. "Nope, but it's only two blocks. We can call ahead and someone can go get it."

"And y'all think Alaska is remote," Ford teased. "You have to drive for your pizza? May as well be with me up there. All right, so we need a designated driver else someone has to walk to pick up pizza."

"I'll be the designated driver," Noah said. "I'll do anything to not have to wield a paintbrush."

"Painting isn't your kind of dirty is it, Hot Rod?" Ford snickered.

"Shut up," Noah said, even as he laughed at the old nickname.

"For the record, I take exception to the fact that Noah picked out a Chevrolet truck to turn into a bed. Then again, all the Fords are probably on the road, getting something done."

Jackson and Noah both groaned. The old Ford vs. Chevrolet digs had been going on between them since high school.

"I've got you figured out though, Noah. You were afraid of putting a Ford in there because the kid might see the word Ford on the tailgate every day and think of me. You want to be the favorite. I get it."

Without fail. Things always ended up a competition when the four of them got together.

Jackson said, "Yeah, well, you could have come up with the plan and sent parts."

"No one asked me." Ford wiped his wet hands on the back of his pants, and then repositioned his ball cap.

"That's because I was afraid Billy would end up sleeping in an igloo if I asked you." Jackson nudged Noah and laughed.

"Alaska isn't all igloos, polar bears, and ice fishing, you know. Y'all are watching too much reality TV."

"That's probably true, but still," Jackson said. "You're not really the carpenter of the group. Plus, Noah offered when I told him what I was thinking about doing."

"I'd have given my right arm for a bed like that when I was a kid," Ford said. "When we get it done, I call dibs on test-driving it for sleepability."

"You always call first dibs," Noah teased. "I bet that means something. You probably need some kind of therapy or something."

"Funny."

And it was funny, because out of all of them, Ford was probably the sanest one. They'd all gotten college degrees, none of which were being used, but Ford had at least used his college degree to supplement his income so he could remain flexible enough to do the things he loved. He'd taken the reins of his uncle's company and quadrupled its size in record time by leveraging the internet and social media. That tiny Tennessee company turned into a nationwide product distribution center. Now they shipped their exclusive beef, turkey, venison, and bison jerky worldwide. And Ford hadn't wasted any time hiring someone to work that company so he could take off to explore the country.

Ford had been the first to succeed in business. First to leave Tennessee. And always first to call dibs. That was Ford in a nutshell.

Too bad Noah hadn't left Nashville when Ford had. He could have avoided that first disaster of an engagement altogether. He wouldn't be surprised if some of those folks were still harboring ill feelings toward him for calling off that wedding, even though Jenny was happily married with three kids now.

"If you're still standing after the bachelor party, we'll let you sleep in the cool bed." Noah shot a glance toward Derek. "This guy never could hold his liquor."

Ford stopped what he was doing. "We're doing a bachelor party?"

Derek shrugged. "I thought Angie said y'all weren't doing that?"

"Why wouldn't we?" Noah said.

"I don't know. No one said anything."

"It's an unspoken rule. Man-law." Noah looked to the others for confirmation, but neither Jackson nor Ford looked overly interested in the prospect of a party-hard ruckus out on the town. This was going to take some doing.

"We aren't going to be doing a bunch of stupid shit the night before the wedding," Jackson said. "I already told Angie there wouldn't be any shenanigans."

"Why'd you go and do that?" Ford asked. "You know Noah throws the best parties ever."

Noah had planned to have one hell of a throw down. Had even found a couple places they might go, but now he was having second thoughts.

"I don't want to feel like hell on my wedding day," Jackson said. "It's like a hundred degrees and I'm going to be nervous, all I need is to spew, hungover, on Angie's high-dollar wedding gown. Not the kind of memorable day I want to give her, or the example I want to set for Billy."

"That's cool." Three days ago Noah would have felt differently. He hit town determined to save Jackson from Angie's clutches, but Jackson was happy. It was plain to see. Angie was great and when Noah saw Jackson with Billy, he'd be lying if he didn't admit he was a little jealous. "You've got a whole lifetime ahead of you. We don't have to start it off on a drunken stagger."

Jackson's expression softened.

Noah propped the old bed rails from Jackson's spare bedroom between the truck cab and the tailgate, then pulled a tape measure out and started a list of the bolt sizes he'd need to put this together. "I think we can mount the tailgate to a couple of painted six-by-sixes to give it a good sturdy frame."

"That'll look great," Jackson said and the other guys nodded in agreement. "You said something about license plates as the lamp shades. I've got the old lamps from that room. Ford, do you think you could do something creative with that?"

"Sure thing." Ford gave a little two-finger salute from the bill of his ball cap.

Jackson handed him the stack of license plates.

"I'll get some paint the color of the truck so we can paint the dresser to match, and we'll use the car emblems on that."

"Billy has a ton of cars and trucks. Matchbox types, some Tonka trucks too. What do you think about some shelves to get those off the floor? You ever step on one of those barefoot? Those hurt like heck."

Noah winced. "I've never stepped on one, but my dad used to say that all the time. I can't tell you how many times I was put on restriction for that as a kid."

Derek spoke up. "I have an idea for some shelves. Ford and I will take care of those. But for now we're going to get that painting done."

"Cool." The two of them went inside, and Noah turned to Jackson. "Can I have the keys to your truck? I want to go get these supplies. We'll have this room done in no time."

Jackson tossed his keys to Noah. "I really appreciate everything. You've really come through. But then, you always do."

Maybe that was because he didn't have someone else trying to sink her nails into his free time, or making him feel bad for doing something on a whim. Being single had its privileges.

Chapter Seven

Noah drove from Jackson's house back to Main Street. He parallel parked along the street at the end of the block. This town was so different from where he lived back in California on the water in Malibu, but not so different from where he'd grown up.

People smiled as they walked by, and he found himself nodding and saying hello back, falling back into those casual feelings of his youth. The tall building that housed the hardware store was tucked between a law office and the corner pharmacy.

Noah had his doubts that he'd get what he needed here. It looked like a pretty small place from the outside, but as he opened the door and stepped inside, his hopes increased. The storefront was narrow, but it seemed to go on forever. This building must take up the whole city block from front to back.

The old building had character. The fourteen-foot ceilings were maximized with floor-to-ceiling shelving along the outside walls, and one of those old brass rail ladder systems like you'd normally see in a library so you could get to the taller shelves. The place seemed to be stocked to the gills.

Hand-painted signs hung from chains labeling what inventory was on each aisle.

He stood staring at the sign, trying to decipher where he needed to go.

"Can I help you find anything?" The gravelly voice came from somewhere beyond, but Noah didn't see anyone.

"Bolts?" He answered loud enough to be heard.

"Up one aisle and to the left."

"Thanks, man." Noah followed the instructions and stood facing a wall of dark pecan-stained wooden cubbies. Or maybe they were just dark from years of use. Either way, there were boatloads of them.

He was tempted to count them and do the math to see how many bins really were in front of him. Even the big-box home-improvement stores didn't seem to have this many items in their inventory of bolts and hardware.

Each slot held a box of bolts, nuts, or other fastener. Some of the boxes were factory labeled, others labeled with permanent marker in shaky print. Some new and shiny, others weathered and peeling. He started going through the old bins of bolts, looking for what he needed.

Sliding the bins in and out, the contents shuffled like coins dropping from a slot machine. It didn't take him long to figure out the order of things. Then, he easily put his hands on the bolts he needed. Counting them out, he started grabbing nuts to match, spinning them onto the end of the long bolts, one by one.

"What are you doing here?"

He glanced over his shoulder toward the feminine voice, out of habit mostly, because it wasn't like he knew anyone around here. He hadn't expected that the woman had been addressing him. Megan stood there in worn-out blue jeans and a white tank top. The way her sunglasses were pushed on top of her head, loose tendrils of brown hair fell across her cheek. Her wide smile was easy, and her eyes danced playfully.

"Hey there. I'm getting some supplies for a project I'm working on."

"You haven't been here but a few days and you've got a project?"

"Jackson and the guys, we're making something."

"Something besides trouble, I take it." She eyed him with curiosity. She'd clearly already passed judgment on him.

"I'm not the kind of guy who gets into trouble."

"Because you walk a straight line? Or because you're good at not being caught?"

"How did I make such a bad first impression with you? Was it something I said?"

"No. I was just asking."

He nodded slowly. *Why do I even care what she thinks?* He felt this unexplainable need to set her straight. To fight for his own honor. And that was a first. "You can trust me. Just like you're keeping things on task for the bride, I'm doing the same for the groom."

"That's comforting. I guess I should thank you."

"That'd be nice. I mean, we are kind of on the same team. We could even help each other."

"I was going to check in with y'all tomorrow and be sure everybody had picked up their tuxes, and that Jackson had a gift for his bride."

"Now you can just ask me." He put his hand out. "We'll keep this wedding on the rails, partner."

She shook his hand. "I plan to do exactly that. So, partner, what is it that you boys are working on that is keeping you out of trouble?"

He wished he'd just said hello. Now he was kind of stuck. *Awkward.* "Can't tell you. It's a secret."

Her lips pursed in a cute little pout. "I can keep a secret."

"Sorry. Man-law. Can't tell a girl." He shrugged.

She narrowed her eyes. "Is it a surprise for Angie?"

"Guessing is as bad as telling." He zipped an imaginary zipper across his lips and shook his head.

"Fine." She walked on by, and he gently grabbed her arm.

"Not so fast. What are *you* doing here?"

"It's a secret." She raised her shoulders and let them drop with a cocky jerk of her head.

"That's not fair. Mine really is a secret. A surprise. You don't want me to ruin a surprise, do you?"

"Well, as long as the surprise isn't for me, then I don't think you'd be spoiling it. I can keep a secret."

"That's not the point."

"Isn't it?" She raised a brow.

She had a point. No one would know that he told her, if she kept her mouth shut. But then women were notorious for not being able to keep a secret. At least all the ones he knew were.

"Tell you what," she finally said. "I'll tell you mine, if you tell me yours."

"I have a feeling yours isn't as good as mine."

"Guess you'll never know."

"Fine."

The smile stretched from ear to ear. No way he could resist that.

"I love secrets," she said almost bouncing with excitement.

"No." Noah shook his head. "I'm not falling for that. You have to tell me your secret first."

"Okay, but you can't change your mind. A deal is a deal."

"The mantra of my life." And he planned on making another deal with her soon.

"No covert operation. Not a secret or a surprise. Just air filters for the air-conditioning unit, and a few other little things I need for the shop."

"That's not a secret."

"Who says what's a secret?

"So, you're picking up stuff for your candle factory?"

"Yep." She pushed the hair away from her face. "Although the term *factory* is used rather loosely."

"When are you going to let me come over and see you in action?" Her head was puzzled by new thoughts. Was he flirting? "There's not all that much to see. Seriously, my factory is really just a small operation."

"Nothing wrong with starting out small."

"I don't have any plans to get bigger. I like the size of my business. I'm perfectly comfortable financially, and I've got one assistant who can keep things rolling so I can drop and travel when I get the urge. It's kind of perfect."

"Sounds like it. I'd still like to see it." He couldn't let this opportunity pass. "And I'd love a personal tour of that fancy car of yours too. You don't see cars like that every day."

"Happy to show it to you. Whenever you like. Just say the word."

"How about now?"

She looked stunned.

"I won't be long. Look." He showed her his list. "I only need to find a couple more things and then I'm done. I can't stay long, but I'd love to see your place."

"Well, okay. I guess I could wait for you. I have to get Mr. Owen to get my stuff for me. I'll meet you at the counter."

"Perfect." He practically ran through the aisles, collecting the things on his list like he was on some kind of million-dollar scavenger hunt.

It wouldn't take him long to see that car and verify that it really was in as good of shape as it had looked through the window. Please, please, please, don't let it be ruined with aftermarket junk. That would break his heart.

He glanced at his watch. The guys would wonder what was taking him so long, but they'd just have to forgive him.

They would survive a little while longer without his help. He was dying to get his hands on that car. The sooner the better.

~

He couldn't stay long? That sounded perfect to Megan. She could be polite. Show him around and then get on with her day.

She walked over to the counter to wait, hitching herself up onto one of the old metal barstools that were usually filled by men gossiping.

"Megan Howard. How're you doing, you beautiful young thing?"

"Hi, Mr. Owen. I didn't even see you sitting back there. I'm good." He seemed to have shrunk. As a little girl she'd always thought of him as a tall white-haired man. Now he looked more like a gnome that had been here as long as the building. Centuries maybe.

"You still making those girlie candles?"

"Yes, sir." His wife was one of her best customers. "Business is good."

"That's good. They sure make my house smell nice. Put the wife in a good mood too. That's always a plus. What do you need today?"

People swore her candles had mood elevators in them, but really it was just all stuff found in nature. "I need a new filter for my air conditioner, ten-by-twenty. And some four-foot fluorescents."

He pushed himself up out of the chair and grabbed a filter from the rack behind the counter. "Just one? Cheaper by the multipack."

"Just one. I'm hoping I'll finally get a new unit soon."

"You'll save a bundle when you upgrade that old system." He paused, like he was trying to remember what the other thing he was looking for was. "Okay. And a box of fluorescents."

"Yes, sir."

He shuffled down an aisle, and then she heard the same rhythm of scuffling leather against concrete coming back. He held the carton of bulbs under his arm like a football. He laid her items on the counter, and then opened the big journal that stayed on the desk. She sat patiently as the old man wrote in her purchases, painfully slowly. But the monthly billing was convenient, so she went through this ritual every single time she came in.

Noah walked up to the counter and put his things down, then handed Mr. Owen a paint chip. "I need a quart of paint this color too."

Mr. Owen closed the journal, and then took the paint chip. He held the paint chip up, squinting at it, then laid it down on the counter and put his magnifying glass over it. He mumbled the color code to himself and scrawled it in big letters on a scrap of paper. "No problem. What are you painting?"

Noah glanced over in Megan's direction.

"Yeah, Noah. What are you painting?" She fluttered her eyelashes, overdoing the innocent look.

He pressed his lips together. "A piece of furniture. Wood. I don't want to have to do much sanding, so whatever you think."

"I've got just the thing." Mr. Owen left to mix the paint and Megan leaned against the counter. "Furniture, huh."

"Yep."

"Must be for Angie."

He grinned. He was enjoying toying with her.

"Why else would it be a secret if it weren't for Angie?"

"For me to know."

"And me to find out?"

"I didn't say that."

"Maybe it's unspoken. Ya know. Like the man-law."

Mr. Owen walked back over to the counter with the quart of paint. "Got everything else you need, son?"

"Yes, sir."

Megan thought Noah's eyes were going to fall out as Mr. Owen carefully looked at each item and wrote out a sales slip. "Old school," he mouthed to her.

Finally, Mr. Owen finished writing up the sale. Noah had paid cash, which resulted in a painfully slow count back of change before they finally got outside.

"Lord. I could have made that paint with crushed berries in the time he took to write it up."

"Things are slower in small towns."

"That? That in there? That wasn't slow, that was like reverse. Is it yesterday?"

His grin was playful and showed off his dimple. Had she always found dimples this sexy?

"Nope. Still today," she said with a laugh. "You coming with me or not?"

"Where's your ride?"

"I walked. It's just around the block."

He pointed toward Jackson's truck parked at the curb. "Hop in. I'll drive. That way I don't have to backtrack when we're done."

He was in a hurry. "Fine."

Noah put her box of fluorescent tube lights and air conditioner filter in the back seat of the crew-cab truck, and then held the passenger door for her.

"Where to, madam?"

"Up to the next corner and turn left. Then two streets and I'm on the right."

There was no traffic, and since it was just a few blocks, there wasn't even time for small talk.

"Over there? Balanced Buzz?"

"That's me."

"Sounds like a medical marijuana shop. What kind of candles are you burning? I guess that could be considered aromatherapy." His laugh carried.

"Not that kind of buzz." She fluttered her hands out to her side like wings. "Like bees buzz. I use beeswax. All natural. All the way."

"Ahh. Okay." He pulled into the driveway. "You drive a Karmann Ghia?"

"I do. I love this car. My daddy bought it for me in high school."

"Your daddy was quite the car guy, huh?"

"A car guy. A real estate guy. An into-everything guy."

"You never wanted a new car with all the new bells and whistles? Usually the types who are environmentally conscious are driving those little micromobiles like a Fiat or Prius. Saving the environment. You doing all the bee-buzzing candle stuff, seems funny you're driving that."

"I limit my carbon footprint in other ways. Besides, I can work on this car. Daddy taught me everything I needed to know to keep it going. It's a fun ride, and a convertible. What more does a girl need?"

"That sounds like a loaded question." He pulled the truck through the canopy and parked to the side of her car. "This okay?"

"Yep." She opened the door and hopped down out of the truck. She grabbed her stuff out of the back seat, and then headed straight for the front door. When she opened it, Noah was still hanging back, checking out her little car.

"She's in good condition." He ran a hand down the fender. "Not a speck of rust."

"Thank you. I did have it repainted a few years ago. It's been a great car, though."

"This was always one of my favorite years, although the '57 had a nice low sleek look. It's a '72 right? This was the last style change before they quit production."

"I know," she said, trying not to sound snippy. What? Did he think just because she was a girl, she didn't know cars?

He looked up and his gaze met hers. "Nice-looking. A fun ride."

Was he talking about the car or her?

"Come on in. I'll show you around."

"What inspires a girl to live in a gas station?"

"A deal too good to turn down, and a little imagination." She walked inside and put her stuff down on the repurposed church pew in the entry hall. "Maybe a lot of imagination. Honestly, my dad was a hot mess, but he knew real estate and boy, he could grab things at a steal."

"Everyone's got their gift."

"Yeah, well, Farley Howard was known as one of the savviest real estate dabblers around these parts for a long time. That is until he retired."

"What happened then?"

"He went flat-out crazy. Long story. He used to flip properties for big profit. Anyway, by then he wasn't buying and selling like he had been, and Daddy signed the deed to this place over to me."

He followed her.

"It's like my dad knew when the timing was right to move the properties. The golden touch, people would say. This place was a gift to get me started out of college. Told me that it had all the potential to bring great things to me whether I decided to live in it or sell it. I wasn't too sure when I first got it. But I love it now. I can't really imagine living or working anywhere else."

"Show me around."

She strolled down the hall toward the open space with the long wooden tables. "This is kind of a work area. I use it for projects, get-togethers. Whatever." She turned to the left and walked down the hall, opening a glass door to a room that was nearly all white, except for playful little bumble bees painted along the walls in random spots that all led to the vat where she boiled down the honeycomb. "This," she said, "is where the magic happens."

He leaned in. "Looks like a laboratory."

"Candle making is very scientific. I think that's why I like it so much. It lights both the creative and analytical sides of my brain. I used to do a lot of painting, but that was a long time ago."

"You paint too?"

Why'd she even mention that? Pulling the door closed behind her, she pointed to three large framed canvases across the way. "All of those are mine."

"You did these?" He stepped forward and looked at them closer. She saw him look at the signature in the corner.

"Yes. That is my signature." She pulled her hands to her hips. "Really? You think I'd lie about something like that?"

"I don't know. Guess I never met someone that really painted something that I liked before." He stood looking at the detail of the car in the painting. "You're really good. You sell these?"

"No. I have a whole studio full of work. I still dabble once in a while, but just for fun."

"I want this one. It's the DeSoto."

"Yep." She had several that anybody would recognize as the DeSoto, but this one had been an abstract she'd messed around with. Just a small section of the car, but it created an interesting exercise in light and shadow—one that did have a way of captivating anyone who passed by. "You recognize her lines."

"From a mile away." His voice held a tone of admiration that made her fidget.

She was always a little uncomfortable when people looked at her work like this. It was a little like being naked. Her whole soul out there for the viewing. And this, the painting, was a part of her life she couldn't relive. There was a reason she'd kept most of her paintings tucked away behind a closed door. And she wished now she'd left them all there.

He ran his hands along the shiny chrome frame. She'd picked it out because it looked like the bumper on the car.

"The frame is nice too. Pretty."

"Guys love shiny things. I do too. Seemed like a good fit." She tried to hide her discomfort with the joke. Being so uncomfortable with people ogling her artwork was part of how she knew painting wasn't her path. Kevin, Megan's ex, had been her buffer for that. He'd made her believe in a dream that wasn't meant to be. As much as she'd loved painting, she didn't want to show or sell her work. Can't make money like that. And it didn't matter anymore. She hadn't been able to pick up a brush with artistic intent since Kevin died. And thinking of him now disturbed her.

A rush of anxiety assailed her. "How about I show you the inspiration? The car."

His face lit up, and he dropped his attention from that painting faster than a kid turning his nose up to spinach.

Relieved to get off the subject of her art, she practically race-walked to the garage bay and flipped a row of light switches. The dark glass panels that lined the whole wall brightened, and light danced on the shiny curves of the automobile—metal and flawless paint.

That view still made her heart smile. Daddy's loving touch had been the last one on this car. If she'd only been able to bring herself to offer up the plan of the limo instead of the Adventurer. Knowing the car was going to be out in the elements, and probably get dirty, this weekend still made her gut ache. But somehow her friendship had to win this battle. She knew Angie too well. If one little thing didn't go off just right, she'd start worrying that it was some kind of sign.

Noah walked slowly toward the glass. Almost trancelike, he blinked.

She opened the French doors to the garage, and Noah walked right past her like she wasn't even there. Making his way around the car, he pulled something out of his pocket and held it along the fender of the car.

"What is that?"

"Sorry. Occupational hazard. It's a magnet. If a car is full of Bondo, it's an easy way to know without getting all up under the car." He slid the magnet in his hand across the car, taking his own sweet time. "This is one beautiful car."

Daddy would have loved the compliment and Noah's obvious appreciation for his favorite car.

"How many miles?" he asked.

"Twenty-seven thousand seven hundred and forty-two."

He laughed. "Approximately?"

"There was one previous owner, but there weren't more than like a few thousand miles on it when Daddy got it. Daddy said that that wasn't even enough miles to be real love."

"My granddad had one of these. Exactly like this. I mean, exactly."

"I didn't think they were that popular."

"Wasn't as much that they weren't popular as it was there were not many made, so you just don't see them around. Especially the convertibles."

"Daddy would take me out on drives. We had a lot of good memories in this car. My mom never did care for it, especially with the top down."

"Do you mind if I pop the hood?"

"Not at all. It's a V-8."

"I know." He was almost curt with the response.

Well, excuse me.

He lifted the hood and leaned in. A soft whistle filled the air. A swirl of pride coursed through her.

"This is one sweet car." He shut the hood and then took the bottom of his shirt and wiped his fingerprints from it. "Really nice. Do you know what you've got here?"

"I do." Her nose tingled. The memory tugged at her, threatening to pull her down. "The last memory I shared with my daddy. She's a beauty."

He looked like he was getting ready to say something, then he walked back over to the door where she was still standing. "This was a Mobil gas station?"

Relieved for the shift in conversation, she said, "Yeah. Did the red Pegasus give it away?"

"Pretty much. It's cool how you've worked in the memorabilia around here."

She flipped the lights off and closed the door behind them. "Man, you should have seen this place when I first got it. One heck of an eyesore. Out of business for going on forty years, the dust on top of years of grime had piled up so thick, we had to scrape everything down before we could even begin to start cleaning it."

"Grease and dust can build up quick. That's why I'm such a stickler about cleanliness in our shop."

"It took a while, but I had help from my friends. I'm pretty resource-ful. Bartered with contractors, worked for two months straight cleaning up, trucking off old parts and junk just to get the place prepped for repair and renovation."

"Well, you'd never know to see it now."

"I wanted to embrace its previous function as a gas station rather than try to camouflage it. That never seems to turn out well. So I shopped auction houses and went to swap meets to find just the right memorabilia to decorate with, trading some of the finds from the garage to recoup my investment."

"Ever go to the big one in Pennsylvania?"

"Yes! Got some great stuff there. Who knew people would pay for old oil cans."

"You'd be surprised. I love all the old memorabilia. They have a whole day set aside for that stuff at the big auctions every year. You ought to meet me at one of the big auctions some time. There's one coming up in Scottsdale. It's a blast. I'll bring you in on my VIP."

"That would be fun."

"You could even sell your car there."

"Oh, I'll never sell."

"Never? That's a long time." He laughed. "Show me the rest of the place. I'm assuming you don't sleep in the car."

"No. I have an apartment on this end of the building."

She gave him a quick tour through her place.

Noah leaned into the doorway of her bedroom. "That red Pegasus headboard. Is that sign vintage?"

"Yes. It was here at the gas station when I got the place. There were a bunch of old signs. It was hard to pick what to keep and what to sell, but that Pegasus caught my eye right off. Besides, it was too darn big to haul anywhere. It wouldn't even fit in the bed of a pickup truck unless we stood it up and I was afraid it would get broken."

"Really cool," he said. "There's a lot of that kind of memorabilia at the auctions I go to. Real Americana stuff."

"You should've been here back when I got the place. We'd be so filthy at the end of the day going through all the old, oily, greasy stinking mess that we used to tease that we needed to build a car wash just to get us clean."

Noah grinned. "I can imagine. Did you make that old gas pump lamp out of things you found here?"

"No, the glass-cylinder visible gas type pumps that had been part of this station were long gone by the time I got it. There were a couple old metal ones that some guy paid me pretty good money for. They looked like junk to me, but they more than paid for that one."

"When was this place originally built?" he asked.

"Nineteen thirty-three. At least with the building being mostly block there'd been surprisingly few problem with the building structurally."

"The thirties makes sense," Noah said. "The exterior has that almost art deco design to it."

She turned and led him back out to the living room.

"I like this place and I like you, Megan Howard."

A blush rose, heating her cheeks. People usually teased her about her odd choices, but Noah seemed to get it.

He looked at his watch. "I got to run. Think I could get a rain check to come see the rest of the place?"

"Sure."

"Cool. I love this place. It's really great. You've done amazing things with it, and I'm blown away by your talents."

"Thanks. I'll admit when Daddy signed over the place I wasn't very appreciative, but I've really grown to love it."

"I can see why. It suits you."

He made her nervous when he held her gaze like that. "Out this way," she said, trying to recover. "But you said you'd tell me your secret."

He got to the door and stopped. "I did, didn't I?"

"Yes. Are you as good as your word, Noah Black?"

"I am." He pointed his finger at her. "Not a peep. Especially not to the other girls."

"What is it?"

"We're all working on a room for Billy. It'll be a huge surprise for Angie too. All Jackson's idea. He's really excited about it."

"You're kidding? That is too sweet."

"Yeah. We're making him a bed that looks like a truck."

"He will go wild. That kid is one hundred percent grade A boy, and does he love trucks. I take that back. He loves anything with an engine in it." She suddenly felt closer to Noah. "Jackson's the best. Angie will cry like a baby."

"Good tears. But I hope I'm long gone before the tears fall. I'm not good at seeing a girl cry, no matter what kind of tears they are."

"Oh, they'll be good tears, and I promise you I will not mess up this surprise. It's too good."

"You know," he said. A crease formed across his forehead. "Since you're in the know, anyway, maybe you could help out."

"How's that?"

"What if you paint a mural in the room? Just a couple cool things on one wall, make it look like the truck is at an old gas station, or driving through the countryside. Take some creative license."

"Really?"

"Yeah. Why not? Wouldn't it be fun?"

"Actually. Yes. It would be. I'd love to be part of this surprise. Billy is the best kid."

"Great. Well, the guys are priming and painting today. I'm putting the bed together. Why don't we get together tomorrow? Can you swing some time in your schedule?" He walked to the door.

"Totally."

"Where's your phone?"

She turned to the old church pew behind her and took her phone out of the top of her purse. "Here."

He typed in his number. "Text me. And if you want to sketch. I can try to paint in some of the big spots to help get it done quicker, if that will help." He handed her the phone back.

She stuck her hand out to shake his. Because it was awkward to be exchanging phone numbers with him. It wasn't like a date, but still a little weird.

He shook her hand then tugged her in and dropped a kiss on her cheek. "Deal."

"Deal," she uttered.

He walked out the door, leaving her still reeling over that tender little kiss. Not a sexy one, but damn if there wasn't something hot about it.

She leaned forward, watching his long stride as he headed for the truck.

Or maybe it was just him.

Chapter Eight

Megan stood there, watching Noah pull away. She raised her hand and waved. What had just happened?

It was nothing. He was just being nice. Maybe that's what California boys do. It was a kiss on the cheek for heaven's sake.

She went back to the worktable and put the boxes of candles on her work cart and wheeled them out to her car.

Loading the boxes of candles into her car to take them over to Katy and Derek's for the reception, she kept thinking about Noah's short visit.

She put the cart up and locked the door. Just across the bridge that rose above the creek, she peered over the side. The water was low again today. No surprise. With little rain and record heat, water was at an all-time low. She put on her blinker and slowed a little. The right turn onto Blackwater Draw Road always came up quicker than she expected. She still had misgivings about this stupid road.

Even after all of these years.

When she was a teen, guys loved to scare the girls by driving down this dark twisty road and turning the lights out. She'd been in the car with a group of friends after a football game when her boyfriend thought it would be funny to try it. She'd screamed, begging him to turn on the lights. Only, when he flipped the lights back on, the surprise was on him, because a deer was right in front of them. He'd slammed on the brakes, sending her reeling across the car, and banging them both up pretty good. It was a stupid thing to do, but fortunately no one was seriously injured. She'd never forgotten it, though.

The trees hung over the road, heavy with summer leaves, like a tent. It was the heavy foliage that made this road so dark at night.

Once she made the elbow curve, Piney Creek Lane was on her right. Only now, there was also a sign for the retreat. There had never been a sign at the end of the lane for the inn before. It had been a well-kept secret. Now, that Derek and Katy would be catering to folks from all over the nation, they were making changes. Like this sign. Simple. Elegant.

Lonesome Pines Inn
~ A Healing Retreat ~

Fashioned in the same tradition as all of the business signs in Boot Creek, it was black with bold lettering. The pop of color against the chalkboard-like black background mimicked the look of those art pieces where you covered every square inch of a paper with the most vivid colors in your crayon box, then covered it in black paint. Once it dried, scratching the black paint revealed the surprising rainbow of random colors. It was Naomi who had started that tradition in this town. She'd once been well known for her art in that media. Megan had a feeling those signs were one thing that would probably never change in Boot Creek. It was part of the charm of the town.

She'd heard that Katy had commissioned someone from back in Atlanta to make the sign as a gift to Derek.

Things are probably feeling real for them now.

Derek's dream was coming true. It wouldn't be long before they were fully operational. A good thing for everyone in town.

The last time Megan had driven down this lane, it had been a potholed, mucky mess. Today the road was level as her car crunched through a fresh layer of gravel—dust wafting up behind her.

She parked her car in front of the door. It was hard to think of Lonesome Pines as anything but Naomi Laumann's home. It was a landmark—part of Boot Creek history. The fame of Naomi's late husband's brother, Dillon Laumann, and all the stars he and her husband, Marshall, used to bring to their tiny little map-dot of a town had made this place a big deal.

Things were changing in Boot Creek. It made her a little sad. But Lonesome Pines had never looked better. Katy and Derek's personal touch showed on the porch, which now flaunted huge hanging baskets of bright blue petunias.

Katy came out front. "Can I help you carry something?"

"Yes. That'd be great. The place is looking great." Megan pushed her sunglasses on top of her head, and took one of the boxes out of the trunk and handed it to Katy. "Think you can carry two?"

"Sure." Katy lowered her arms and Megan stacked another box on top.

Grabbing the other two, they headed for the porch.

"Last night was so much fun," Katy said.

"I had a good time too. What'd you think of Jackson's friends?"

"Nice guys. Very different. Kind of a weird combination of guys to have all been best friends. Wonder if they were always that different?"

Megan had wondered the same thing. She could picture Noah and Jackson teasing Ford as a thirteen-year-old boy, but then again it was hard to say. As confident as she was now, back in high school she'd been kind of a loner, preferring to spend her hours with a sketch pad rather than on center stage like Angie, but they'd still been besties.

Katy balanced her boxes against the house and her knee as she twisted the handle on the screen door and threw it open.

Megan caught it with her foot and held it open for Katy.

"Thanks." Katy led the way in and down the hall to the left.

Megan stopped in her tracks. The foyer looked completely different. "Oh my gosh! I always knew this place was huge, but this is the first time I've ever seen it without all the stuff in it!"

"I had the same reaction. And Naomi didn't even take all that much from here. But moving the antique desk and the boxes and boxes of memorabilia she had displayed really opened up the place. The fresh paint made a big difference too."

"It looks great. Feels *very* different."

"Yeah, I think it's starting to take on its new purpose."

"Where do you want these?" Megan asked.

"Let's put them in this first room to the right there. I've been starting to line things up for Saturday in here. For a simple reception, it sure has a lot of components."

"These things have a way of taking on a life of their own."

"I don't mind. It's good practice for the festivities we'll offer a few times through the year."

Megan and Katy placed the boxes on a table near the door. On top of the bed, there were stacks of white tablecloths and boxes of napkins.

"Y'all having fun without me," a voice came from down the hall.

Katy ran toward the door. "That's Angie. She said she was going to come by this morning."

"She probably doesn't know what to do with herself since yesterday was officially her last day at Blue Skies Café. I don't know what they are going to do without her."

"Hey girl," Katy called out as they walked toward Angie.

"I just brought the wedding favors over," Megan said.

Angie's lips formed a perfect O. "How'd they turn out?"

"Beautiful," Katy said.

"Of course they did. I can't believe in less than a week I'll be Mrs. Jackson Washburn and on a plane to Tahiti."

Megan snapped her fingers. "I knew I was forgetting something." She pretended to write on an imaginary notepad. "Pick up coconut bra and sunscreen." She dropped her hands. "'Cause you know it's the maid of honor's job to be sure the bride makes good fashion choices."

"What would I do without you?"

"Beats me. But on a happy note, we're only days away and the checklist is nearly complete. Not even one hitch in the plan so far."

"Could y'all knock on some wood right now? I don't want any hitches . . . not even one."

All three girls knocked on the dark wood trim.

"That was loud enough to ward off all evil," Katy said.

"Good," Angie said. "The guys are all going to get their tuxes checked today so that Carla can do any last minute adjustments. Jackson says he's got all of that under control, so I'm letting him go with it."

"Great. I'll check that off my list."

"Well, maybe you could check in. You know, just to be sure they're all taken care of."

"You've got it. I had them on my list for Wednesday, so I'll keep that on the schedule."

"Perfect. Do you girls want to get together tonight? Jackson said he and the guys have plans."

"Oh, great. 'Guys on the town' is always trouble." Megan cocked her head. "Then again, at least if they're determined to get into trouble, they're doing it early in the week. We'll have time to bail them out of jail."

"They aren't going to get into any trouble. Derek's going to be with them. It'll be fine," Katy added.

"You think? I kind of got the impression Noah could cause some trouble," Megan said, thinking about that feeling he'd stirred up in her earlier.

"But he's cute," Angie said. "And from what Jackson says, he makes a pretty good living. Turned his hobby into a big business. Must be nice to get paid to play."

"Probably a *player* too," Megan said. "I know his type."

"Be nice, Megan," Angie said. "One of these days you're going to have to lighten up and give men a chance to show you who they are before you shove them in a category."

"Not today—I'd thought we'd still be working on things for the big day, but we're so caught up why don't we do a girls night?"

Katy brightened. "Y'all can come over here. We just set up the new media room. We can pop in one of our old faves or see what Hallmark Channel has on tonight."

"Works for me. I'll text Flynn." She pulled out her phone and worked her fingers over the keys. "She's in."

"That'll be good." Angie bit down on her lower lip. "So, can I ask y'all about something?"

"Sure. What's up?" Katy moved toward the living room. "Come on in and sit for a minute."

"I don't know if I should be worried or not, but I had the oddest conversation with Jackson this morning."

Red flags snapped in Megan's mind. "Odd how?"

"Well, you know the guys are moving all my stuff into Jackson's house when he and I leave, right?" She sat down on the couch and pulled a throw pillow to her chest.

"Yes. Lucky for you. I hate moving," Katy said. "Not having to do your own packing is the best gift ever. Do you know what a moving company charges to do that?"

"No idea."

"It's a lot. Of course, no telling where things will end up if they unpack the boxes for you."

"I told them to put all the boxes in the garage, grouped by location. Since Jackson and I are combining households, no doubt there'll be stuff we won't need. I already donated quite a bit to the women's shelter."

"We'll help you go through the rest of it when you get back." Katy sat down next to Angie.

"What's got you concerned?" Megan was determined to get them back on track. Red flags were nothing to ignore. Maybe she was the skeptic of the bunch, but someone had to be the voice of reason.

"Right." Angie looked away for a moment. "Maybe it's not really a concern. It seemed out of the blue. Just kind of hit me funny."

"I'm sure both of you are going in about a million directions right now. Nothing like trying to play host, plan a wedding, get ready for a move and a honeymoon, and work, and raise a kid all at the same time."

"Put it like that . . . I need a nap," Angie said.

Megan folded her arms. "Me too, and I'm not doing any of those things. Probably ever! Are you stalling?"

"No. So he asked me if I'd ever consider moving."

Megan straightened. "You mean, like, to another town?"

"Or another state," Angie said. "We'd never really talked about that before and I have to admit I felt a bit cornered by it."

"I would have too," Megan said.

"I don't really know why, though." Angie leaned against the wall. A worry line appeared as she squinted. "There's nothing tying me to Boot Creek. I mean all y'all are here, but we'd be best friends no matter where I lived. It surprised me that he just brought it up."

Katy stepped closer. "Does he have a job offer in another place? I mean it's not like he grew up here. He kind of just wandered into town, if I recall."

"Right. No. He said he was curious." Angie shrugged. "Should I be worried?"

Megan relaxed. "I wouldn't sweat it one bit, Angie. I can tell you what I think this is."

"What?"

"Those friends of his. They are trying to put doubts in his head. You heard Noah's backhanded speech the other night at your going-away celebration." Megan took a step back and raised an imaginary beer in the air. *"Skills he wouldn't need if he stayed single,"* she said impersonating him with exaggerated swagger. "Please."

Angie leaned forward in laughter. "He did not act that douchey."

"It was in the subtext."

"You like him." Angie's mouth dropped wide. "You think he's hot."

"I do not like him. He's hot. No question there, but he's one confidence point away from gold chains and an open shirt."

"Oh, he is not. He's super sweet."

"He's not that bad. I'm just teasing, but I'm not interested. You are mistaking me for Flynn. But seriously, what is it about men? It's like there's this unspoken pact to try to keep each other from making a commitment. Do y'all think they teach that in gym class while they are telling us about our periods?"

Katy dropped her face into her hands and groaned. "I hated that talk. I can still remember coming out of that classroom thinking all the boys were now thinking about us having periods. Why did I think they told us all the same thing?"

"Relax. I'd put my money on Noah stirring up trouble. That guy is the poster boy for being single. I don't know what his problem is." And as soon as it came out of her mouth, she wondered why she'd just said that. He'd been nice to her.

"Some girl probably broke his heart once."

"Jackson told me that Noah had been engaged before. I bet she broke it off. Or left him at the altar."

Katy pulled her hands to her heart. "Oh, my gosh. He'd be scarred for life."

"He probably deserved it then." Megan pushed her hair back over her shoulder.

"You sound bitter," Katy said. "I thought I was the only one that had a recent past bad enough to make a person feel that way. But then Derek swept that stuff aside so fast I barely had time to pout about it. Something in your past I don't know about?"

"No. I just hate that men manipulate women for their own agendas."

Angie inhaled a deep breath. "It was a long time ago, Katy. Megan's not sharing the whole story, and it's not likely it even matters. But can we at least agree that all men are not like Kevin?"

Katy's mouth took an unpleasant twist. "Sorry. I didn't know."

"It's fine," Megan said, but it wasn't fine. When it came to Kevin, her feelings were just as confused and bruised as the day he died and the ugly truth started seeping out. That he'd not only lied, but stolen from her. "In my head I know that, but I just can't forget it. I never want to feel that way again. And you're right, Angie. I can't go casting those stones against everyone I meet. Just because I don't want to be in a relationship does not mean that it's wrong for someone else."

"My ex broke some big trust, but they aren't all that way. It's not always a gamble," Katy said.

"Fine. But no one ever broke Noah's heart."

Angie started smiling. "How do you know that?"

"I asked."

"Really? When? And how the heck did that come up in casual conversation?" Katy and Angie grinned.

"Stop grinning like that. It was nothing." Megan regretted saying anything. "It came up last night. No one is that hell-bent against marriage without some reason. If that reason is in the form of an ex-wife or a broken heart, I get it, but there's that whole breed of self-centered bachelors that require quick and early screening. I screened him."

"If you're not looking for a man, then why are you screening them?" Angie's eyebrow rose so high it practically hid behind the swoop of her bangs.

"Public service."

"You want someone in your life. Admit it."

"No. I'm different. It's in my DNA. I'll never marry."

"How can you even say that?" Katy asked. "Spinsterhood days are over."

Angie said, "You don't really believe that. Tell me you're joking."

"Look at my parents. They couldn't make it work. If I take after my mom, then I'll let a man walk all over me. And I almost did. Look what happened with Kevin. I was absolutely clueless about what was going on. I will not put my guard down like that again. And if I take after my dad, well, we all know his story. So why bother? I'm a divorce waiting to happen. No, thank you. Besides, I have a good life with a lot of freedom to do as I please. I like that. Why mess up a good thing?"

"It can't be that bad," Katy said with a laugh.

"Whatever." Angie rolled her eyes. Megan hated it when Angie did that. "You're just jaded. You never think straight when it comes to relationships. Kevin's faults were Kevin's. Not yours. And I still think if you ever let your guard down long enough to feel something, you'd feel differently."

"That was deep, Angie. If I let my guard down to feel, I'll feel something. No kidding. That's the whole idea. Back to the real question at hand."

"And off of the subject of you?" Angie said in a mocking tone.

"Exactly. Would you, Angie Millwood-Drinkwater-almost-Crane, ever consider living anywhere else?"

Angie let out a long sigh. "Boot Creek is all I've ever known. I didn't even get to go away to college like the rest of you did. My whole support system is here. But my life will be with Jackson and I adore him, and so does Billy. I know we'd be fine no matter where we were."

"Then all is well," Megan said and Katy nodded in agreement. "Okay, so we're doing girls night here tonight?"

"Yes!" Angie raised on tiptoe. "Please. It'll be great. I'll bring stuff to make margaritas."

"And I'll make my special *queso* dip," Katy said.

"Great. I'll bring some chips," Megan said. "This will be fun. It's been too long. You want us to pick you up, Angie?"

"I'll probably come over early and help Katy."

"Okay, we'll be here around seven. That should give Flynn time to visit with her grandparents and get them fed before we come over."

"This is perfect. Y'all are the best friends. You're keeping me sane this week," Angie said.

"I'm pretty sure that's our job."

"And our pleasure," Katy said. "I can't wait to fire up the media room. Derek went hog wild with it."

"Great. I've got to run. I've got work to do today if I'm going to be playing with you gals all night." She turned to leave then stopped and turned back. "Angie, don't let those boys cast any doubts. I know I may not be the marriage advocate of the group, but I do believe you and Jackson are going to have a wonderful and long-lasting relationship." And Megan meant it, but now those words had her worried. Not about whether Jackson was holding something back, she really didn't think that was the case.

But did she really have a problem that was going to keep her from ever trusting someone? She'd never thought of it as a problem before. She was happy. Wasn't she? Had Noah somehow gotten under her skin? Maybe a teeny bit? Were the girls right?

She got in her car and headed home with that niggling worry dancing in her mind. Was there more happiness out there that she was missing out on? She tried to picture her life differently. Imagining herself in Angie or Katy's position, with a man who loved her and didn't mind showing it. A true partner in every way. Could there be someone out there for her like that? She couldn't even picture it.

She cranked up the radio.

I'm perfectly fine with that.

Chapter Nine

Megan had tossed and turned half the night. In her dreams, Noah's eyes—*those gorgeous, dark chocolate eyes that seemed to lock in like he was gaining access to her mind*—had the power to access her thoughts.

Her pulse quickened. That dream had been sexy. Really sexy, and now that was a little awkward. How was she supposed to act around him after what she'd seen in that dream?

It was odd enough to meet a guy who seemed to be her doppelgänger from a behavioral standpoint. They had a lot in common, but the last thing she'd expected was to be dreaming about him. She wasn't even interested in him. In anyone.

Lord, help me.

This probably wouldn't have happened if she'd talked to the girls about Noah last night. But she was afraid she'd slip up and ruin the surprise about Billy's room. And they'd been drinking. She sucked at keeping secrets when she'd been drinking.

Besides, they'd have jumped to the wrong conclusions for sure. She wasn't interested in him like *that*. She just found him . . . interesting. He made her smile, and that was fun. Nothing wrong with fun.

But one thing did bother her.

Everything Noah had said mirrored her thoughts and beliefs exactly, but she questioned that. He'd seemed aloof, and a little too overconfident in what he'd said. Did she seem that way to others? She hoped not.

She remembered in psych class talking about how the things that trigger a negative response in you are the very things you need to work on.

Great. Now I'm psychoanalyzing myself. And based on one semester of a class I barely paid attention in. If that didn't spell trouble, nothing did. And Kevin is not like every man that I'll meet in my life? How can someone who'd been gone for so long still influence me so much?

She got out of bed and checked the weather on her phone. Another scorcher.

~

With a pair of denim shorts and a T-shirt from the annual Blackberry Festival on, she tugged her hair up in a clip and then tucked her ball cap into her big purse. She'd want that when she was painting later, but her mom would have a fit if she wore a hat into a restaurant.

Mom has a lot of rules. She'd probably have a conniption over her not being dressed up to meet with Flynn and her grandparents for tea at Bella's this morning anyway, but really no one else would even be there. Not like the queen was going to show up for a spot of tea. It was Boot Creek for goodness sake. And she had things to do today.

The heat hit her the instant she stepped out of her house, the humidity hanging from her like a winter-weight poncho.

She walked up the street and over to Bootsie's Bouquets to pick up Mom. They'd walk over to Bella's together from there.

Just as Megan crossed the street, her mom walked out of the store, looking at her watch. "I was getting ready to go ahead and walk over without you. Thought maybe I got the plans mixed up."

Megan knew better. It was her mom's way of putting her on notice for pushing the timeline. Mom always liked to be early. Poor Daddy had gotten the brunt of that passive-aggressive behavior when Megan was a kid. Now she was the sole recipient.

Lucky me.

"We've got plenty of time. Come on," Megan said, hooking her arm through her mom's. "How are you this morning?"

"Good. I have an order of flowers coming in this afternoon. I'm trying a new place. Can't wait to see how they look."

"That should be fun." And just as she lifted her gaze from the sidewalk, Noah came walking toward them wearing a car-show T-shirt that showed off well-defined muscles she hadn't noticed before.

"Megan?" The beginning of a smile tipped his mouth as he lifted his chin. "Good morning."

Mom tugged on her arm. Megan knew she was dying to know who the good-looking man calling her name was.

"We are bumping into each other all over the place," she said to him as they got within just about six feet of one another.

"Sure are. Am I going to see you today?"

Why did she find him vaguely disturbing? Like she wanted to see him, but didn't? "I was thinking I'd text you when I'm on the way."

"Looking forward to that."

"Noah," Megan said, trying not to screech from the pressure her mom was applying to her bicep, "this is my mother. Everyone calls her Bootsie. She owns the flower shop next door. Noah is in the wedding."

"Hi, Bootsie. Very nice to meet you. Noah Black." He offered a nod.

Mom tittered like a schoolgirl. "You must be the one from California? You're too tan to be the Eskimo."

He laughed politely. "Yes, ma'am. I'm the Californian, by way of Tennessee anyway."

"What part of Tennessee? I love Nashville. Country music is my favorite."

"I grew up just outside of Nashville. In Franklin, home to lots of the biggest country music stars."

"You're so lucky."

"Well, I haven't been back in a long, long time." Noah said. "I'm surprised we didn't meet the other night. I can see the resemblance between you two. Megan obviously gets her good looks from your side of the family."

"Thank you," Bootsie said.

Megan watched her mom nearly coo at the compliment. "We're off to meet some friends. I'll catch up with you later," she said, steering her mom forward before she tried to invite him along.

"Sounds good," Noah said.

Megan forged ahead.

"He is delightful."

"He's nice." When Megan glanced back over her shoulder, he was standing there, watching her walk away. A little tinge of excitement raced up her spine.

"I think he likes you."

"He lives in California."

"But he's cute. You think he's cute, don't you?" Bootsie exhaled a long sigh of contentment. "Well, I think he's really very good looking. You could do worse."

"Thanks, Mom." Why her mom wanted to always fix her up with someone was beyond her. Look how bad her marriage to Dad had ended up. Why would she want that for her daughter? Of all the people who should understand why she wasn't hot to trot to get into a relationship, you'd think it would be Mom.

They stepped inside Bella's to see Flynn and her grandparents already seated at a table. The white tablecloth looked pristine against the dark wood of the walls. The table was set with perfectly matched china and goldware. Very elegant. A three-tiered porcelain tray held an assortment of bites to eat along with the requisite tea.

One level was nothing but scrumptious looking pastries in an array of colors—lemon yellow, strawberry red, an amazing carrot cake, and brownies with a dark chocolate glaze the color of Noah's eyes.

Noah's eyes? Stop.

She glanced over at Flynn who was staring at her. Megan hoped she hadn't just said that aloud. She smiled and grabbed a lemon bar and held it to her nose, inhaling the citrusy sweetness.

Like her candles, each delicious nugget she picked up teased her with appealing aromas—herbs, fruits, and chocolatey sweets. She inhaled the tangy lemon and burst of sugar, maybe even a tiny hint of lavender, before nibbling the tasty bite.

Sweets and savory sandwiches were passed around the table as they chatted. Bootsie and Flynn's grandparents filled in most of the conversation. As they started getting deeper into a conversation about the economy and the local mill closing down, Megan leaned over to Flynn and tapped her on the hand.

She looked up.

"What do you think of the groomsmen?"

Flynn's features became more animated. "I think they're great." Her brow wrinkled. "Don't you?"

"Yeah." Megan shrugged. "Of course, I mean they are all really different, but nice. I . . ."

"What?"

"They'll be gone at the beginning of the week. I don't know. I was just wondering if you were kind of interested in Ford? I mean, he seemed to be interested in you, but he lives in Alaska. That would just be crazy, right?" Or even if it was just California.

Flynn picked up her cup and took a sip of tea. "That's just geography. If it's meant to be, it'll happen no matter what. I'm going to enjoy the moment and not even think about it. Just let things happen. Kick a few doors open. If it's right, they won't slam back on my hand."

"And you're okay with that?"

"Why not?"

Why not? Good question.

"Is this about me or about you?" Flynn asked, casting a direct challenge.

Megan stuffed a tiny quiche in her mouth to keep from having to answer. Unfortunately it was spinach and some kind of weird cheese that was more pungent than tasty. Thank goodness Flynn's grandmother pulled them right back into the conversation. Perfect timing.

She hadn't been here but a couple of times before, but Flynn was very close to the family who owned the place. He'd been a chef in Asheville, North Carolina. A big deal. But Megan was more the pizza-and-beer type. She could only do so much of this pinkies-up tea stuff, despite her mother's wishes.

An hour was about the length of Megan's sit-still span, and that had passed about twenty long minutes ago. She kept waiting for a moment where she could gracefully exit, but the conversation seemed to drone on without anyone taking a breath.

Finally, Bootsie stood. "Oh, goodness. I'm having so much fun that I've lost complete track of the time. I have a shipment coming in. You will forgive me, won't you?"

Her mother looked panicked. But for once, Megan did want to thank her.

"We all understand," Megan consoled her. "I'll walk you back to the shop."

"You don't have—"

"I don't mind at all." She shoved enough to cover her mother's and her own tab into Flynn's hand. "Should be enough for the tip too." She stood and pushed her chair in. "It was so great to catch up, and Flynn, I'll see you tomorrow at the spa."

"You sure will. I can't wait."

Megan waved and herded Bootsie right out the door.

"Slow down, Megan." Bootsie said, half out of breath. "We're not in that big of a hurry."

Megan slowed down, and then it came: "What else do you know about that handsome Noah? I can't stop thinking how nice he seemed," Bootsie said.

She had half a mind to lie and tell her that he was out of prison on probation. That would shut her up. "Don't know much about him. Just that he's a car guy."

"Like your dad."

That's all she said, and Megan wasn't sure if that was meant to be good or bad. But since she didn't drone on and on trying to talk her into pursuing him, she was perfectly happy with whatever it meant.

She kissed her mom on the cheek. "Have a good day, Mom. I'll talk to you later."

Bootsie unlocked the shop and took down the "Be Back In Thirty Minutes" sign that had been hanging in the door for the past hour and a half and probably would be back up in a little while when Bootsie took her lunch break. You could set your watch by Bootsie's lunch hour. Hungry or not, she'd take that break.

Megan walked back to her place and loaded up a box with paints and brushes. She grabbed a box of chalk, a couple of pencils, and a sketch pad out of a drawer on her workbench.

She carried the box to the front door, and then set it down while she put on her hat. Checking herself in the mirror, she went back to her bathroom and applied a little mascara, which led to a little foundation and a little blush too. Some lip gloss and she was finally satisfied, if not regretting that she even cared.

She texted Noah, and he responded right back.

Megan: Sorry it took so long. Still need help?

Noah: Come on over. The guys went out to lunch, but I'm here.

Megan: Need me to bring anything?

Noah: Just your smile.

Can't paint with a smile. She shoved her phone back in her purse and carried her box of supplies out to the car and put it in the passenger seat. An unexpected swirl of excitement coursed through her as she got in her car to head over to Jackson's house. Probably just the thrill of being part of the surprise.

But as she pulled into the driveway, that swirl picked up speed when Noah walked out. He'd changed out of his jeans into a pair of cargo shorts and a black T-shirt. A T-shirt that fit him just right. The logo, silver-foiled California Dreaming Restoration, had her doing a little California dreaming too.

"I brought some paints and stuff," she said as she got out of the car.

"Great," he said. "Can I carry something?"

"In the passenger seat." With guns like that he could carry her stuff anytime.

He walked around and got the box then led her inside.

"Billy's room is going to be the one at the end of the hall."

She followed him, and then stood in the doorway with him. An empty canvas. The walls had been primed and painted a soft buttery yellow, giving the room a sunshiny look. Blue painter's tape still covered the power outlets and wood trim.

"Is it dry?"

"Yeah." He tugged a piece of blue tape from the switch inside the door. "I was getting ready to put the plates back on."

"Well, let's figure out what and where we're painting. No sense in having to tape things up twice."

He stepped into the room. "True. I was thinking we'd just paint that one wall. I'm going to put the bed right here." He looked like an airline attendant showing passengers the lighted exits as he motioned where the bed would go. "A dresser here."

Megan agreed. The wall he'd pointed to would be the focal point of the room. "Great. Did you have something in mind? I was thinking maybe a gas pump like the one in my house, and then we could do a sign with the prices that also includes a section with chalkboard paint. He could draw there if he wanted to."

"That's a cool idea."

"I brought some chalkboard paint with me." She pulled her hands up on her hips, imagining what it would look like.

"Maybe a garage-bay door with 'Billy's Garage' written over top?"

"That would be cool. What color palette are we working with besides the yellow on the walls?"

"I'll show you."

She hesitated a moment, watching him in profile. He was handsome, and although her first impression had been of all swagger, there was a fun boyish charm about him too. An old feeling, one she'd kept under control, prickled at her senses. Suddenly noticing every angle, smell, and move that he made. She let him guide her out of the room and to the garage. He blocked the doorway. Then pushed the door open and stepped aside, creating a grand gesture. "What do you think?"

The truck bed took up the better part of the garage. With the tailgate as the footboard and the cab as the headboard, it was no mistaking this was going to be the bed of any boy's dreams. And this was way more safe to concentrate on than the way Noah smelled or looked in the sunlight right now. "I think he is going to be thrilled. That is my favorite style Chevy pickup. And the color. I love it. Was that a stock color?"

"Tropical Turquoise."

"It's great. I bet it was bright as heck back in the day. The worn look just makes it that much cooler. This is the best bed ever. It's going to be like sleeping in the bed of a truck."

"I know. I'm pretty happy with how it's turning out. Look I used the taillights as decoration on the chunky wooden frame."

"Wouldn't that be cool if they worked?"

"Already thought of that. I rigged up a switch right here by the rail. He can use them like a night light if he wants to."

"You've thought of everything." And she wondered what kind of attention to detail he would put into a night out together. Not that she didn't appreciate spontaneity, but she'd always been a sucker for the tiny details too.

Looking at the blank canvas, she wished Jackson had told her about the project himself. She could have been working on this a week ago. "I'm going to sketch something out. This is going to be great. It's going to be bright and playful."

"Do you need my help?"

"No," she said. "Not really."

"If I can be helpful, I'd be happy to help. Especially where you might have big areas I can't screw up."

"Thanks, we can make quick work of it that way. Let's get started." Megan snapped her fingers, all that Noah-talk from Mom and then Flynn's comments had her mind thinking things it really had no right to be thinking. "I meant to bring a paint tarp. Do you know if Jackson has one around?"

"That we've got. There's one still folded up in the closet that we used when the guys painted yesterday."

"Perfect. Then I'm going to go sketch something out real quick."

"I'll get us something to drink. Water, soda, beer?"

"If you've got a cold beer, that'll be perfect."

"My kind of gal."

The quick comment landed on her like a butterfly. Unexpected and soft, its wings slightly tickling her. Nice. Megan went back to Billy's room and sat on the floor. The sketch came easy. She knew exactly what she wanted to paint. The ideas flowed like they hadn't in so long.

Noah walked in with two beers and stood looking over her shoulder. "I like it. This is going to make the room."

"I'm pretty sure that bed is going to make the room, but this will be pretty cool. I'm going to need a few pints of paint, though. Think you could run to the store and get them while I sketch things out and get started?"

"Sure. Give me a list."

"I just need a few basics. I can mix to get pretty much the colors we need, but can you get him to mix a turquoise about four shades lighter than what you got for the dresser, to use for the sky? That should anchor the color scheme of the room and tie things together."

"I'm your beck-and-call boy. Just tell me what to do."

That would be a first. Entirely different from Kevin, who used to be the one making all the plans. Some that she'd never known were even in progress. "Oh, you know what. I had another idea. Do you have a ladder?"

"Yeah. I'll grab it. What else?"

She scribbled what she needed on a piece of paper and handed it to him. "You can get all of it at the hardware store."

"The hardware store? Aw, man. Maybe it's the old man's day off."

"Mr. Owen? He never takes a day off." She could see the discouragement all over his face, and boy did she sympathize. Not that she was about to admit it.

He looked down at the list. "Of course, he doesn't. I'll be back . . . eventually . . ." He turned and then stopped in the doorway. "What am I thinking? I don't have a car."

"Take mine. Keys are in it."

He left and then came back with the ladder. "Here you go. See you shortly. Well, in a while."

She sat there until she heard him leave. Then she raced over to the ladder with a small jar of glow-in-the-dark paint and a skinny paintbrush. She climbed the ladder and straddled the top. Carefully, she painted tiny stars in the shape of the Big Dipper, and then scooted the ladder and did the Scorpio constellation and Leo. Those were the only ones she knew by heart. She reached out to the sides dotting a few random stars."

The paint was colorless, just little wet spots. She scooched the ladder and filled in a couple empty areas with scatters of various-sized stars. It might require a little fill-in work once they saw them in the dark. She hoped it worked.

She hopped down from the ladder, then fished around in her box of supplies for her chalk to start marking out the mural in broad soft strokes.

After a few minutes, she stood back, taking it in.

If she'd ever had a son, she'd have done something just like this for him. She marked a few spots on the drawing she'd done on the sketch pad for the areas that Noah could start filling in, like the sky and the concrete block of the garage. She could come back in, and contour and shade. It would save time.

By the time she heard Noah pull back up to the house in her car, she had the life-sized gas pump well under way. The pop of fire engine red was going to draw the eye right in against the yellow and dingy turquoise of the bed. She let her brush glide against the smooth surface. She never tired of watching the colors come to life beneath her strokes.

"Whoa!"

Megan turned to see Noah's mouth hanging open.

"That looks three dimensional," he said stepping into the room. "Damn, you *are* good. Just how long have I been gone?" He turned his wrist, looking at his watch.

"Thank you." It wasn't that difficult of a thing to paint, and she knew exactly what one looked like since she had one in her house. It'd be different if it had been something she'd never seen before. But it did feel good to be creating. It had been a while.

"Got everything on the list." He handed the large paper sack with the hardware store logo on it to her.

"Great. Can you bring me a big glass of water?" She dug through the bag and laid everything out on the tarp.

"Sure thing. Ice?"

"No. A plastic cup of tap water. For the paint." She lifted her almost-empty beer. "I'll stick with the beer to drink. I need to water down the paint."

"Gotcha."

She took a small clear plastic bucket from her box and mixed in some of the lighter blue paint.

He came back with a large plastic cup of water and two beers.

She accepted the cold beer and took a sip, then took the cup of water and tipped a small splash into the paint bucket and stirred it until she got the consistency she wanted. "This will be perfect." She dipped the brush into the paint and then made a few long sweeping motions across the wall. The motion came with a natural ease. A comfortable rhythm.

Megan dipped a nearly dry brush into the cup of water and then softened the lines she'd just painted. Then, she stepped back and turned to Noah. "Okay, you paint everything above those blue lines with this." She extended the cup of watered-down paint his way.

"You make it sound so easy."

"It is." He looked doubtful. "You can't do anything I can't fix. Trust me, if I was worried I wouldn't let you help. Go to it."

He sucked in a breath and picked up a brush. "Well, one thing I can promise. I'll be faster than Mr. Owen."

"That's not really going to be helpful. Step it up, Buttercup."

"Buttercup? Who you calling Buttercup?"

"You." She tried to concentrate on her work but couldn't help glancing his way playfully. "Chop. Chop. We've got to get this done quickly."

The edge of his smile quirked upward. "Anyone ever tell you that you're a little bossy?"

Anyone? That was an understatement. She came by being bossy honestly. And was dang proud of it. "Hey, you asked for my help."

"I'm not complaining."

"Really? Sounds kind of like bellyaching to me." And during all of that playful chatter, the mural was coming together, just like she'd never stopped painting. A little scary, but more comfortable than not.

"You might not play well with others," he said under his breath.

She smiled, enjoying the banter. "Might be why I work alone." Although he was easy to be around.

He used a large brush to start filling in the blue, and she got to work on the garage and the sign over it.

Using fat rounded block letters, the words *Billy's Garage* now graced a perfect red oval in glossy white.

Megan put Noah to work on the light gray of the cinder-block garage, while she painted the bright caution-yellow curbing around the mock median near the gas pump.

Something plopped against her ball cap.

He did not just drip paint on my head, did he? She slowly looked up at the very moment he sloshed a little too much paint on his brush—again—and dripped paint right on her nose.

"Hey!" She swept the paint with her hand, the slick goop smearing under her fingers across her face. "Careful there, buddy."

He looked down and started laughing. "Sorry." He raised his paint cup up under the brush.

"It's not funny."

Nodding and grinning, he didn't look too sorry. "It kind of is."

She took her brush and dipped it back in her paint and dragged a bright yellow line right down his leg.

"I don't think you know what you started. Mine was an accident."

She stood up. Taking a ready stance. "What?" She rubbed her face on her sleeve.

He laughed, pointing at her cheek.

"Seriously? There's *still* paint on my face. You deserved that."

He thrust his brush forward and made a dot on her arm.

She retaliated with a slash of paint across his cheek, but he already had her looking like she had a case of the gray measles.

"Stop!" She twisted and zigzagged out of his way. "Okay. I'm sorry I started that."

"At least you admit it."

"Well, really you started it, but I didn't let it go. But we better stop before we ruin the mural we just spent hours on."

"You really giving in? Because you look like you're ready to strike."

She giggled. "Yes." She let out a breath and cleaned out her brush.

Noah plopped down on the floor, letting out a huff. "That was fun."

She used a paper towel to wipe as much paint off of herself as she could. "I think I need another beer," she said. "And less help."

"Aww, are you firing me?"

"No. You're a good helper, I guess."

He pulled his shirt off and found a dry spot, reached out, and smudged the paint from her cheek and her arm. "It really was an accident. The first time."

His stomach was perfect. So perfect that she had the urge to stare, take in every ripple and the texture of the skin so she could later recreate it. But he was so close, stroking her cheek . . . softly. She took in a deep breath and swatted at his hand. "You don't have to do that. You're going to ruin your shirt." Only it wasn't his shirt she was worried about. She was having a little too much fun with this guy. She didn't want to give him the wrong idea.

"I don't care. I have another one. We buy them by the case at the shop." He dabbed at a spot of paint on the back of her leg.

His touch was strong yet gentle.

Wanting to tell him to stop, she struggled with herself because truthfully, she was enjoying his touch. But before she could win the battle of her own mind, he stopped and tossed the shirt across the room.

"Back to work," he said.

"Now who is the bossy one?" she teased. Although having him boss her around wouldn't be the worst job she'd ever had. She went to work, glancing back to take another look at his fit physique.

~

Two hours later they had the main portions of the mural filled in. All that was left was for Megan to finish some of the shading and details.

He stepped back, still watching her work. "This blows my mind. I can't believe how fast you are."

The easy feeling had returned. Was it that just enough time had finally passed? Or was there something about *this* project, maybe the purpose behind it, that made her feel one with the paints again? The edges of her mouth tickled, as she realized she was smiling. "It turned out exactly how I wanted it to. You can clean up the tarp and all of that stuff. I'll just use my tray for the rest of the colors. I won't make a mess. There's only a little fine-tuning left to do."

He stepped in closer, resting his hand on her shoulder. "I can't thank you enough for agreeing to do this." He leaned into her space. Speaking quietly. "Running into you at the hardware store was a really good thing. This is ten times better than I'd hoped."

"I'm glad you let me be part of it." *Was he going to kiss her?* She resisted pulling away.

The front door slammed open and the guys came in, hooting and hollering. "Dude. Where are you?"

He pulled back, and she turned back to the mural.

"I didn't tell them you were coming. It's going to be a surprise," he said, racing to the hallway.

She wiped her sweating palms on her shorts, catching her breath from the almost-kiss just as Jackson and Ford herded Noah back into the room and crammed into the doorway.

Jackson pushed Ford out of the way. "Oh my gosh. No way."

Megan smiled. Their reaction was all she needed.

"Amazing."

"Did you do this? I know Noah didn't do it."

"I helped," he said, looking to her for confirmation. "Didn't I?"

"He was an excellent helper. He takes direction well."

"That's a first," Ford said. "Trust me. Noah has never taken direction from anyone. Much less from a woman. You must have superpowers."

"It's true. He's untrainable," Jackson said. "This looks professional. I thought you made candles."

"I do. I used to paint a little too."

Noah grinned. "You should see the paintings in her house."

Ford swung around and stared at Noah. "In her house?"

"Long story." Noah's face reddened.

"Oh I bet it is, Hot Rod," Ford said.

"Hot Rod?" Megan looked to Noah for an explanation.

"Another long story. Shut up, Ford." Noah's face pinkened.

Megan enjoyed seeing him squirm, a little embarrassed, and her mind raced with possibilities of what that old nickname may have grown from. The dimple on his cheek deepened, and that was kind of cute. Cute? No. Sexy. Way sexy.

"Come on, you guys. Let's load the bed in the room. I want to see this thing put together."

"I'll just finish up in here," Megan continued to work on the mural as the guys bickered and joked around, making long work out of the short task of moving the bed into the room.

The bed looked great alongside the mural.

She stood between the painting and the bed, detailing the lines of the garage and shadowing the images. Billy would never notice the difference, but she'd know. It was her commitment to finish anything she started that wouldn't allow her to stop at *good enough*.

Jackson left to get the box spring.

"We're going to go with Jackson over to Criss Cross Farm for a cookout. You coming with us to his old stomping ground?" Ford asked Noah.

"Think I'll pass. I'll work on the room some more. You don't mind giving me a ride back to the inn, do you, Megan?"

"Not at all." Only she caught the glance between Ford and Noah when she answered. What was it between those two?

Noah grabbed Ford by the arm. "Come help me bring the dresser in. I'm going to paint it in the room so we don't have to move it later."

"Okay, man. Hey that hurts."

She could hear Noah as they went down the hall saying, *Hot Rod? You really had to call me Hot Rod in front of her? What the heck? Want me to tell her your nickname? Yeah. I didn't think so.*

She couldn't help but smile. Boys were always boys. They just turned into boys in men's bodies at some point.

Chapter Ten

Noah came back into the room with a stack of newspaper and a bag of supplies.

Megan didn't even acknowledge him as she made tiny, wispy lines on the detailed mural.

He watched her graceful hand sweep across the page. Gentle strokes that created an image with just a few well-placed lines.

He wouldn't mind having this same scene on a wall in his workshop. Something like that would probably cost a fortune, but it would be cool. Maybe he could talk her into coming out for a visit and doing some painting for him.

He tucked newspaper under the dresser and spread the tarp around it. Pulling a screwdriver from his back pocket, he popped the lid on the paint and stirred.

"Wow, that has a strong smell," she commented.

"I guess I should crack a window." He turned on the ceiling fan, and then walked over and opened a window. The heat rushed in.

"Not sure if being high or hot is worse," she said.

"I hear ya. We'll see how hot it gets. It won't take long to paint this." He went to work on the dresser, and it didn't take long to get the first coat on.

"You know," she said. "I think if you give it one more coat, and then we distress it a little, it'll really look better than all shiny and new."

"Scuff up the edges a little?"

"Yeah. We could even water down some brown paint and use it as a glaze. I mean, if you want. I don't mean to be telling you how to do your project."

"No. It's a good idea. I like it."

She smiled, making a quick movement with her shoulders. "Good." She put her brushes in the cup of water and started closing lids and stacking things back into her box.

"You're done?"

"I think so. Did I miss something?"

Not a thing. "No. It's great." But he wasn't really ready for her to leave. "Help me with something else?"

"Sure. What ya got?"

Noah pointed to the roll of bubble wrap on top of his things. "Take a look in that for me. See what you think."

She picked it up and reached her hand inside, looking serious. Pulling out the stack of chrome badges, her expression lightened. "Neat." She shuffled through them. "They're all different."

"Yeah. I'm thinking now it may have been easier if they'd been all the same, but that's what I had laying around. In my mind I was trying not to persuade Billy to my favorite cars, exposing him to an assortment."

"Or a diverse addiction," she said, joking.

"True," he laughed. "Hadn't considered that." He stepped back and dabbed paint on a spot he'd missed. "Thought we might be able to use them somehow on the dresser. What do you think?"

"It goes with the theme." She held one up and squinted, as if trying to imagine what it'd look like on the dresser.

"Think we can come up with something that doesn't look tacky?"

"It'll be cute. Plus they are shiny. Boys love shiny stuff. Especially chrome."

"You trying to tell me that girls don't?"

"I do. But I'm not most girls. Most girls are going to prefer diamonds to chrome."

"Point taken. Different shiny. Kind of like that whole *Women are from Mars; Men are from Venus* thing."

"I think you have that backwards," she said with a grin.

"How about *men are for chrome; women are for diamonds*? Now that would have been a title people wouldn't mix up. It's way more clear."

"Maybe you can write that book."

"In my spare time." He filled in another block and squatted to start another area.

"Right. We all have so much of that," Megan said. "Although I'll admit, a chrome ring might be kind of cool."

"See. There's hope. Maybe chrome is the new middle ground. Maybe I should start making some calls and start my own line of wedding rings." *Did I just use the word* wedding *in front of a woman? What the heck am I thinking? She'll be humming "Wedding March" if I'm not careful.*

"Don't let it go to your head."

"Hard not to. You know women are a big mystery to us." *That's right. Make it general. Not about her. Safer.*

"Trust me, it goes both ways. We don't understand y'all any better than y'all get us. We just don't make it public knowledge. We're better at keeping secrets."

"Hey."

"Hey, I wasn't the one who told the secret about this room."

"You tricked me into that."

"Tricked you? Oh no. I don't think there was anything tricky about it." She sat cross-legged on the bed, watching him paint.

"Fine. I see how you are."

"What are we going to do about the dresser?" She held up the VW and Mercedes badges. "With all of these?"

"Finish painting it and then I think we use the badges right down the center of each drawer. Smallest to biggest. That work?"

"Works for me." She started organizing them in a pile by size. "Tell me, what exactly do you do at California Dreaming Restoration? Do you just gallivant around the country looking for cars to fix up?"

"First off all, I don't gallivant. Ever. No gallivanting. No traipsing. Nothing so haphazard, I can assure you."

"Pardon me. You know what I meant. Do you buy and fix up cars, kind of like a car flipper, or is this company just your way to write off a really expensive hobby?"

"Yes, and yes, and sometimes people gallivant over to me and ask for my services."

"Best of both worlds, I guess. You must stay really busy."

"I do." *And when I get my hands on that Adventurer, it'll probably fall into the really expensive hobby category, but worth every dollar.*

"Do you have employees?"

"Yes."

"How many?"

He did a quick count in his head. Administrative, mechanics, paint and body, the core team, not including the lawyer and accountant. "About eighty."

"Eighty?" She fumbled the VW emblem, sending it rolling across the floor.

He put out his foot to stop it, then leaned over and tossed it back to her.

She caught it midair.

"Nice catch."

"Thanks. That's a big company. A lot of salaries. A lot of responsibility for people's livelihood."

"I'm a responsible guy. Did I not mention that?" As much as she loved that car, he'd have to build her trust so that she'd want to sell it to him. Although spending time with her wasn't really that much of a chore.

"Maybe I thought you were kidding." She scooted off the bed and walked over to the dresser. She held the Mercedes and VW badges up to the drawers. "What do you think?"

"That'll look good," he said, but when she tipped her face toward his with a smile, he stalled out.

"Yeah. I like it too." She leaned casually against the closet door. "I thought you were a small business person like me."

"I think we have a lot in common." He took a piece of sandpaper out of his bag and ran it lightly along some of the edges, exposing some of the brown finish below. "I also think we make a good team."

She looked uncomfortable. He'd said too much. Hell, he wasn't even sure where half of that had come from, but it had been a good day. A really good day. He'd never met anyone quite like her before. But then hadn't he thought that when he'd met Jenny, later proposed, and regretted it like hell? And then Diane too. Was he really going to fall for that again?

"I think I was wrong," she said.

He sucked in a breath. "About?"

"I don't think the dresser needs a glaze. I like it with a little distressing on it. I think you're about done."

"Excellent." He turned and gave her a high five. "Could not have done this without you."

"I wonder when Jackson and the guys will be back," she said.

"Not sure. Why?"

"This room looks great. But if we have time, it would be great to get everything put together. Do you know where the sheets are? I can help you make up the bed. We can surprise Jackson with the finished room."

"Yeah. He bought new sheets, pillows, and stuff. They were in the garage. He didn't want Angie to see them. Let me go get them."

Noah left and came back with three big shopping bags of stuff. "Don't let it get around that I was ever seen with this many shopping bags. This size purchase should only be done online and arrive in boxes."

"I'm on the same page with you on that one. Let's see how he did." Noah unloaded the bags.

Megan looked impressed. "These are nice. Yeah. This will work. He got a comforter too. And this little truck pillow is cute." She motored it across the air, making engine noises that made him laugh. "I think maybe Jackson might have wished for a bed like this of his own once. He seemed to know exactly what to buy."

"You don't know how close to the truth that is."

"How do you know?"

"Because I had a car bed when we were kids. It was the envy of all my friends. He loved that thing. He wanted one exactly like the one my dad built me, except blue. Mine was red."

"Which is why you picked blue for Billy's bed, isn't it?"

"Guilty."

"So this isn't an original idea? You had a pickup truck bed?"

"Oh, no. My dad wasn't a car guy. He was a carpenter. He built me a race-car bed. MDF. Thing probably weighed like a ton. He'd routered out the grooves for the doors and wheels. My mom painted it. She did a great job, not as good as you would have, but all the guys envied that bed. It was very cool."

"Sounds like you had a great childhood."

"I did. But I was always closer with my granddad than with my parents. He was the one who got me into cars."

Megan pulled the sheets out of the package and carried them over to the bed. Noah got on the other side and they made quick work of making the bed, pulling the comforter on top. He slipped the pillowcases over the pillows and tossed them to her. She placed and pouffed them until it was perfect.

"I bet this bed is even cooler than the one you had," she said.

"A whole lot cooler. And mine was never made. Boys aren't that neat."

She jumped onto the mattress and flung back onto the freshly made bed, looking sweet as all get out lounging there with her hair splayed across those perfectly placed pillows.

He swallowed. "Yeah, my bed never looked this good," he said, hoping she didn't hear his voice shake slightly. Because she looked damn good laying there.

"This is just like laying in the bed of a truck on a moonlit night."

"That sounds romantic." And he had the sudden ache to be in the middle of a dark field with this beautiful woman right now.

"Probably taboo for a man like you, huh?"

"No. I have my moments." He climbed onto the bed and stretched out next to her. He pulled his hand up under his head, crossing his legs at his ankles. "Looks more like a sunny day," he said, pointing to the overhead light. "At high noon."

"You're right. It does. You like surprises?" she asked.

He rolled over onto his side, facing her. "I do."

"I have one for you." She pointed to the overhead light. "Turn out the lights."

He leapt from the bed. She was shy. No problem. He flipped the light switch and in one froggy leap was back on the bed next to her. He pulled her into his arms and ran his hand up her back. Nuzzling her neck, inhaling the sweet smell of her.

She pushed back. "Stop it, Romeo . . . or should I say Hot Rod?"

"What? You said—"

"I'm not the surprise. Nothing's going to happen."

He dropped a kiss on her nose. "Oh, come on. Stuff could happen. You might like it."

"On your back, Hot Rod."

He turned over. Maybe she wasn't as shy as he'd thought. He was glad it was dark so she couldn't see him grinning.

"Turn your attention to the ceiling," she whispered into his ear.

Her breath warm on his neck, he looked up. "You are something else, Megan Howard." He turned to try to give her a kiss but she met his face with her hand.

"Again. I'm not the surprise, Noah." Her hand rested on the scruff on his chin, and she turned his face toward the ceiling. "Do you see it?"

"I—"

"On the ceiling."

She wasn't playing hard to get. And he liked that about her. "Hey, are those stars?"

"Yep."

"Were they here before? Jackson has stars on his ceiling?"

"No silly. I did that while you were making time with Mr. Owen this afternoon."

"Killing time, more like it. How'd you do that? Hey, is that the Big Dipper?"

"Sure is."

"That's neat. This is almost as good as laying under the real stars." He lifted up on an elbow. "I'm tempted as hell to steal a kiss from you right now."

"You don't have to steal them."

"No?" He rolled over onto his stomach, his nose to hers. Wanting to kiss her so badly.

"Nope." She reached up and kissed him.

He liked her confidence and the aggressive nature of her kiss. She knew what she wanted, but he had no intention of letting her set the pace. He took the reins, slowing her down. Deepening that kiss, teasing her. Raising the stakes.

A sweet sigh escaped from her as he pulled away, sucking on her lower lip.

He felt it too. "You're hot."

"That's because you're an excellent kisser. And it's summer. Everyone is hot."

She liked messing with him. That confidence turned him on. "Not that kind of hot. Hot like you're beautiful. And you're fun. And you wickedly keep me off balance all the time." And this wasn't part of the car plan either. She really was a different kind of gal. And she had his full attention.

"Wickedly, huh? I've never been called wicked, but I think I like the sound of that." She kissed him on the cheek. "You are welcome. Now turn the light on before things get out of hand and we get caught by the guys. That's not the honor I want to be maid of, thank you very much."

"You sure? It might be worth it. I'm a gentleman. I won't tell. It'll be our little secret."

"I have no doubt."

"Let me show you." His hand lightly grazed her bare arm. Goose bumps raced beneath his fingers.

She took a quick breath in. "No."

He paused, but it wasn't easy. "No? It feels right. No?"

She shook her head. Her nose bumping him. "Let's not, but I think we've just proved that there's nothing cooler than a truck bed," she said. "I wouldn't mind having this in my room."

"It's kind of a turn-on. I was thinking the same thing. Maybe I could build you one." He sat up. "I never met a girl who got cars as much as I did. And I've met a lot of women."

"I'm sure you have. I was a daddy's girl. Daddy always wanted a boy, but all my parents had was me. And Daddy and I shared his love for cars."

"Sorry for your loss. I know you must really miss him."

"Thank you. It was unexpected. I mean, it's not like he was sick." Her words trailed off and the room became quiet.

The mood shifted from hot and playful to somber. And he didn't want to ruin the day, nor was he ready for it to end. "Are you hungry?" Noah asked, patting her tummy like a drum, hoping to rescue the mood. "It sounds hollow in there."

"I am."

"We didn't even have lunch. Just beer," Noah said. "And I'm the first to say that a high-carb beer is good food, but I at least owe you a meal for hijacking your whole day. Let me take you to dinner."

"I can't go anywhere. I'm a mess. I have dried paint all over me."

"We can stop by your house so you can change. I want to take you to that only nice place in town. Bella's."

"You do realize, even though it's the nicest restaurant in town, it's still casual. The food is swanky. The service great, but the atmosphere is casual. We could just as easily do a simple picnic out on the creek."

"Sounds even better," Noah said. "Come on, let me do something nice for you."

"You don't have to do that. I had fun."

"Me too. And I don't want it to end." And he had no idea those were the words that were going to come out until they had, and he meant them. He drove Megan back to her house.

~

She waved from the door as he left to go back to the inn and get cleaned up.

As soon as he was out of sight, she ran back to get showered and changed. By the time the doorbell rang, she'd just finished blow-drying her hair. She stepped into her favorite cowboy boots, and pulled the bottom of her black boot-cut jeans down over them. The pearls Dad had given her on her sixteenth birthday caught her eye on her dresser. She held them up to her neck, perfect with the creamy white camisole she was wearing.

The doorbell rang again.

She struggled with the pearls, trying to hurry, still trying to connect the clasp as she ran toward the door.

"Coming." Her boots clip-clopped down the tile entry. She slid to a stop in front of the door and swung it open. "Hi."

Noah stood there with a bouquet of daisies.

Her lips bunched. "That was so nice." *How sweet.* "Thank you."

"I want to go on record that I went to Bootsie's Bouquets to buy you yellow roses, but your mother insisted daisies are your favorite."

Mom was probably telling everyone in town. "They absolutely are. What a nice surprise. Let me put these in some water."

"Sure."

His eyes weighed on her as she walked away. A giggle churned in her gut. She felt giddy at the attention. But what would it hurt? He was fun.

She came back with a lime-green mason jar filled with the daisies and set them on the table in the hall. "They really brighten up the place. They're great."

"Glad you like them."

"I do. You ready? I'm starved."

"Yeah, me too. Are we walking or driving?"

Megan grabbed her keys and her purse. "Let's walk. It's just a couple of blocks." She locked the door behind her, and they walked to the corner. Noah grabbed her hand, loosely holding it.

"You look really nice. I like a girl who can pull off jeans and pearls," he said. "And it looks good on you."

"Thank you." She had to take extra long strides to keep up with him. The sun was still bright, and the air so steamy that dinner in the air-conditioning at Bella's sounded much better than the picnic she'd suggested earlier. She was glad he'd insisted.

One of her best customers, the gal who owned the boutique down the way, hailed her from across the street. Megan waved in response.

"This way," Megan said when they got to the next corner. "Just on the other side of the street."

He moved at an easy gait, for him. Looking around, taking in her small town. She wondered how it looked to someone who hadn't lived there their whole life.

When they got to Bella's, Noah held the door for her.

A white-shirted waiter met them at the door. "Two? Are you Mr. Black?"

"Yes."

"You called ahead?"

He shrugged.

Nice touch.

The waiter took them to a quiet booth near the back, and laid the menus on the table. "Something to drink?"

"I'll have a beer. Megan, what would you like?"

"I think I'll start with one of your famous blueberry slushy drinks like you guys do for the Blackberry Festival."

"Excellent choice," the waiter said.

"You've got to try one," she said to Noah. "Bring two of those."

"Still the beer, sir?"

"Oh, yeah. I might need a chaser for something that fruity."

"Yes, sir." The waiter hurried off and was back with their drinks before they'd even taken a good look at the menu.

The waiter slid the two bright purple concoctions in front of them, and then put Noah's beer next to his.

Noah shot her a glance. "Looks kind of girlie."

"You're going to love it. Trust me."

"We'll see."

The waiter stood there at the table. "I have specials tonight. Can I tell you what they are, or do you know what you want?"

"We'll listen to the specials," Noah said.

"Excellent!" The waiter beamed with excitement. "We have a wonderful appetizer today. Fried green tomatoes with a dollop of homemade pimento cheese, arugula, and a crispy pork belly crouton with a ginger sesame drizzle."

"We're so in on that," Megan said.

"Also, our special entrees this evening are: espresso braised short ribs on top of mascarpone polenta, crispy sweet potatoes, and smoked shiitake jus; and fried mustard pork tenderloin with creamed corn and wilted greens with a corn cake." He held his pencil to the ready. "I got to sample both dishes earlier this evening. Magnificent."

"Then, I think I'm going to have the pork tenderloin special. I mean, how can you go wrong with fried pork loin?" said Noah.

"True. And honestly I don't think I've ever heard of anyone getting anything here that they didn't like. It's that good."

"For you, ma'am?"

Megan giggled to herself. The waiter knew her, although he hadn't shown that he did. He'd worked for her mom for almost a year. Clearly he was excited about his new job and eager to impress. "I'll have the short rib special."

"Great choices. I'll be out with your appetizer shortly."

"Thank you," Megan said.

Noah waited until the eager waiter moved along and then leaned forward. "I want to show you something." He pulled out his phone and swept his finger across the screen a few times and then got up and slid into the booth next to her. "I'd forgotten I had this on my phone."

He handed his phone to her, leaning in as she took a look.

The picture was pretty fuzzy, but the car was easy to make out. It was the spitting image of the one in her garage. He hadn't been kidding that his grandfather had had one just like it. Same color, of course—there weren't but a couple of choices back then, and it looked like the same year too. The young boy standing next to the car looked like he had an attitude.

Long hair, parted down the middle, hung nearly to his shoulders. His arms were folded across his chest like he hadn't been too willing a participant in the photo shoot. One foot stuck out, his long, skinny leg bent awkwardly like he just wanted whoever was taking the picture to hurry the heck up so he could skedaddle on out of there.

She pinched her fingers against the screen to zoom in. She glanced up at him and back down at the picture. "Take that smile off of your face." She looked again. "Now look like an angsty teenager."

He laughed, then frowned and grumbled.

"Oh, yeah, now I see it." She handed him the phone back. "So funny that we both have history with that kind of car." The years had treated him well. He was a much more handsome man than he had been a boy. But then, her old pictures and hairstyles weren't all that great either.

"Yeah. My aunt found that picture in my granddad's stuff and had it scanned and sent it to me years ago. She's techno-savvy for an old gal. My dad doesn't even have a smartphone."

"It's hard to believe anyone can make it without a smartphone these days. But it's like no one gives you their full attention anymore."

He leaned in closer, nudging her shoulder. "You have mine."

Could he say the right thing any better if he'd been scripted? He was too good to be true.

"I had fun this afternoon, and the room looks great. Have you ever thought of doing murals for hire?"

"Me?" Where'd that come from? She couldn't tell him that story. That was baggage better left unclaimed. "No. I just mess around now. I let that dream of becoming an artist to make a living go a long time ago."

"Why?" His eyes slightly narrowed. "You're really good."

"People don't make it in that world. Not without a lot of sacrifices. I've learned that I like to be able to change my plans on a whim. Get up and go when I want to. Or not. And my art is personal. I paint what I want to paint. I'm not commercial enough. I'd starve with that attitude trying to be an artist. And I'm not the nine-to-five type, so the candle business really suits me and my creativity quite well." Fortunately he didn't seem to notice the tremor in her voice.

"If you ever change your mind, I'd love you to do a mural for my shop. I think my people would love it. It would really brighten up the place."

"That's a very nice compliment." And it had been fun to work on that mural for Billy today.

The waiter brought their appetizer.

Noah slid one of the fried green tomatoes over to his plate, using his fork to cut through the layers and take a bite. "Now that is way better than it sounds."

"I thought it sounded good."

"That's because you grew up in the land of pimento cheese and fried tomatoes."

"Tennessee isn't that far away."

"True, but my mom wasn't a real Southern cook. She came from an Italian family, so I was well fed in a different way."

"I do love Italian food, but nothing beats old-fashioned Southern cooking." She took a bite. He was right. It was tasty, and she wasn't a fried-green-tomatoes-eating girl most days.

"Did you ever sell any of your paintings?"

"Yeah. I did. For a while there I sold quite a few, but I had someone selling them for me back then. I don't like that part. The asking for money. It stole from my creativity. I love the creative part. I don't like the marketing and sales and business of it." And that was more than she'd usually tell anyone about that.

"I can understand that."

"I work just as hard with the candles, but the science of figuring out the right colors and scents appeal to my creative and analytical side. Plus my art was so personal. Everyone likes candles. Not everyone wants a big honking painting of a car, or a landscape, or whatever."

"Will you show me more of your work?"

The waiter placed their meals in front of them and offered them fresh cracked pepper. A few well-placed twists, and he was off again.

She picked up her fork. Noah was probably just making small talk about her art.

"Maybe after dinner?"

Had she missed part of the conversation? "What?"

"You'll show me more of your paintings. I'm interested in seeing them."

Was he just being nice? "Nothing to really see. They're all pretty much in the same style as the ones you've already seen, but I have a bunch in my studio."

He looked pleased as he pressed his fork down into the salad. "Cool. I'd really like that."

She wasn't one to play a lot of games. It wasn't her style. She put her fork down. "Really? Why?"

He stopped chewing, and blinked.

Megan smiled politely. "I mean people say stuff like that all the time and don't even mean it. I was just wondering."

"Oh, well." He placed his fork down. "I'm not people then. Because I don't say things to just be polite." He held his hands out. "What you see here is what you get. And yes. I want to see your paintings. I'm intrigued. Unusually so, I might add, because it's not like I know a thing about art."

Interesting.

"But I know what I like."

His gaze held hers.

The art? Or me? But those words didn't come out of her mouth.

"And I am interested to see what else you've done."

"Then I'd love to share that with you. I haven't even done much with them lately. It'll be fun to look through them again."

"Good." He held up his slushy. "A toast to being genuine and real. I like that."

She raised hers. "I like that about you too. It's rare to find these days."

He took a sip, then slugged back his beer. "You're telling me. You don't know how refreshing it is to be able to sit and chat with someone who is being straight up about things. Not trying to impress. Not trying to psychoanalyze me. Just enjoying the moment."

"I do know what you mean. This is very nice."

"Did you know," Noah said, "that there were only sixty-two DeSoto Adventurer convertibles made that year?"

"Like mine?"

"Yes. And I'm telling you, it's rare to find one that someone hasn't painted or ruined with some other kind of mods. I've been looking for one for years."

"That's hard to believe. What are the odds that two people who don't know each other and both have a history with one of those sixty-two cars end up as best man and maid of honor in a wedding?"

"I don't know. But I'm sure it's like the lottery. Slim to none."

"How did your dad come to fall in love with that DeSoto?"

"I'm not entirely sure. I was just a little girl when he got it. Mom was never a fan of it. Said it was too darned big. Not that he would have let her drive it anyway. I don't think anyone ever drove that car. Ever. But him."

"You've never driven it."

She shook her head. "Never."

"Really?" He looked shocked.

"No. Daddy always drove. I loved riding in that car with him. He was always so happy driving it."

"Good memories."

"The best."

"Those cars were ahead of their time if you ask me. My granddad taught me everything I know about cars on his old DeSoto Adventurer. I loved that car as much as he did. Or maybe it was Granddad that I loved so much and the car is just part of that."

"I know how you feel." And it was neat to meet someone else who might actually understand how much this car meant to her because of her relationship with her dad. "So, did you get your start as a mechanic?"

"Not really." He looked like he hadn't really considered that before. "Well, no. I never worked as a mechanic, turning wrenches in a garage, except on personal projects. My car fixation was driven by my relationship with my grandfather and his love for cars. He taught me everything and I loved it. So, I *can* fix cars, but mostly I'm a collector and restoration guy. We cater to a pretty exclusive clientele. Not really a mechanic-type garage."

That would explain his clean hands. He didn't look the grease monkey type. "Just how exclusive?"

"Think of me as the car guy to the rich and famous."

"Like anyone I'd know?"

"Yes."

"Interesting." He'd skipped the opportunity to name-drop. He wasn't going to kiss and tell. That scored him a point, even if it was only because he'd had to sign some type of nondisclosure or something. That earned him credibility with her.

"Tell me about your candles. How'd you get into that?"

"The candle part was a little by accident. I used to just be into the aromatherapy stuff. People count on my blends to help them through things."

"Like what? Like magic?"

"No. Like different aromas help different things. Everything from respiratory ailments to headaches, and stress and falling in love."

Amusement rose in Noah's voice. "And you don't think a candle that is supposed to help you fall in love is magic?"

"Other people might think that. In fact, many of my clients pretty much do believe it's magic. I even kind of used to believe it, but now I'm not so sure it's not the Hawthorne effect."

"Could be," Noah said. "But I am a believer in the value of holistic methods. Aromatherapy included."

How California of him. Not like any of the guys around here would admit to that. "Me too. Just not that it's magical. It's more scientific than that. I get beeswax from a local beekeeper. He actually pays me to take it. And I mix all of my oils myself too."

"Good for the bottom line."

"Yes, it is, and I do everything from beginning to end to purify the wax I use in my candles. There's a lot more to it than people think. It's a combination of science and art."

"I'd like to see you in action."

She cut her eyes his way to see if that was meant to sound like a come-on, but he looked sincere. "You are awfully curious about me." Did that just come out of her mouth?

"I admit that you've got my attention. I've never met anyone like you."

"Thank you. I think."

"It was meant as a compliment." Noah put his napkin in his lap. "I'm stuffed. That was one of the best meals I've had in a long time."

"Told you it was top notch."

"And even that blueberry concoction wasn't bad. A little sweet and tangy for my taste, but it was good."

"We have this huge blackberry festival here every year. It's what our little town is known for—blackberry everything. You should try to come next year."

"I just might do that."

The waiter brought the check. "Everything good? Dessert?"

"No, thank you, we're set." Noah slid his platinum card into the folio, and the waiter stepped away. "Your place?"

A flurry of butterflies took flight in her stomach. "Sure."

The waiter brought the receipt and Noah tipped generously and signed the receipt. "Let's head on out then."

He held the door for her and they stepped out on the sidewalk.

"We must have been in there a lot longer than I realized," she said. The sun had set and stars filled the cloudless night sky. A soft breeze stirred. "It feels great out tonight."

"Sure does." She lifted her chin, toward the stars.

"Too bad we don't have a truck bed. We could be out under some real stars tonight."

He'd had the same thought. "Yeah. Good night for it." She dropped her head to his arm. "So what's it like where you live? I mean, I know Los Angeles, but are you right in the city? Out in the suburbs? Near the water? Do you have stars like this?"

"I'm not right in the city. LA is big. My shop is out toward Calabasas, but I live in Malibu."

"On the beach?"

"Yes. Great view."

"I bet. I've always loved the beach. But I've only ever been to the East Coast beaches. Mostly the Outer Banks here in North Carolina."

Malibu sounded pretty uptown, and she was pretty sure she could name at least a couple Hollywood stars who had mansions in Calabasas. "Aren't you afraid of earthquakes?"

"No. Not really. It's not any worse than tornados, or hurricanes. You can't run from them."

"Well, at least with hurricanes you get some notice."

"That's true, but most people don't heed the advice or evacuate anyway."

"There's always a few. You're right."

"Have you ever been out to LA?"

"No. Never had a reason to go. I've always thought it would be fun to see the Hollywood sign." She wanted to say Malibu, but that would sound like she was asking for an invite so she kept that little tidbit to herself. "And drive up the coast with the water on the wrong side. I'm an Atlantic girl. I think it would be cool to see the Pacific."

"You'd be inspired. It's so different. You'll have to come visit me."

"Maybe I will." She looked both ways and then they crossed the street over to her house. The soft-lit solar lights gave the place a glow, and her Karmann Ghia sparkled under the lights of the canopy. She dug into her handbag for her keys, and then unlocked the front door. "Come on in." She held the door as he came in and then closed the door behind him.

She hung her keys on the hook next to the door.

Noah did a double take. "You have a DeSoto key ring. Is that the one with the key blanks folded inside?"

"Yeah," she said taking them back off of the hook. "It's really clever, isn't it?"

"Sure is. Never actually seen one like that." He held the keys in his hand like they were a fine piece of jewelry. "Really cool."

It was fun to have someone else as enthusiastic about the car as she was. No one else seemed to really understand.

He hung the keys back on the hook and followed her down the hall.

She opened the double doors on the right hand side.

"The more I get to know you, the more I realize how much this place suits you."

"I like it."

"What's your favorite space here?" He sat down on the couch. "Mine would be the garage. Hands down. Especially if it had that car in it."

"Yeah. *Especially* now that the car is here. But I have a secret spot. It's still my very favorite. I've never shared it with anyone. Not even my friends. Not Angie or Flynn even. Only the contractor knows about it."

He looked worried. "Now you have me curious."

She paused. Lord, he probably thought she had a sex den or something. Now this was awkward.

"You going to show me?"

"I think so, but first I'll show you the rest of my paintings like I promised. They are in my studio."

"Great." He stood and followed her to the room in the far corner. The whole wall slid, almost like a secret room, but really it was a barn rail door with the rail hidden under a soffit the same color as the wall. You didn't even notice it from across the room.

"I know artists who would kill to have a space like this."

She'd once felt that way. Thought it was her perfect place to create. But she'd lost that inspiration. That desire. Things were different now.

He walked over to the large wooden bins with the stacks of completed canvases arranged by size. None of them small, though. She did work on the big scale. Always. The smallest being twenty-four by twenty-four.

"You did all of these?"

She nodded, wishing now the incomplete piece under the drape wasn't sitting on her easel. She hoped he wouldn't want to look at that one. She hated showing anyone work that wasn't complete.

"These are great." He flipped through them, stopping more than once to really look closely and comment on color or intensity. "You have enough here to open your own gallery."

She laughed out loud. "If all it took was paintings to open a gallery, anyone and everyone could have one."

"You're good enough, Megan. I'm serious."

She shrugged off the compliment. She didn't even really want to hear it. She'd been told a million times that she had skill, but it hadn't gotten her where she needed to go. Or maybe it had, but after what had happened with Kevin, how could she trust that part of her life again? It was too much to risk.

"You have enough automotive-themed drawings to have a show."

She was not going to go into it with him. She couldn't, so she just sucked in a breath and hoped she could get him out of there.

"This is my absolute favorite." He tugged out a twenty-four-by-thirty canvas.

Daddy's car. The whole car—tip to tail—and parked right in front of this building. The old Mobil Pegasus was even still on the front of the building at the time. She wasn't living here then. She'd been home from college break.

"It's perfect."

"Nope, there's one thing amiss." She hugged her arms to her body. "I could have fixed it, but I kind of like making a game out of it. My dad had this painting. He made a buttload of money betting people they couldn't figure out what was different."

"Try me."

"Okay. Bring it with you."

He carried the framed canvas and followed behind her.

As they approached the garage door, she stopped. "You a betting man?"

"Oh, yeah."

"Good. Let's make a bet out of it. Daddy will get a little laugh from heaven," Megan said.

"Sure." She liked it when he smiled like that. "What are the stakes?"

"If you figure it out—I'll show you my special place."

"If I don't . . ."

"Then, you have to place an order for custom candles for California Dreaming Restoration. A big order." He could afford it. If Daddy had taught her anything, it was not to miss an opportunity.

"You're on."

"All righty, then." She pushed the door open and flipped on the lights.

Chapter Eleven

Noah locked his knees against the rush of adrenaline attempting to toss him off balance as the light flooded the room and reflected from that car in the middle of it like a shiny gem. *I want this car. More than anything.*

He propped the painting on a giant toolbox that graced the far side of the room. Probably full of anything but tools. He was dying to open one of the heavy drawers and see. It looked to be one more treasure from this building's past.

Noah considered himself an expert on this car, but he didn't notice anything out of place on this painting. And he had an eye for detail. This bet was right up his alley.

Being pragmatic about his approach, he started at the front and worked his way down the car. Comparing the painting to the car.

After making his way up and down the car three times, Megan spoke up. "Are you ready to give in?"

"You'd like that, wouldn't you?" He stopped and stood next to the painting. Leaning against the toolbox. "No, ma'am."

"All right. I've got all night." She watched with smug delight.

"Don't need it."

"Really?"

"Really." He couldn't help but curl his lips into a smile. "I know what's different."

"You only get one guess."

He folded his arms across his chest. "That car is missing the gas tank flap on the left side."

Her mouth dropped open. "I can't believe you got it. No one ever figures that out."

"I know this car." He turned and picked up the picture. "And I still love this picture. It'll look great over my desk. What'll you take for it?"

"It's not for sale."

"Why not? It's just sitting back there collecting dust."

"I don't sell my paintings anymore."

"How about you think about it?"

"I don't think I'll ever change my mind."

He put it back on the toolbox. "Well, it's not entirely fair that I took that bet." He shoved his hands in his pockets. "I know cars better than anyone. If you really don't want to show me your secret place, I understand. It wasn't a fair bet." He'd much rather stand here next to this car anyway. He'd spent the better part of his years living and breathing to find a car like this. Right down to the original gold bullet hubcaps. Standing here today was what had been his ultimate goal. He could still hardly believe he was here. Touching it. Hearing its stories. And if Megan was here too, so much the better.

"A deal is a deal. I'd have made you order those candles."

"Who says I won't. I just hadn't thought of it yet."

"Don't be a suck up," she said playfully.

"Hey I like nice smells."

"I don't make a new-car-smell candle."

"I know what aromatherapy is. I happen to have a love-hate relationship with peppermint."

"That's good for all kinds of things. Nausea, indigestion, as a liniment, and to relieve itching from poison ivy or even herpes. Don't have herpes, do you?" She leaned back against the door with a shifty grin on her face.

"No." He laughed. The girl was ballsy. He'd give her that. "No, ma'am. I have a clean health card. I promise. I hate it because it reminds me of the liniment they used on my shoulder. College football. Love it because my grandfather was always eating those puffy sugary peppermints."

"I love those mints too." She picked up her pace heading back toward the front door.

Is she escorting me out? Did I insult her? It wouldn't be the first time I'd said something that pissed a woman off, but I didn't mean to . . . this time. He retraced the conversation, but then Megan stopped in the hallway and opened a closet.

Well, it looked like a closet, but it wasn't. It was a set of stairs.

He pointed to the metal stairs. They looked almost like diamond plate. "To the special place?"

She grinned.

"Nice. I feel like I'm in a mystery movie or something."

With each step there was a loud clang. You couldn't tippy-toe up these things easily. The metal echoed in the cinder block cavern. When she reached the top, she placed her finger on an electronic keypad.

"Don't tell me that it's fingerprint access control."

"Okay. I won't."

"I may be falling in love with you." He'd said it as a joke, but it wasn't all that far-fetched. This girl was his kind of girl.

"Oh, there will be none of that, my friend."

A girl after his own heart.

"Yes, ma'am."

She pushed her shoulder against the heavy metal door and stepped outside. "My secret place."

He stepped onto the rooftop behind her.

"It's everything I need when I need to get my wits about me." Megan walked across the sparsely decorated space. She opened the door of a weatherproof unit. Inside, a wine chiller, full of beer, glowed a bright blue. "Beer?"

"Nice."

She took two out and popped the tops on the old-fashioned bottle opener attached to the side of the door, then handed him one.

The only thing up there was a double chaise lounge. She lifted the canvas tarp from it to show him.

"This is great."

"It's better when the mosquitos aren't swarming." She swatted one on her neck.

He swatted one on his arm. "They are hungry little critters, aren't they?"

"Yeah. Not a good night to hang out here."

"Maybe another time."

"Maybe," she walked to the door. "Let's go inside before we're eaten up so bad we itch through the whole wedding ceremony on Saturday. Angie would kill us for that."

"That wouldn't look good, would it?"

She let him go ahead of her and she closed the door and locked it.

He went down the stairs, his steps sounding heavy, hers softer right behind him.

He wasn't ready to call it a night.

He hoped she wasn't either.

There was an awkward moment when she closed the secret staircase behind her. If he didn't say something now, he'd be out the door.

"Mind if I stay and have another beer with you?"

She hesitated, and his ego took a slight blow, like he was getting ready to get the kibosh.

"I'd like that." She gave him a smile that sent his pulse racing.

They went back to Megan's apartment, and Noah couldn't help but glance down the hall to the left toward the garage where the DeSoto was parked. That car was going to look so good in his collection.

Megan set her beer on the coffee table, then sat on the couch.

Noah sat down beside her, a respectable distance from Megan. His arm slung over the back of the couch, he turned to face her. "I've really enjoyed being with you tonight. Thank you."

"Me too. You're easy to be with."

A loud pop made Megan groan.

"What was that?"

"My air-conditioning." Her voice broke. "Sit tight. I've been baby-ing this old system these last few weeks, trying to not put a new one in until next year. It keeps tripping the breaker."

She jaunted off with a confidence that let him know she'd handled this situation a time or two. But nonetheless, he said, "Need me to look at it? I'm pretty handy."

"Thanks, but no. I've had the electrician jury-rig it to get me through. I'm riding on borrowed time here. The holidays are always a big quarter for me. I'll replace it after that. I won't need it in a few more weeks anyway."

She needed the money. Sweet. That would make the big dollars he was getting ready to offer her for that car even more appealing. His hopes soared. It really was going to happen. Any other car he wouldn't have any doubt at all, but this was the one car he just couldn't seem to get.

She came back into the room and raised a hand in line with the vent overhead. "Sorry about that. See. It's working fine now."

"You have the magic touch."

"Good thing. It's going to cost a lot to do it right. I want to put my apartment and the workshop and storage all on separate zones. The candles need to maintain a constant temperature and humidity level.

Plus, if down the line I decide to rent parts of it out, I can already have those services on separate boxes."

"Good planning." And just as he was going to suggest she sell the car to pay for it, she sat right next to him on the couch.

"I'm glad I met you," she said.

He couldn't tell her exactly what he was thinking. Not without getting slapped, so he squelched those thoughts and took it down to a gentlemanly pace. "Meeting you has been a really nice addition to this trip."

Didn't she know her perfume had his nerves sizzling? That if she tossed her hair back one more time, he was going to kiss her perfect neck? But damn if he would screw up his best friend's wedding by making it with the maid of honor. He couldn't take the chance of misreading a little innocent flirting.

She leaned in and kissed him.

And all bets are off. He smiled, lowering his mouth to hers. Eager to really kiss her like she deserved to be kissed.

She arched into the cradle of his arms, taking in the heat of his kiss.

"Nice," he said. "Very nice. You're trouble, young lady." He leaned back, determined to keep his wits about him.

"I guess you'd better leave then." But the look in her eyes was a flat-out dare.

He squeezed his eyes shut and dropped his head back. "You don't know how much I don't want to leave. But if I don't, it might get really awkward on wedding day."

She giggled. "I'm not the one getting married. Now that would make it awkward."

"Oh, yeah, that would be bad." He ran his finger under her chin. He wanted to experience all of her.

She caught his finger playfully in her teeth, a seductive smile playing on her pink lips. "We're both single adults." Her eyebrow lifted, and that sent his hormones adrift.

"I like you. I want you." He pulled her in for another kiss. "Maybe I could stay."

"You should."

"You sure about this?" Why the hell was he asking? Don't give her a chance to back out now.

She returned the kiss. That was answer enough.

And for the first time in a long time, all those walls he normally kept up, seemed to be crashing down. Because this girl seemed different. Somehow. And as confusing as it was, he had every intention of enjoying it while the moment lasted.

He scooped her into his arms and carried her toward the hall. "Which way?"

"I wondered where you thought you were taking me."

"To the closest spot to lay you down and run my hands up this luscious body of yours, before I completely unravel."

She pointed to her bedroom door.

He pulled his arm out from under her knees, letting her stand.

Her hands slid down his chest as her feet touched the floor.

Leaning forward he brushed his lips at the nape of her neck and made contact with the soft skin between her shoulder and ear.

She gasped. Arching her back as if wanting to get away and be closer to him at the same time.

"Can I undress you?" Not something he'd ever asked before. This little lady was tugging him into new territory. He wanted her, but in a tender way.

Without a word, she nodded, and began working his belt as he undressed her. Slowly caressing her skin, leaving a trail of chill bumps behind his fingertips.

"You're beautiful," he said, laying her back onto the bed and stretching out beside her in no hurry.

He looked into her eyes and then shifted up on an elbow to look into her eyes, kissing her softly on each of her eyelids. "You're not like anyone I've ever known." And he didn't really even know her yet. But he wanted to.

"You've been a surprise too," she said.

His lips caught hers as his warm palm made a path between her breasts and then slowly but firmly continued to her belly and over the parts of her that were warm and lifting to meet him. A guttural groan escaped as he sucked in a breath and trailed kisses from her mouth to meet his hand.

Roaming her every curve with his mouth in his own sweet time, he settled his cheek against her soft inner thigh.

Megan pushed her fingers through his thick hair while he kissed his way up to her belly and the sexy curve between her breasts and back down again. She squirmed, pressing herself up against him.

She felt a rush of desire, and at this moment she didn't care who won—her head or her heart—as long as it didn't make her stop.

Closing her eyes, she tried to relax. She gulped in a breath of air, her body wanting to retreat from the feeling of losing control, but wanting it even more. She pressed her eyes closed. Seeing the colors, feeling the rhythms and the music in her head that let her enjoy every moment.

She reached for him, guiding his face to meet her parting lips. Her breaths matching his with each kiss. Each push. Every increase of intensity.

Their breathing grew heavier, hearts pounding, as they both moaned in anticipation of what was to come. Noah rolled Megan over flat on her back, pausing only a moment as he smoothed her hair out on the bed around her, tracing his hand over her face, her lips.

"I want you." He'd fought the feelings, pushed them aside thinking they couldn't be real, but they were. He needed Megan. He wanted her. She made him feel alive in a way he'd never felt before. Honest and true.

She mouthed something that never made it into words. Instead, she pulled him back into a kiss. Her body responded to his warmth. She inhaled his sexy scent, awareness tingling through her.

As if he knew, his strong hands eased over her curves.

Her body reacted to the connection, bucking as she gasped. Her back arched as if she had no control of her body as it danced its own rhythm to his every move.

A perfect beat, and it climbed in intensity, but he was in control of the pace. Forcing her to give in to the pleasure and let go completely.

Breathless and sweating, she rested her head in the safe cradle of his arm.

~

Blinking her eyes against the sun, Megan turned over and picked up her phone off of the nightstand.

Nine fourteen.

And a reminder.

The spa. This was the morning she, Angie, Katy, and Flynn were all meeting at the spa for a day of pampering. Good lord, she'd set the thing up. How could she have forgotten?

She looked over at Noah, tan all the way to where the sheet covered his lower half. That had been one night to remember. Somehow waking him and shooing him away so she could meet the girls at the spa seemed tacky.

She slipped out of bed and quietly got dressed.

I can't just leave him. She grabbed a piece of paper from the hall, jotted a quick note, and then tiptoed back into her bedroom.

He hadn't moved.

She laid the note on her pillow and left.

Holding her breath until she made it all the way out to her car, she let out a sigh of relief. She had just enough time to still make it to the spa on time. If she hurried.

Thank goodness the other girls were riding separately. That would have been awkward as heck if someone had called with him lying there right beside her in bed.

No. The girls did not need to know that she'd slept with the best man. Before the wedding? Nearly a complete stranger? No, ma'am. That was a little tidbit of information that she'd keep to herself. He'd be gone next week, and that would be that.

She'd planned to stop and pick up some supplies while she was in Raleigh this morning before meeting up with the girls, but those plans had been chucked after that first toe-curling kiss from Noah. And if she showed up late, it was going to be hard as heck to keep her night with Noah from the girls.

Pushing her car to make up some time, her wheels squealed out of the turn on the on-ramp. She loved driving her VW. It handled like a dream. Kind of like Noah last night. She smiled. Satisfied and ready to see him again.

She pulled into the parking lot with just a couple of minutes to spare. Thank goodness she hadn't gotten a ticket. She'd deserved one fair and square, but it would have put her late for sure.

She checked herself in the mirror. Her lips were swollen from way too many kisses, and her cheeks were red. Whisker burn from that sexy scruff. A small price to pay for one heckuva night.

Hopefully she'd be able to hide it from the girls until after the facials. Then she could blame the products.

Katy pulled into the lot just as Megan was getting ready to open the door. She waved and waited for her.

"Glad I'm not late," Katy said. "Derek was in one amorous mood last night."

"Must have been the full moon." Whatever it was, she hoped there was more to come.

"Can't believe how fast the days are going," Katy said. "Can you believe the wedding is almost here?"

"No. For the longest time it seemed so far off. Now I feel like it's snuck up on us."

"I'm so ready for this day. I need to relax," Katy said.

As soon as they walked into the spa, a herd of red-lipsticked, white-coated, clinician-looking types practically attacked them.

Angie and Flynn were already sipping mimosas. "Hey!"

"Looks like y'all have a head start on us," Katy teased.

They were led back to a room that had already been set up for their group. Up to six people could get facials, manicures, and pedicures at one time in the luxurious room. On one wall stacked stone reached from floor to ceiling in soft weathered tones of tans and blues with water trickling down into a pond.

The room glowed with soft light, and Megan felt a little like she was in the middle of this weird water ballet as the white-coated women all seemed to descend at once—leaning them back in their plush leather chairs and clicking on the lights and steam machines.

She closed her eyes. Last night things with Noah had gotten steamier than this facial. As the aesthetician cleansed, exfoliated, and lathered luxurious creams into her skin, Megan couldn't help but smile with Noah Black still on her mind. She wouldn't soon forget last night.

Her chair was electronically moving to the upright position. When she opened her eyes, the other girls were being moved too. Flynn on her left and Angie on her right, they all had pink glowing skin.

"Do y'all feel as relaxed as you look?" Flynn asked.

"I hope so," Angie said. "And we haven't even gotten to the massages yet.

A new crew of four white-coated women filed into the room. They filled the footbaths with warm water and blue foamy suds then pressed the buttons on the electronic panels on the massage chairs.

"Now this is what I'm talking about," Angie said as the rolling massager made her arch and ebb like a possessed woman. "I totally should have put one of these on my bridal registry."

"We should go in on one together," Megan agreed. "We can keep it at my shop."

"Or the inn," Katy offered.

"Or the B&B," Flynn said. "I think we'd fight over it. Maybe this isn't a good idea. Megan, what did you do to your leg? That looks painful."

"What?" Megan twisted her hip. A swatch of turquoise paint looked like a gnarly bruise. She'd roll with it, only as soon as the pedicurist massaged that lotion into her leg, it was going to disappear. Awkward.

"What's wrong?" Angie leaned forward in her chair.

"It's nothing." Megan hoped they'd let it go. "Y'all relax."

"That is not nothing." Flynn's forehead creased in concern. "It's got to hurt like heck."

"It's paint. I must have missed it when I was in the shower."

"Paint?" Flynn and Angie both leaned forward.

"Stop speculating." Megan knew they'd leap to conclusions. At least they hadn't noticed her lips. The kissing would be way harder to explain away. "I was working on a project."

"That's great!" Angie reached across and grabbed Megan's hands. "You have so much talent. I'm so excited that you're painting again."

"It's not like that. I'm not."

"But you can. I mean. It's a start. Right?" Angie looked so hopeful. But either way this story was going to disappoint. She wasn't going to paint. And she wasn't going to be with Noah. So she just let it go, closing her eyes and hoping they'd do the same.

"This is quiet time." Megan looked at the gal who had pulled her rolling chair up to start on her pedicure. "Right? Tell them to be quiet and enjoy this."

"Enjoy," the woman said softly. "Your friend is a little bossy."

"Oh, great. My own girl is turning on me." But Megan was glad because the joke seemed to get everyone focused on relaxing instead of her.

A few minutes later, Katy said, "Megan, I didn't know you were an artist. I mean, I knew you were a craftsman, but the painting . . . I hadn't heard that."

"It's old news," Megan said.

"Is not." Angie turned to Katy. "That mural on the side of the building at the intersection of Cabot and Main. Megan did that."

"You're kidding? That is so pretty."

"And paintings. She even won some art shows. Used to even sell some pieces."

"I had no idea. I'm so impressed. You've got to show me your work," Katy said. "We should display some of it at our place. For the retreat."

"That would be perfect," Angie said. Her voice was rising the way it did when she got excited.

"Y'all slow down. I'm not painting again."

Angie leaned over to Katy. "She only paints when she's totally in love with someone or something. A guy broke her heart. Hasn't painted since."

"If you think you're whispering, you suck at it. I'm sitting right here."

"I just thought she should know."

"The two are not connected."

"Nothing is that coincidental, Megan. We all know you were absolutely heartbroken. Kevin was your muse. Or he stole your muse when he left. Whatever it was, he stole your gift to the world."

She wasn't having this conversation. That was old news. She'd moved on. All of that was fine right where she'd tucked it safely away. Not to be tempted or destroyed again. "Lord, Angie. Don't be so melodramatic. It's not like I was making a living at it. The candle business is what I was meant to do. Let it go."

Flynn had her eyes closed, and her head leaned back, but it didn't keep her from jumping in on it all. "Someone's touchy," she sang.

Megan couldn't believe she'd missed that paint. Good lord. And Noah hadn't mentioned it either. Probably because he put it there. Not that she hadn't deserved it.

"It's probably the wedding that has inspired you," Angie said. "Weddings are so romantic. Besides *he* was a long time ago."

"We're not saying his name again."

"I didn't."

"I know. I'm just saying. Maybe."

"Maybe it's the wedding, but it wasn't a painting like you think. It's just a little project." And that wasn't a complete lie. It kind of was the wedding that had inspired her, because it was Jackson's surprise wedding gift to Angie that had kicked off that whole chain of events. And Noah asking her to be a part of it. And spending time with Noah hadn't been half bad either. Probably because they both had the exact same values and views on life and relationships.

Megan peeked over toward Angie, who was staring at her with a knowing look. Angie knew her so well.

"You know, Megan, Jackson was saying that Noah couldn't quit talking about you the other day."

Megan's hopes soared. Only she wasn't sure why. It wasn't like she was looking for anyone. She was completely happy the way things were. "He'll be in California next week. Don't be silly."

"Yeah, besides," Flynn added. "I think Noah was out on the prowl last night. So he must not be interested in Megan. He never made it back to the inn."

Megan felt like a squirrel in the middle of a highway, unsure of which way to dart. "How do you know?"

Flynn's hands moved with her words as she began to explain. "Well, he wasn't there when I went to bed. And he wasn't there for breakfast with the other guys."

"Maybe he got up early. Went for a run or something," Katy said.

"I guess it's possible," Flynn said. "But don't you think the guys would have said something if that was the case?"

"He could've been over at Jackson's," Megan said.

"No," Angie said. "Jackson would have told me. I talked to him last night and he was already in bed. He didn't mention anyone else being there this morning either."

Quit trying to cover for him. You're just looking guiltier. She picked up the color-key chart for the nail polish colors, hoping no one would notice that just-been-laid look about her. Because right now she felt like it was written all over her face.

"We don't have to pick colors, remember? We're all getting the same thing," Flynn said.

"Yeah, I was just looking. To look." *To hide. What I want is to crawl in a hole and hide. I can't believe I slept with him. I don't even know him. And he'll be gone next week. What was I thinking? Am I crazy?*

"Ford is really nice," Flynn said, out of the blue. "I'm glad I'm walking down the aisle with him."

"You're welcome," Angie said.

"I'm glad you've found the perfect guy, Angie. I think I'm going to quit looking for a while. I feel like I'm trying so hard that I'm scaring the good ones off."

"You have been a little ummm . . . overzealous," Angie said with kindness.

"I know. I was thinking about that last night. I just want what you and Katy have so badly."

"It'll come. In the right time. You're so busy getting the B&B back up and running. It's not the best time for a relationship for you right now. Things have a way of working out at the right time. Be patient."

"I'm trying," Flynn said. "Y'all have to help remind me of that."

"We will," Megan said. "I will anyway."

"I knew you would. Aren't you always the one who reins us back in? You're lucky to be so happy by yourself. To not need anyone."

She didn't. But she sure was thinking it might be nice to have someone around. If that someone was like Noah. But then again, how many Noahs were out there in the world? And then of those, how many were near Boot Creek? Slim pickings at best.

Angie spoke up. And Megan knew that she would. "Flynn, calming down and not trying so hard does not mean that you give up the dream of finding your soul mate. It will happen. Look at me. And I have a child. I really didn't think I'd ever find someone who could love me and Billy the way I wanted. And then there was Jackson."

"And Derek. I was in the middle of a meltdown when I bumped into him. So, not the right timing, but I think fate will bring you together if it's right. No matter what. You just have to be open to what the world is putting in front of you."

"How do you even know when it's right, though?" Megan asked.

"You'll feel it," Angie said.

Katy's voice was soft, dreamy. "His kisses will send your every nerve ending tingling like a sparkler, and you won't be able to think straight. Your insides will be like the inside of a snow globe and your cheeks will hurt from you smiling—all the way from your heart to your lips. It's incredible."

"Sounds impossible."

"Don't be a Debbie Downer," Angie said.

"You're going to have yours one day. I'm telling you. No matter how hard you try to avoid it, you will find love and you will not deny it."

"We'll see." Megan wasn't going to jump into that express line.

"Me too?"

"Definitely, you too, Flynn."

Megan remembered exactly how Noah's kisses had felt. Emotion shuddered through her just at the memory. "His kisses will make me feel like a sparkler?"

Angie swatted at Megan's arm. "Stop laughing. You'll see. Okay, maybe not like a sparkler, but, like, tingly. And fabulous. Oh, you go ahead and laugh. When you've really been kissed, you'll know it."

She bit her lip. She contemplated spilling the truth, but the truth was she could identify with that stupid sparkler reference. "I kissed Noah last night."

"What?"

"He was with you? That's where he was? All night?"

"Oh, my gosh. And you let it go this long without saying anything?" Flynn could catch flies in her mouth it was dropped open so wide.

"Do you like him," Katy asked.

"I like him," Megan admitted. "I definitely like him. At least the way he kisses."

"He's so cute," said Flynn.

"And he's also going back to California. Not really a smart move, but I don't regret it. Not one bit."

"Don't discount it so quickly, Megan. I told you Jackson said Noah can't quit talking about you."

"That," Megan pointed out with a finger stabbed in each of their directions, "does *not* mean he likes me like that."

"Doesn't mean he doesn't," Katy sang out.

"How was the kiss? Tell us," Flynn begged.

"Oh. My. God." Megan lifted her foot out of the water and curled her toes. "Like that. And it wasn't one kiss. It was dozens of them and they were all the toe-curling kind. Every single last one of them."

"Holy shit. Megan. I can't believe it. But I'm happy. I'm excited for you," Angie said. "Wouldn't it be so cool if we were married to best friends?"

"Calm down. I'm going to be sorry I told you."

"Did it feel like fireworks?" Flynn teased.

"Yes, it kind of did," Megan admitted with a laugh. "I swear we are so immature. Good thing we aren't in a spa in Boot Creek. The whole dang town would know by now."

"Who says they don't?" Angie added.

"Not a word of this to anyone else, y'all. He's going to be leaving town. It was a horrible slip up. It just kind of happened. It all started so friendly, and then I went a little nuts. I don't know what was I thinking."

"That you're an adult and you are allowed to have some fun," Flynn said. "Good lord, Megan. It's one guy. One time. You hit it off. Nothing to be ashamed about."

"Y'all know that I've never slept with a guy I barely knew. Never." She gave them her don't-mess-with-me look. "No one better breathe a word of this to my mother."

"Megan. You're not sixteen," Flynn said laughing.

"I feel it."

"Yep. That's another sign." Katy pressed her lips together. "I'm telling you. That first day I met Derek. I had butterflies. Was giddy. It was ridiculous. I was like a schoolgirl with her first crush. I know exactly what you're feeling, Megan."

"See. And it worked out for Katy." Flynn's eyes were wild with excitement. "How was it? He's so hot. I bet it was hot. So did he just show up and you kissed him?"

"No. It was very nice. He even brought me daisies."

"Which means your mother already knows." Flynn pointed out.

"True. She is the only flower game in town." Megan scowled. "But she doesn't know the rest."

"She's probably at home hoping right now. Come on, really? You're thirty."

"I'm not thirty yet." Megan had heard the almost-thirty speech from her mother about a hundred times too many. Megan's clock wasn't ticking, but her mom's was ticking loud enough for her to scare away men for a country mile.

"Well, close enough. So what'd you do? He showed up with daisies and you kissed?"

"No. It wasn't like that at all. We'd bumped into each other earlier. He wanted to see the candle stuff. I said he could come over. He showed up with flowers. We went to Bella's. We talked. Enjoyed a great meal together. It was nice. And we'd spent . . ." She caught herself right before she spilled the beans about the project. *Pull yourself together, girl. You can't ruin the surprise. It's just too good.* "He wanted to see the car. His grandfather had one exactly like Daddy's. Same year. Same color. Everything. We have a lot in common. I don't know. It was nice."

"From what Jackson says," Angie said, "Noah's whole life is cars. His work. His play. His passion."

Oh, he was passionate all right.

Katy leaned back and closed her eyes. "Nothing wrong with building your career around your interests. I mean, we're all doing that too."

"Yeah, but we're small scale. He's in a whole other league." Megan still couldn't get her head around how big his company was. She'd meant to look it up on the internet, but she hadn't had a moment to spare yet. Now she was itching to do it. She wanted to know more about him.

She wanted to be in his league. Or did she? A flash of her walking down the beach with the Pacific Ocean lapping at her ankles as her gauzy blouse blew in a gentle breeze, and Noah, tan and smiling, walking toward her in the California sunshine. He has that look in his eye. The one that he used when he said she was hot. Like he was going to explode if he didn't say it out loud. Walking hand in hand with her, he opens the door of a bright yellow hot rod for her, then gets behind the wheel and drives so fast it makes her squeal with excitement, taking the curves fast and making the beautiful view flash by as they cruise the beach highway.

What would that really be like?

"Ladies?"

Megan snapped out of her little Noah daydream. They'd already spent too much time talking about Noah. Instead of relieving the emotions she was struggling with, they were just encouraging her and making her even more curious.

The hostess at the spa led them to the locker room, where they each changed into white waffle weave robes.

Then she guided them all to where the next part of their spa treatments would be done, and handed them each a glass of champagne. The row of thick-cushioned tan recliners filled one wall with bubbling water below them. The water changed from pink to purple to blue and back through the rainbow again.

"How do you know when you find your soul mate?" Flynn asked.

"Don't look at me," Megan said. Although she was beginning to believe she might have just experienced it.

Chapter Twelve

Noah hadn't had any luck getting Megan alone during the wedding rehearsal. She'd been with the girls or talking to the photographer or on her phone the whole time.

Now he sat, staring at her from across the room at the rehearsal dinner. He'd much rather be back at Bella's having dinner alone with her. Or back at her place having *her* for dessert. But for now, watching her bop back and forth through the room talking to everyone and taking care of business wasn't all that bad of a second option.

She lifted her chin and waved.

He was running on all eight cylinders now. Truth be told, he'd been running in high gear ever since he woke up in her place alone. He'd taken the opportunity to go out and take another look at the Adventurer. It was sweeter than he'd ever imagined. Right down to the matching numbers. It was the real deal. A rare find. As he'd stood there looking at that car that morning, all alone in her garage, it was like nothing else existed. Everything he'd wished for had just fallen from heaven.

Noah gave Megan a chin nod back, anxious for time to talk to her. He'd be leaving on Tuesday, and tomorrow was the wedding. It might be his last chance to really have any time with her. Plus, his bet with Jackson was that he'd have a deal on that car before the couple headed off on their honeymoon.

He pushed up from his seat and walked over to where Megan was talking to Flynn's grandparents, Suz and Rich, from the airport.

"Good to see you two again," Noah said.

"I still can't believe that you are in the wedding party with our sweet Flynn," Suz gushed. "It has to be some kind of fate or destiny or something."

"Good to see you." Flynn's grandfather, Rich, extended his hand. "Suz and I told Flynn how helpful you were, but don't mind Suz. She's just a hopeless matchmaker. Can't blame her this time though. Not many guys your age would've given us a second look or concern."

Noah shook his hand. "Small world, isn't it?" And he wasn't just thinking about bumping into them, but also that this trip put the car of his dreams right on his path. And Megan, well, he wasn't sure how the heck she played into it, but he'd figure it out soon enough. "Hope you don't mind if I steal Megan away."

"Not at all," Flynn's grandparents said in practiced unison. Probably from years of being together.

Megan let him lead her away. "It's going to be a beautiful ceremony."

"I'm sure. Want to get some air?"

She looked a little surprised, but then nodded. "Sure. Yeah, I've been going all night." She pointed toward the door across the way. "There's a meditation garden out that way."

They walked outside. It was still warm, but without the sun it was tolerable. They sat on a concrete bench next to a small bubbling fountain.

"I can't stop thinking about your paintings," he said. *Or you. Or that car of yours.*

"Flattery will get you everywhere," she mused.

"I'm serious. I was thinking that it would be really cool for you to come out to California and do some paintings of the cars in my collection. Maybe some of the new jobs we're working. We could sell them. I know my clients would go crazy for them."

She smiled politely.

He'd had a slew of ideas. "We could do a calendar. You could even do a specialty line of your candles that use your prints as the label on the jars. Kind of two arts in one package."

"Thank you. That's really sweet." But the conversation just hung there.

"But you don't want my advice?"

"I'm sure you're trying to be helpful, but I told you, I'm doing fine with things the way they are."

"You don't want to grow your business?"

"I don't paint anymore." All of the peacefulness of this meditation garden couldn't keep the past from howling in her memory right now.

"But you're an amazing talent."

"I like my simple little candle business. It pays the bills. It's plenty." She looked off and sighed. "I want to be free to do things."

"Like what?"

"Well, I don't exactly know yet, but as the opportunities come up, I don't want to be tied down with tons of timelines or commitments. Besides, if you get too big for your britches, things don't go your way. I prefer a simple life, thank you—not be tied down by anything. Not a business, family . . ."

"A man?" *There was more to this story. She was way too cocksure, like she'd recited this a million times.*

"That too. And yesterdays. There are some yesterdays I just don't care to repeat."

He looked into her eyes. A woman scorned, or just a woman who was a lot like him? He wasn't sure. Maybe there'd been too much stress with being an artist. "I understand your philosophy. I play more of the go-big-or-go-home route, but just the same, I'm not looking for someone to chain me down either. In fact, I'm not looking at all."

"Exactly." Lightning bolts seemed to dance in her eyes. "Finally, someone who seems to get it. I swear, it's a breath of fresh air. I know what's ahead of me. I'm comfortable with it. Why can't everyone else just let me be with that?"

"Probably because they think there are bigger things for you. But you can't predict what will happen tomorrow based on every yesterday."

"What do you have against yesterdays?" She glanced heavenward, almost as if the question was for someone else. Not him or anyone of this earth.

He let the silence stand for a moment, until she looked at him as if waiting on an answer.

"Nothing," he said. "I'm who I am because of every yesterday. I'm just not going to base my future on them. You seem to be building a wall around your future so that no one can get over. Aren't you afraid you'll miss something ahead?"

Her eyes narrowed, a slight tilt to the curve of her lips. "Were you trying to get over my wall?"

She definitely had his attention. "You're different. I'm curious." *And you scare the hell out of me.*

"Well, I don't think I need to worry about you. You don't seem the relationship-seeker type."

"I'm a type now, am I?" He wasn't sure whether to laugh or be offended. "I'll have you know that I've been in a couple pretty long relationships. Been engaged twice."

"Really? But you didn't get married. What made them leave?"

"They didn't leave me."

"See. Not the relationship type."

"I called off those engagements, because they changed. Not me."

"You sure about that? You are the common denominator there."

"Positive. Once I placed that engagement ring on her finger, everything changed. Second time, just the same as the first."

"Why'd you break it off?"

"The rules changed. Their attitude changed. Suddenly all the things we'd done weren't interesting. Maybe they wanted the lifestyle or the money and not me, or they were chameleons willing to act like what they'd thought I wanted. They were good at it if that was what it was." *And damn if I didn't learn from that mistake. Or have I, because right now I'm thinking all kinds of things.*

"Sorry that happened to you. Twice."

"Me too. So you can see why I might be a little hard to get close to. Most girls aren't interested in the things I'm interested in anyway. And then there's you." His heart clenched, wondering how she'd respond to that.

"Me?"

"You're different. I really like that. You're confident. Secure. Fun. You even like cars."

"I sure do."

"If you sold me the DeSoto, that could solve a lot of problems for you financially."

"Why do you seem so worried about my financial stability?" Her lips bunched, and not in a happy, I-want-to-kiss-you way.

"I'm not worried. I like the car. I'd totally buy it from you."

"Not . . ." She stood up, looking across the way.

"What is it?"

"I thought . . ." She walked forward and then turned, wide-eyed. There wasn't anything peaceful about the man Megan was focused on, and he was heading their way. At least they'd been out here when he showed up. "It's Angie's ex, Rodney. He's here."

Noah jumped from the bench and laid a protective hand on Megan's arm. "What's he doing here?"

"I have no idea. But it's not good news. He always spells trouble." Her chest heaved with each breath.

"Calm down. We'll get him turned around and out of here before he sets foot inside the building."

"He's coming this way right now," she said.

Noah stood there. "I'll handle this."

She stepped back as Rodney got closer.

"You the sorry ass getting ready to marry my wife?" Rodney asked, flailing his arms as he spoke.

"I don't think you were invited," Noah said.

"You gonna make me leave?"

Megan's heart pounded. She could smell the whiskey on Rodney's breath from where she stood. If he made a scene, it would ruin the mood for the whole weekend. "Rodney, you just go on back home. Y'all's divorce has been long over. You've got no reason to be here."

"Thought I should warn the poor sucker who was going to marry her," Rodney said. "You him?"

"No one's interested in what you have to say. Why don't you get back in your truck and leave? You don't want to make a scene."

"I ain't making a scene. I'm gonna save that sonofabitch some damned heartache's what I'm gonna do." Rodney staggered and Noah caught him by the arm.

"You have no business here tonight."

Rodney raised his chin. "I got business. My son is in there. I'm his father. His dad. That kid's always my business."

"You don't want him to see you like this. Come on, man." Noah spun Rodney around and grabbed him by the arm. "You've had about one too many. Want me to call you a cab?" Noah paused, looking Rodney right in the eye. "Or a cop? Your choice."

Rodney pulled his arm back. "Don't need your help."

Megan had dialed 911 and requested assistance when Noah first approached Rodney. Even though the goal was to get him to leave, she couldn't let him drive off drunk either. She looked up, and she couldn't believe what she saw. Rodney was already halfway back to his truck. Noah was still standing where he had been, just off to her side.

"Thank you so much, Noah. I called the police. I hope they get here before he gets that truck started."

"Clearly he's not over her."

"It's been a long time. He was an awful husband and father. Angie would die if she knew he'd shown up. Can we not tell her?"

"Fine by me. You can tell your friend or not," Noah said. "But I feel like I have to let Jackson know. He has a right to know. Especially if this guy might show up again."

"If Jackson knows, he needs to tell Angie. They can't start their marriage with a secret."

"But we can keep a secret from our friends? That doesn't seem right."

"You're right. Tell him. Let *him* tell Angie. He can assure her everything will be okay . . . or not. Up to him."

"Yeah, we'll let them figure it out," Noah agreed.

A police car pulled into the parking lot and right up in front of Rodney's truck.

Megan went back over and sat on the bench. "Poor Billy. He's still young, but I have a feeling Rodney is always going to be a problem for them. I'm so glad he has Jackson to look up to now. They make a good family."

"Yeah. I've never really thought I'd have kids. Don't think I'd ever heard Jackson talk about it either, but watching Jackson with Billy, I can see that it was meant to be."

"I know. And that cool room makes me almost want a kid." Megan pondered and then shook her head.

"I bet you'd be a good mom."

"Thank you . . . I think."

"Maybe you'll have a little girl who looks exactly like you someday. I bet you were an adorable little girl."

"I was awkward. And a tomboy."

"You want to have kids?"

"I've never thought I'd have children. Maybe if I met the right man I'd think differently. I'm not against it. I'm just not one of those girls with a clock ticking. If it's meant to be, I'll know it. But I'm not the marrying type."

"That's the first time I've ever heard a woman say that about kids. Do you really mean that?"

"Yeah, I do. My parents ended up divorced. Daddy marched to his own beat. He'd always been an embarrassment to Momma the way he drove around in his big white pickup truck with six-foot American flags flying from the two back corners of the tailgate. I personally thought it was kind of funny. He seemed to be having one heckuva time. But people in town were used to the behavior and, after a while, they barely even stared when he cruised by waving. He'd become the self-proclaimed welcome center for Boot Creek."

"That's kind of funny."

"Mom said he wasn't like that before he retired. She said retirement gave him a touch of the crazies."

"Or just the freedom to be he who he really was," Noah said.

"But he wasn't the man Bootsie had fallen in love with, and try as she did to be an understanding wife, eventually it got so bad that she'd left him and moved into the upstairs of the bakery."

"That had to have been hard."

"It was. Especially when not two weeks later Daddy had hooked up with a bleached blonde dancer from the go-go club up off the interstate. She's not but a few years older than me. He sold the house, gave Momma her half, and bought himself a big house in the next town over."

"Ouch."

"Yeah, Momma divorced his butt so quick. But Daddy was high-functioning crazy. Using his retirement money to gamble his way into that little dancer's heart. But through it all, Daddy had never risked losing that car."

"Can't blame him."

"I don't want to end up like either of them. And sometimes people fall in love for all the wrong reasons, but one of you is completely in the dark." Her eyes clouded. "I can't go through that. And it's not even just my gut, look at all the data I have."

"That's yesterday's data."

"It tells a story."

"It's history."

"I had a bad feeling about Rodney all along, but Angie wouldn't listen. If she had, she could have avoided that whole heartache."

"That was Angie's path. Not yours. And she got Billy out of all of that. And now Jackson. That doesn't seem like such a bad path to me."

"I love Jackson for her. But you didn't see the hell Rodney put her through. And he did treat her good before they got married. I can see how she didn't see it, but I had that feeling."

"Probably made her stronger. The great mom that she is. The thoughtful partner. The partner that will stand up for herself, and Jackson loves that about her."

"He does. Doesn't he?"

"Yeah. Never thought I'd see him like this. But it suits him."

"That's what's important." She nodded with a smile. "And Angie is over the moon happy." She paused. "How about you? You seem to have the same views on marriage that I do. Why is it okay for you and yet you question me?"

"Double standard. You're right. I apologize."

"I'm not asking for an apology."

"I want to be me. I love my life. The creativity of building the cars. The excitement of the projects. Starting with a mess and creating something that dazzles the mind."

"Won't keep you warm at night."

"That *is* a problem."

She cocked her head. "Somehow I doubt that." And why was she wondering what it would be like to wake up to that face each morning?

"There you are," Jackson said. "We're ready to head out. Angie's hanging here awhile. You coming with us?"

Noah hesitated, but he got up. "Yeah. Sure." He looked back to Megan. "Good talking to you tonight."

"I really enjoyed it." Her smile was easy. "A lot."

Me too. He nodded toward Jackson, in their unspoken agreement that he'd tell him about Rodney showing up. "Yeah. I've got this." He gave her a wink as he walked away.

He walked inside with Jackson. Ford and Derek were hanging by the door where Jackson had parked.

They all got in the truck, and Noah said, "So, there was a visitor tonight. An uninvited one."

"What are you talking about?" Ford asked.

Noah directed his words to Jackson, but was glad to know that all four of them would be on the same page. "Angie's ex showed up earlier. Drunker than hell. Wanting to share advice with you."

Jackson spun around. "Are you kidding me?"

"Nope. Megan spotted him while we were sitting out there talking. I had a quick chat with him and sent him on his way. Not sure if he'll show up tomorrow, but we probably should be prepared for it."

"He's an ass."

"I gathered that. And a little crazy eyed. And he's big by the way."

"I don't care how big he is."

"Easy to talk big and bad, but he's that kid's dad and no matter what a jerk he is, he's going to be in y'all's lives until that kid is eighteen. Hell, maybe longer."

"He's not a father to Billy. And, trust me, I'm crystal clear on the custody agreement. That loser doesn't even care."

"You will be a great stepfather. I know you will be, but Jackson, don't you kid yourself into thinking it's going to be this cozy three-person family, because that guy is going to be swooping and stirring shit whenever he damn well pleases."

"I don't doubt that he'll stir up trouble. But that was part of the package from the start. She's worth it."

"Okay. I'm just saying."

"I know. Noah, I hope you meet someone who turns your every belief on its head one day. I know what you're saying and I know that you mean well, but I love Angie. She makes me feel like my life is worth living. I want to wake up every day and see her face. I want to raise Billy, and if having those two in my life means that I have to pay the price of some bad days . . . it's a small price."

"I'm honestly happy for you. And Angie really does seem great."

"I knew you'd like her."

"I do. I think she's good for you." Noah couldn't dispute their obvious connection. "Now, that doesn't mean I feel any differently about marriage. I'm still not a believer. I'm not drinking the Kool-Aid, but I do believe *you're* happy. And I'm proud to be your best man."

"That's all I can ask of you, man."

Only it was easy to say that he wasn't drinking the Kool-Aid, but something in the water here in Boot Creek must be doing something, because he was having some serious feelings about Megan in just a few short days. No woman had ever made him feel this way. This right. Right enough that he didn't even care if he couldn't get the car. As long as he could get the girl. It was like a late-night, alien-body-snatching B movie.

He looked out the window into the dark countryside. *Probably a crop circle out there right now.*

Chapter Thirteen

Megan took a deep breath in and let it out. The meteorologist had hit the nail on the head—for once. The heat wave had finally offered a reprieve and the skies were brilliant Carolina blue against cotton-candy-like clouds.

A perfect day for a wedding.

Perfect for a couple to start their happily ever after.

And yet Megan felt like she could cry or fall apart at any moment.

If it wasn't so darned early in the morning, she'd pour herself a drink to calm down. But that wasn't going to solve the problem.

She could have solved the problem last weekend, only she'd chickened out. Now she had no choice but to get in that car and take it over to the church.

It's a car. This is ridiculous. This is not a big deal.

But it didn't matter how many times she said it. To herself or out loud up on the rooftop patio. It felt huge.

Still in her pajamas, she sipped coffee from a tall mug. The morning air was fresh, and the birds seemed to be pretty happy about it too. Squirrels chattered, and the sounds of Boot Creek waking up and getting to work on a Saturday morning reminded her she'd already been sitting there too long. And she wondered how much her opinion of this nice morning had been influenced by the time spent with Noah. He'd buoyed her mood and sparked interests in things that she thought she'd set aside for good. But anxiety coursed through her, making her muscles ache.

She had no good reason to feel this way. Dad had been the one to say yes to letting Jackson and Angie use the car to begin with. He'd trusted Jackson. Why couldn't she? Angie was her best friend and her dad had treated her like a second daughter. He'd have loved to have been here for this wedding. He'd originally been the one that was going to give her away. It had worked out fine that Derek would do it. They were as close as any two friends could be.

She'd washed her hair before coming outside, and now it was nearly dry. A tangle of curls, but Flynn was doing all of their hair in updos for the wedding anyway. She'd stalled just about as long as she could.

With her mug in hand, she went downstairs and turned off the coffeepot and put her mug in the dishwasher.

She changed out of her pajamas into a pair of yoga pants and a loose fitting baseball-jersey-style shirt that had BLESSED across the front in a bright blue, swirly font, the same color as the sleeves. She slipped her feet into a pair of flip-flops and picked up the tote bag she'd packed with all of the things she'd need to get ready at the church.

Dread filled her as she walked toward the garage. Her hand slipped on the knob as she twisted it, her palm sweaty.

She flipped the light switch.

Daddy's car was now hers. This car made a statement. It was the perfect representation of Daddy. Big, audacious, shiny with unexpected strength and charm.

She walked in and set her bag down next to the car.

Not once, ever, had she driven it. Daddy had always done the driving.

Anxiety swept over her.

Keep moving. Just do it.

The huge metal-and-glass overhead door that opened to the back parking lot was an old manual-pull type.

She walked over and wrapped her hands around the weathered rope pulls. She tugged with all of her weight. It was in working order but was always hard to get moving. The first few inches were a booger-bear every time.

One day I'm going to be able to afford an electric opener for this thing.

She gave it one more good tug. The pulley and gravity finally took control, sending the door rolling up with a clatter.

On edge, she jumped back, even though she'd gone through the routine of opening this door dozens of times. But it was her own fault that she was now in this position. Had she been brave enough to confide in Angie about the car and told her about the limo, she probably would've understood. Not that even she herself really did. It didn't make sense, and in her mind, she knew it was an over-the-top desire to hang on to an old memory through a car, but it was there. And it felt all too real. And regardless . . . it was too late to change it. *Calm down.*

Licking her lips, she walked back over to the car to open the driver's-side door. Standing there, she stared inside. She let her hand rest on the gold ragtop. He'd held up well. A strong car. Like Daddy. He always made an entrance. An impression.

She smiled, an image of her father laughing in her mind. Daddy had always had a way of filling a room. She loved that about him. This car kind of did the same thing. It made a lasting impression.

It was only right that Daddy would have wanted Angie and Jackson to start their new life together driving off in this car.

Jackson was everything she could've wished for her best friend in this world. *I'm almost a little envious. What would it feel like to be loved like that? To have someone there to spot me through every good and bad day?*

I'm stalling.

But what was the harm? She'd given herself plenty of time that morning. And that had been easy, since she hadn't been able to sleep a wink last night.

Walking around the car, she allowed her hand to glide across the smooth finish. As shiny as if it had just come off the showroom floor, her hand smoothly swept around each curve of the car. Tracing its contour. Remembering the Saturday mornings she and her dad had spent hand washing it and using the special chamois he only used on this car. It was an all-day affair. Not that it ever looked dirty to her.

That painting Noah had fallen in love with was still on the toolbox where he'd left it. Flaw and all. Her little secret. But she'd shared it with him. Her secret spot too. Easy to share secrets with someone who will be over twenty-five hundred miles away in a few days. Someone she'd never see again.

Why do things have to be so complicated?

She studied the painting. It had been done a long time ago. Another lifetime. Like someone else's lifetime ago.

Get a move on, girl.

Carla had taken all of the bridal party dresses over to the church, so all Megan had to take was her makeup and shoes. An easy morning with the girls, playing dress up and supporting Angie on her big day.

What kind of maid of honor am I, having doubts about the car now? She felt selfish and silly.

She straightened and marched over to the driver's side of the car and picked up her tote bag. She shifted it up on her shoulder and then wrapped her fingers around the door handle. Just standing there. The thrum of her heartbeat echoed in her ears. She'd never opened this door before. Not even when they'd delivered the car.

Tears filled her eyes.

She looked toward the ceiling. Wishing Dad was there or would somehow give her a comforting sign. She'd only ever sat in the passenger's seat. She'd liked it that way. She'd never even asked to drive it—perfectly happy with him being at the wheel.

She could picture Dad sitting there with his arm out the window, smiling in her direction. Them laughing. The wind pushing against her hand as she chased the air with her open palm.

Pulling the door handle with one quick thrust, she opened the door and tossed her handbag into the passenger's seat. She closed her eyes, dropped behind the steering wheel, and let out a breath.

"It's fine. I can do this." Maybe saying it aloud would make it so.

Every yesterday in this car had been a special one.

Stretching her legs out, her feet didn't reach the pedals. Her heart hiccuped at the thought of moving it from where her dad had set it. One more thing to leave behind.

Jackson had offered to pick it up, but she'd insisted on doing it herself. She regretted that now. If she'd let Jackson pick up the car, he could have left the seat right where it was. He and Daddy were about the same height.

She grappled around under the seat for a lever or a button. She wasn't even sure how to move it.

The steering wheel felt wide and skinny compared to her little car.

"I miss you, Daddy. Why is it so hard to let go of yesterdays?"

"Maybe because they were that special."

She spun around, sucking a breath so quickly that she choked. The unexpected answer scared the bejesus out of her. She placed her hand against her chest. "Noah? What are you doing here?"

He stood next to the car. His hands on his knees, peering in from the blind spot just over her left shoulder.

His brown eyes locked with her own. "Maybe we don't have to forget yesterdays, just be able to live with them. I know it sounds simple, but damn it's taken me a long time to figure it out. I'm kind of hoping you're coming to the same realization."

"Easier said than done," she muttered, turning away from him. "How'd you get in?"

"Door was open. We don't have to be over at the church until later. I was jogging."

She glanced back again. "Yeah, I see now; you *are* a sweaty mess. It's a good morning for a jog. Why are you here?"

"Thought I'd stop by. I knocked on the front door. You didn't answer, but as I was leaving I noticed the garage-bay door open. You okay?"

"You been standing there long?"

"A little while," he admitted.

Then he knew she wasn't okay.

"Hey, tomorrow will be better. Every day will be a little better."

"That's just it, Noah. I don't want to leave my yesterdays behind." *Maybe some of them, but not these. Not the ones with Daddy.*

"You can't enjoy what's ahead of you if you're focused on what's in your rearview mirror."

What? Was he some kind of philosopher all of a sudden? This wasn't helpful right now. Don't cry. Do not cry in front of him. She resisted the urge to dab the dampness from under her eyes, tilting her head down, hoping to hide any tears that resisted her constraint.

"What are you doing?" he asked.

"Contemplating."

"Contemplating what?"

"Why I've been sitting here for ten minutes, and can't bring myself to turn the key in the ignition."

Noah pulled the door open and crouched down next to the driver's-side door.

"I've never driven it before. Daddy was always the one in this seat."

"You know how to drive a car. I've seen you."

"This is different."

"It's your car now. He wouldn't have left it to you had he not trusted you with it. That I know for a fact."

"I know." She barely heard the words they'd come out so quietly.

He tapped his hand along the window track, then loosened her hand from the death grip she had on the steering wheel. "What can I do to help you, Megan?"

She looked into his eyes as he squatted there beside the car. She felt at ease in his presence. She barely knew him. But just like the other day, she felt at ease when she'd shown him her paintings—the little peek into her past, and her secret rooftop escape.

"Get in and drive."

Did she say what I think she just said? "Drive?"

"Yes." She let out a breath. "Drive. I need to take the car to the church. I can't reach the pedals. I can't do this. Just drive. Okay?"

"Here, I can help you adjust the seat." He reached in to help her. She slapped at his hand. "No. It's right where Daddy left it last."

He froze, raising his hands like a criminal under arrest. "Okay."

"I don't want to move the seat. I know it sounds dumb. You're the right height. Humor me. Okay?"

"Absolutely," he said.

She scooted over to the passenger seat. Nothing ladylike about the way she was crabbing over across to the other side; in fact, it was a bit comical. Good thing she wasn't in her bridesmaid dress.

He slid into the driver's seat. The smell of her perfume and shampoo lingered, teasing his senses.

This car. This girl. Almost too much.

He turned and smiled at her. She looked like a teenager sitting there. Young, vulnerable, even though he knew better. "Tell me about the last time you were in this car."

"I always rode shotgun. This is my spot." She patted the leather seat. "Daddy drove. Top down. No matter what the weather, hot or cold."

"Your hair blowing in the wind?" He could picture her soft beach waves blowing carefree in the breeze, whipping and lifting. It made him want to run his fingers through her hair. He resisted though, grasping his hand against his own forearm instead.

"No." She leaned over and dropped the glove compartment open. A cute laugh escaped her. "It's still here." She reached in and pulled out a hot-pink bandana. "I always tie my hair up in this."

She stared at the rolled fabric, stroking it softly with her fingers. A sweet smile played on her lips.

"Do it," he said.

"What?"

"Let me see." He looked into her eyes. "Your hair pulled up."

She lifted the bandana and spun it behind her neck, pulling the waves of her brown hair into a cute pinup girl look.

"Beautiful." More beautiful than he could've imagined. It sure wasn't hard to spend time with this girl.

A tinge of pink chased from her cheeks to her chest. She pulled her feet up into the seat and wrapped her arms around her knees. The behemoth of a car was wider than she was tall.

"You look tiny in this car," he remarked.

"I know," she laughed. "It's huge, but I have enough memories related to this car to fill the entire front and back seat."

"That's a lot of good memories. You ready?"

She lifted her shoulders.

"Want to put the top down?"

"Do you know how?"

"Do I know how? Girl, you are talking to the expert on this year and model." He reached up and pulled straight down on the two latches at the windshield header.

Megan looked impressed.

He pushed the top by hand to free it, then reached below the dash and flipped a switch, holding it until the motorized top had lowered into the well. With all the grace of a ballerina, the top hid itself completely.

Megan's pout had turned into a smile. "Pretty uptown for an old car."

He started the car. Its throaty rumble sounded as healthy as any he'd ever heard. Megan's dad had shown this ride real love. He hadn't neglected her. He opened the door.

"Where are you going?"

"The cover for the top should be in the trunk."

She sat back looking relieved. Oh, he had no intention of leaving her and not driving this car. Short of a heart attack . . . that was not going to happen. The cover was in the trunk just as he'd expected. He quickly snapped it over the top and jumped back into the car. "Let's go."

"You know the way?"

"I think so. I mean, there aren't but like seven streets in this town."

"Give or take a few."

"And we were just there last night for the rehearsal." He tapped the side of his head. "Car guys have excellent internal navigation systems."

She rolled her eyes, but that was a huge improvement over the look on her face a few moments before.

He slowly backed out of the wide bay, exhilaration flowing through him. "I'll get the garage door," he said.

"No, you can leave it up. No one will mess with anything back here."

He cruised around the building and then gave the accelerator a little punch to get out to the street. He slowed at the stop sign, and then came to a complete stop. "You sure you don't want to drive?"

She shook her head.

"Okay. To the church." Turning left onto Crump Farm Road, he went the posted speed limit. Dying to open it up and really let this car run, how he wished the church wasn't just a few blocks away.

It was only walking distance from the inn where he and the guys were staying, in fact. After driving this he'd feel like running, not walking.

Man, it felt good to be driving this car. He rested his arm on Megan's leg, and smiled. *This. Right here. This was living.*

She smiled back, her gaze lingering as he turned to watch the road.

He flipped the blinker to turn down the street where the church rose on a slight incline.

Megan reached over and placed her hand on Noah's chest. "Don't."

"Don't what?"

"Let's not stop. Let's go for a ride—open her up on the interstate." Her eyes danced, and her smile was playful. Mischievous.

"Really?"

She nodded. A fast and definite yes.

"Hell yeah." He did a U-turn and headed down Main Street. Straight for the interstate.

She struck a confident pose in the seat next to him with that bright pink bandana all tied up in her hair.

Nothing had ever looked sexier.

The heavy car took the tight turn onto the ramp with grace, handling the curves and straightaway like a race car, even though this car was built way before race-car features were part of everyday driving automobiles.

He punched the accelerator, taking the gimme-five-over-the-posted-seventy-mph speed limit, and then pushing right on past it. He let out a wild whoop. "Yeah!"

Megan tossed her head back laughing. "It's heaven."

"Yeah, it is!"

"Faster," she screamed, throwing a fist in the air.

Who gave a rat's ass about a ticket now? It'd be worth whatever penalty they could throw at him. He had the car of his dreams, and a woman that tossed him like a tornado sitting next to him.

He opened it up, letting her roll. Sleek and throaty, the car roared down the highway.

Megan had her head back, grinning ear to ear.

He'd love to be in her thoughts right now.

At the next exit, he slowed the car to the speed limit and then exited, circling back on the interstate to head back to Boot Creek.

"What a way to start the day," he said.

"You saved my morning. Thank you, Noah."

"I'll be your hero any day." And he couldn't wait to get this car to California into his own garage. There wasn't a thing he'd need to do to it. This DeSoto would go straight into his collection.

He pulled into the back lot of the church. "Where do they want the car parked?"

"If you could drop me here, and then park it at the end of the walk-way where Jackson and Angie will be coming out after the wedding, I think that will be perfect."

"What do you want me to do with the keys?"

"Leave them in it."

His jaw dropped. He knew it did. He felt like one of those exaggerated cartoon characters with the bug-out eyes. *Leave the keys in it? She had to be kidding.*

"It'll be fine. Trust me. This is Boot Creek. And it's in front of the church. No one is going to mess with it."

"Okay, if you say so. I know you wouldn't take any chances with it."

"Not in a million years." She opened the door and grabbed her tote bag. "Thanks again for helping me. I don't know what I'd have done if you hadn't showed up, but I'm pretty sure I'd have been a mess by the time I got here."

"Glad I showed up when I did."

She waved and then turned and headed into the church.

He moved the car to the front and got out. A light coat of dust had already settled on the paint. He was tempted to take off his T-shirt and wipe her down to a shine, not that anyone else would notice.

Noah walked down the sidewalk, turning back to glance at the sweet ride one last time before he crossed the street.

Chapter Fourteen

Angie was sitting in a straight-back chair while Flynn twisted, wrapped, braided, and tucked Angie's hair into a beautiful updo.

"Flynn, you missed your calling. I swear, girls with years of practice don't do hair as well as you do."

"Are you trying to build up my confidence before I do yours?" Flynn said through the bobby pins in her teeth.

"No. If mine looks like that, I'm going to be tempted to sleep sitting up in a chair for a week just so I won't mess it up."

"Well, she is the bride. Hers has to be extra super-duper special." Flynn swirled another section of Angie's hair and pinned and sprayed it.

Megan flounced into the chair in front of the big-mirrored vanity across the room. "Man. You get the prettiest dress *and* best hair. No fair."

"No upstaging the bride," Angie said. "That's part of the bridesmaid code."

"Not likely to happen, my friend. Jackson is going to die when he sees you all made up. You look Hollywood beautiful. Flawless." Megan unzipped her tote and started spreading her makeup out on the counter in front of the mirror alongside the other girl's things. Her pile looked meager compared to the others. She could work a paintbrush like nobody's business, but she'd never gotten into the art of makeup.

Katy walked into the room already made up. "I'm the last one here? I thought I was going to be first. I guess y'all couldn't sleep last night either."

"You know I wasn't sleeping. Jackson and I were texting at three," Angie said.

"Me either," Megan admitted, although it hadn't just been the wedding that had kept her awake.

"Guilty," Flynn raised her hand. "We all ought to be a fun crew come reception time."

Megan leaned closer to the mirror and started applying her makeup. "We'll have our second wind by then."

"We'd better," Angie said. "Else Jackson is going to be one bummed-out groom."

"Somehow I think you'll muster the energy for that," Megan teased.

"It's been so weird to not be staying together this last week before the wedding. He usually stays over at my place or Billy and I at his at least a couple times a week. I miss him."

"Y'all are so cute," Katy said.

"Precious. That's what they are." Megan leaned back and checked her eye makeup. "Is this too much?"

Katy turned her by the shoulders and looked. "No. It's not enough. Come here." She reached for an eye-shadow compact on the counter and started dabbing and sweeping. "Close your eyes."

"You're going to do mine, right?" Angie stood and walked over to watch what Katy was doing.

"Yep." Katy took an eyeliner pen and swept soft lines, smudging them as she went. "Look up."

"I better not look like a clown. That feels like a lot of stuff you're putting on me," Megan said.

"Ease up," Angie said. "Katy is so good at this. We practiced mine last week. Jackson went gaga that night. It stays in place and everything. You know I'm like you, not usually much for makeup. It does feel like a lot, but it looks so natural."

"If it's going to look natural, can't I just go *au naturel*?" Megan scrunched her lips.

"No," they all said.

"Got it. Fine."

"Quit making faces," Katy chided.

"Sorry."

"Okay, look at me."

Megan lifted her chin and looked at Katy, then batted her eyelashes. "Beautiful?"

"Very," Flynn said. "Well, you will be when I fix that mop. What'd you do? Dry your hair with the mixer by mistake?"

"Long story," Megan said.

"Get over here."

Megan followed Flynn and sat down in the chair where Angie had been, while Katy and Angie started working through the order of how to get Angie in her getup for the day.

Flynn pulled a comb through Megan's waves.

"Oh, wait, before you get started, let's do the old-new-borrowed-blues with Angie." Megan bounced out of her seat and took a small box out of her tote bag.

Flynn and Katy dispersed and came back with boxes—all of them wrapped in Tiffany blue wrapping paper with white ribbons.

"You didn't have to do this. I think I have it covered."

"Oh no, we're not taking any chances," Megan grinned.

"It was Megan's plan. She rocks the maid-of-honor spot," Flynn said. "We were excited to do this."

Angie dropped into the Queen Anne chair next to a coffee table. "Y'all are going to make me cry before I even get dressed. This isn't fair."

"All's fair in love," Megan reminded her.

"Open this one first." Flynn stepped forward and placed her box on the table. In the top right corner in black script, it read "Something Old."

Katy put one of hers on the table. "Something new," she said, and then laid down the other one. "This one is from Naomi. It's the something borrowed . . ." Katy practically bounced with excitement. "You're going to die. I can't wait to see your face."

Angie laughed. "And I can't open that one first? Really? That's torture."

"Oh, stop complaining." Megan set the last box on the table. "Something blue, and a lucky sixpence in your shoe," Megan said, stepping back to stand with the other girls; they held hands. "Open them."

"I couldn't have better friends. I love y'all." Angie started with "Something Old." Placing the box in her lap, she pinched the end of the white, satiny ribbon and tugged. She laid the ribbon aside, too pretty to waste, then slipped her manicured fingernail under the edge of the paper to unwrap it.

"We couldn't let you go through this life-changing event without all the tokens of good luck for a bride."

"I'd never heard the sixpence part. What the heck is a sixpence?" Flynn shrugged. "Glad I didn't get that one to do."

"It's the wish for good fortune and prosperity, but I had to look it up. I found one on online." Megan shrugged.

"Guess I know what's in that box then," Angie said with a nervous giggle.

Her laughter coming to a halt, as she opened the "Something Old" box, "It's beautiful. It has to be vintage."

Megan watched as Angie carefully slipped her nail into space between the two wings of the tiny gold locket until it opened. Inside there were pictures of Billy and Jackson. "This is perfect. Thank you, Flynn. So thoughtful."

Flynn beamed. "I had the little loop changed so you can use it as a charm instead of a necklace. It's so pretty. So you. And the something old is for continuity." Flynn stepped over and hugged Angie.

Angie shook her head as she focused on Katy. "I'm glad we didn't do my makeup yet." She picked up the "Something New" box.

Katy said, "That one is from Derek *and* me. He picked it out. The something new offers optimism for the future. Derek is always saying that you are the most optimistic person in the world, so you probably don't need it, but you deserve it anyway."

"A gold bracelet? This is gorgeous. Oh, my gosh. I love it. For the charm, right?" She looked to Flynn and back to Katy.

"Yes," Katy quickly added, "But we don't expect you to wear it today. You'll see. There's a theme here."

"Why wouldn't I?" Angie held the gifts in her hand, treasuring them.

Megan interjected, "Because we all know you're wearing your mother's pearl necklace and matching bracelet. Those are special and you should wear them. This is for the happily-ever-after. Keep going."

"Fine. Something borrowed then. You said this is from Naomi?" Angie asked as she pulled the ribbon from that box.

The girls nodded.

"Diamonds and pearls? Oh my gosh, this ring has to be every bit of what? Like, four carats?"

"Only three according to Naomi, but I'm with you—that's one big diamond," Katy said. "It was just sitting in her jewelry box."

"And the pearls have the most beautiful bluish tint." She pressed her lips together, and tried the ring on different fingers of her right hand, settling on her middle finger. "Holy smokes."

The girls were giddy.

Angie held her hand out, wiggling her finger so that the light cast a prism on the wall across the room. "She's letting me wear this for the wedding?"

"It was her idea," Katy said. "I swear, it's like an Elizabeth Taylor ring or something."

She lifted her hand to show them. "It fits perfectly on my middle finger. Amazing. Look how it shimmers."

"Something borrowed symbolizes borrowed happiness, and Naomi said that no one on this earth could have had a more blessed and happy life than her. She wants you to walk in her shoes."

"That is so sweet." Angie fanned her eyes. "This is too much. My eyes are going to be puff bags."

"No worries. The maid of honor has witch hazel. It fixes everything." Megan walked over and got the bottle and some pads from her bag. "Weep on, wedding girl. I've got you covered."

"Thank goodness." Angie picked up the "Something Blue" box.

"Something blue is for love," Megan said. "And fidelity."

"So that's what I did wrong the first time," Angie teased. "Didn't have the right shade of blue."

"No. You didn't listen to me the first time," Megan said. "This time you have my complete blessing."

"He is great." Angie opened the box that held a blue pearl charm by the engraved gold clasp. In perfect tiny letters, her wedding date and new monogram were engraved. She picked up the sixpence. "Am I supposed to put this in my shoe? I'm wearing sandals. That is not going to work."

Megan pointed to the box. "I put a glue dot in the bottom of the box. You can glue it in the arch of your sandal or under your shoe on the inside of the heel or something.

"Good idea. This is perfect. Y'all put so much thought into all of this." She pulled the tissue paper aside. "There's more in this box."

"And the rest of the story," Flynn added in her best Andy Rooney impression.

Two soft blue garters. A slim one and a wide one.

"Two," Megan said. "The slim one is for Jackson to slingshot to the single guys. It has extra bouncy stretchy elastic. The other one is for you. All of your good luck treasures fit into the little pocket sewn into it."

"How clever." Angie stood and hugged each of them one by one. Tears streaming down her face. "I am the luckiest woman in the world."

"Okay, get it out. Because there will be no more crying today." Megan dampened two of the cotton pads with witch hazel. "Hold your breath. This stuff stinks, but it is a freaking wonder drug. Lay back in that chair and let me put these on you while we get everything laid out for you."

"Yes, ma'am," Angie said. "It does stink. I better not smell like this."

"It dissipates. Trust me." Megan and the girls started slipping out of their casuals and into their gowns. Then laid everything out for Angie.

"Okay, let's look at your eyes," Megan said. "Katy, what do you think?"

Katy put her fingers under Angie's chin. "A masterpiece. Let's get this going. I'll do makeup first. We'll all do lipstick last so we don't get it on our dresses. Come over here in front of the mirror, Angie. The light's better."

Angie got settled and Katy got herself ready and then went to work like an expert.

Megan sat in the straight-back chair and let Flynn work her magic on her hair. Less than twenty minutes later, her hair looked like it could be on the cover of a bride's magazine. "Flynn, this is magical. Thank you."

All of them were made up and the girls were in their gowns, except for Angie. "I'm starting to get nervous." Angie balled her hands in her lap.

"You're going to be fine. You're a beautiful bride getting ready to marry the man of your dreams," Katy said.

"What if he changes his mind and doesn't show up?"

"Why would he do that," Megan asked. "That doesn't even make sense."

"It happens. I've seen it. Heard stories."

"I'll go make sure he's here," Flynn said. "I'll be right back."

Flynn breezed out of the door in her soft blue gown and strappy sandals. The old heavy oak door clicked loudly behind her.

"I wonder if Billy is nervous?"

"Don't you melt down on me," Megan said. "I'll lose my maid-of-honor card. I worked hard for this." Megan tried to get Angie to laugh, or at least breathe. She winked at Katy. "There was tough competition."

"Yeah, Flynn and I were just waiting for her to screw up," Katy added.

"See. Don't ruin all my hard work."

Angie reached up and grabbed Megan's hand. "Thanks."

Flynn walked back into the room and closed the door behind her. "This is so exciting. People are starting to arrive. The church looks beautiful. Angie, Billy looks so stinking cute. I wanted to gobble him up in that little suit. And Jackson is so excited I swear he looks like he won the big lottery. Not a worry that I could see."

Angie let out a breath. "Billy was okay?"

"High-fiving and fist-bumping with the guys. He even showed me how he's going to carry the pillow with the rings. He's very proud to be in the wedding."

"My little man."

"Let's get you in your dress, Angie." Megan helped Angie into her gown, and then Katy took over with the last details on makeup. Nothing left to do now but wait for someone to tell them to start walking.

Jackson reached down, picked up Billy, and placed him up in the windowsill. "Now, you're on our level, sport."

"Thanks, Daddy Jax."

Noah loved the nickname Billy had made up for Jackson. He hoped Angie wasn't going to kill them for that, but it had happened in the middle of things this morning after Billy picked up that Noah called Jackson "Jax."

Billy had just stood there letting Jackson put a flower on his suit lapel for an incredibly long time, even for an adult, but the kid had been a trooper. Then he'd looked up and said, "Thanks, Jax." Ford had laughed and said, "you can't call your daddy by his first name," and Billy said. "I can call you Daddy Jax. Okay?"

And Noah wouldn't soon forget the kindness that seemed to fill Jackson's face at that moment. Hell, all of them had traded a look. It was pretty touching.

Jackson had bent down on his knee, eye-to-eye with Billy. "I'd be honored," he'd said.

The waiting around was making Noah stir-crazy. To go from the adrenaline rush with Megan this morning to the dead stop of waiting around in this musty dungeon before the wedding was hell.

"When you think about it, this whole wedding procession thing seems backwards. I mean the girls are the ones dying to get those fancy gowns that cost a month's salary on and be seen like runway models walking down the aisle, and yet they stick us out there for an awkwardly long time before those girls are ever seen." Noah ran a finger between his collar and neck. He had a feeling wherever they had all the pretty girls stashed was a lot nicer than this dark stuffy room they were crammed into.

"Does seem backwards, doesn't it?" Ford agreed.

"Yeah." Derek said, "But you guys won't understand until you've gone through it. Man, seeing your girl that day . . . In all white. Just for you. Indescribable."

"I'll take your word for that," Noah said.

"Maybe I'll be able to describe it. Ask me at the reception," Jackson said with a poke to Noah's ribs.

A knock came at the door. Noah opened it and poked his head out.

"That's our signal. Time for us to take our positions." As best man, he made sure they all lined up in the right order like they'd practiced the night before. And Derek, who'd been hanging with them, took Billy with him. He'd send Billy down the aisle and then hang back to walk his best friend, Angie, down the aisle to give her away.

"Last chance." Noah's brows rose. "What's it going to be?"

Jackson smiled and said, "We're doing this, man."

"Then let's roll." Noah prodded Jackson and he walked out to the altar.

Jackson looked happy, but it felt more like lining up in front of a firing squad to Noah.

The church was packed. At least the air was moving out here, but he was already hot from being cooped up in that room. Jackson looked suddenly pale. And sweating.

"You gonna be okay, man?" Heck, if all those satiny looking bows and flowers on each pew weren't enough to make a man sweat, the fact that there were more people in this church than in a sports bar on Super Bowl was.

Jackson nodded, smiling like he was afraid someone might have heard them. "Yeah. I'm just a little bit nervous. This looks like a lot more than seventy people."

"I can get you out of here."

Jackson laughed. "Not that damn nervous. I love her. I'm excited. I can't wait to make her mine forever."

"Don't call me in five years and tell me I was right."

They fist bumped, and there was a low chuckle from the front row.

"She's a great gal. Don't worry," Noah said. And there it was. Another one of his friends getting married. And being completely sure of it. Not one doubt.

As usual, he stood there with this weird sense of curiosity. He'd never come close to feeling that romantic love that seemed to make his friends get married. Even his engagements had been more of those women wearing him down than something he'd really felt. He felt a little like a naturalist observing some odd phenomenon, detached but totally engulfed in the whole thing as it unfolded in front of him.

Soaring wooden ceilings warm with the patina of time made the big church still feel intimate. Noah felt the pull of the colors and distinct artistry of a large, triangular, stained-glass window depicting Christ as our good shepherd above the baptistery. Another large stained-glass window depicting Mary meeting the risen Christ in the garden dominated the front of the building.

The building was reminiscent of a capsized ship with large wooden beams representing the bare hull. An image that reminded Noah of the words of his grandfather about how important our faith is in the midst of a stormy journey.

And for a moment, Noah felt closer to his grandfather. He wasn't sure if that had something to do with Megan's DeSoto or with being here in this church with that memory. He hadn't thought of that conversation with him in such a long time.

The prelude music flooding the space from the Moller pipe organ suddenly shifted, and the doors opened at the back of the church.

Noah watched with a curious eye as Flynn and then Katy walked down the aisle. Noah felt smug, like the one with all the marbles as his friends, old and new, seemed to look drugged with romance, yet he remained unaffected.

Then Megan stepped into the doorway and began her procession down the aisle.

His mouth went dry. He knew it was her. But she didn't look like the young thing he was cruising down the highway with a couple hours ago.

Her hair was up in a fancy twisty updo just like the other girls, but on her it looked different. Soft. Innocent. Curling pieces had fallen forward to her cheek, that soft cheek.

He felt the incredible urge to rush forward and brush them back. Her eyes were smoky and her lips the softest pink, like a soft rose begging to bloom.

She took cautious steps up to the altar. Her bright pink toenails peeking out from the strappy shoes with each step. The way the soft blue dress moved around her legs, no stockings, her tan legs begged for his attention.

Megan took her spot, directly in line with him, and smiled.

She looked more beautiful than he could have imagined. She was gorgeous all sweaty with paint splotched on her. But this? This he wasn't prepared for.

She wrinkled her nose, her perfect smile turning to a playful grin. Even though her lips were pressed together, he could tell they were quivering slightly.

Excitement. Nerves. He didn't know, but whatever it was . . . it suited her.

The rising sound of a collective *awwww* broke his attention. Beside him, Jackson was giving Billy a thumbs up as the little boy marched proudly down the aisle in his tiny tuxedo with that white satin pillow in his hands. He clutched that thing like it was his favorite toy and someone was going to try to take it from him. He climbed the steps and shook Jackson's hand.

Everyone in the room was smiling.

Billy turned and looked at the rest of the guys with a knowing smile. That little guy knew exactly what was going on and he seemed as excited as Jackson.

I'd have my ring bearer ride down in one of those little cars. Beep beep. What the hell am I thinking? I'm not having one of these.

Noah bent his knees and then straightened them again, those last thoughts making him wonder if he was about to pass out or something. Crazy. He was losing it, but he wouldn't deny that there was a tug on his heart at the sight of stepfather and son. The happiness in that pint-sized little boy's face was immeasurable.

The organist hit those all-too-familiar first four notes and everyone in the church turned their attention to the back of the room.

Jackson got about an inch taller with an audible inhale as Angie stepped out into their view and took Derek's arm.

"She looks like an angel," Billy said quietly, but loud enough that the first few rows were nudging each other.

Derek walked her up the aisle and the music stopped.

Noah could hear Jackson breathing, and Angie looked like she would burst from happiness. He could feel their energy.

"You may be seated," the minister said.

The guests dropped back to their seats, the sound moving the air in a welcome rush.

Noah watched as Derek gave Angie away, and then Jackson took the hands of the woman he loved into his, with Billy standing at his side. Man to man. A family.

And Noah didn't hear one word as that whole ceremony went on in front of him, because he couldn't take his eyes off of Megan. She was focused on her best friend. Genuinely happy for her, even if the bouquets, her own and the bride's, shook in her hands.

He wanted so badly to walk over and step behind her. To wrap his arms around her and whisper, "It's going to be okay."

"I now pronounce you man and wife. You may kiss the bride."

Jackson kissed Angie soft on the mouth, and then twisted her into a dip that had Billy in a fit of giggles so strong that his face was red.

"May I present the Washburn family."

Jackson stepped aside and put Billy between himself and Angie, and they walked down the aisle.

Noah sucked in a breath as he walked toward Megan. He could feel the grin stretching across his face. He probably looked like a dope, but he couldn't help himself.

She wrapped her arm through his, leaning in to hug his arm. Her smile was absolutely contagious.

He could stand to have this girl on his arm again.

For more than three dates.

He reached over and patted her hand with his free hand. "You were the prettiest one here. You even outshined the bride."

She looked doubtful, but said thank you with a laugh. "You clean up pretty nice yourself."

They walked outside and everyone gathered for the official exit of the bride and groom. The DeSoto sat in front of the church, right where he'd parked it, ready for Mr. and Mrs. Washburn. It felt damn weird to know Jackson was married.

A woman walked through, handing out tiny bottles of bubbles for them to blow as the couple left.

"What happened to the days of rice?" Noah said.

Megan's eyes flew wide. "That stuff blows up in birds' stomachs."

"It does not. They eat gravel as grit, for crying out loud. Seriously?"

"Anyway it was birdseed for a while, but our church didn't like dealing with the mess or the weeds that popped up from it. We've done bubbles for years."

"When in the South, do as the Southerners do." He pulled the stick out of the bottle and did a test blow.

"Nice technique," Megan said. "Don't waste them."

"I think we have plenty." He blew a flurry of bubbles her way. One bursting right above her head.

She gave him a warning look.

Jackson helped Billy into the middle of the front seat of the DeSoto Adventurer, and then Angie into the car of Noah's dreams.

A jealous pang went through Noah as he watched Jackson slide into the leather-and-waffle-weave, inset seat of the DeSoto.

Megan swept away a tear. Anyone else that saw it would think that was just the maid of honor insanely happy for her best friend—after all, Katy and Flynn were crying too. However, Megan's smile was about as genuine as the Miss America runner-up. He'd seen her real smile the other night. This was different.

She squeezed his hand, and leaned in, barely moving her lips as she spoke. "Don't let me chase them down and make them get out."

"I've gotcha." He laughed and tightened his grip on her hand. "Smile and wave."

She waved, looking like a beauty queen. "I'm fine. It's okay. It's just a car. Look how happy they are."

Just a car? Good. I hope she just keeps thinking that, because in about an hour, I'm going to make her the offer of a lifetime on that car.

He squeezed her hand.

"Everything is working out perfectly," she said.

"My thoughts exactly." Only he had a feeling they weren't talking about the same things.

Chapter Fifteen

Megan joined the girls to ride over to Lonesome Pines for the reception with Derek. She watched from the backseat of Derek's SUV as the groomsmen piled into Ford's rental car.

"You all looked so beautiful today," Derek said. "All of y'all's tote bags and stuff from the dressing room are in the back."

"Thanks, sweetie." Katy leaned over and kissed him on the cheek. "You look way too young to have a daughter Angie's age." Teasing him for taking on the father-of-the-bride duties. It seemed perfectly natural to Megan. And the truth was, she knew Angie'd asked him to be the maid of honor first. They'd always been best friends, as long as Megan could remember.

"Thank goodness," he said, rubbing his hand through his hair. "My gray hair isn't sparkling is it?"

Katy reached over and ran her fingers through his dark hair. "Just barely."

Flynn giggled.

Megan enjoyed Katy and Derek's interplay. She leaned back, thinking about how Noah had been there for her today. Ultimately, things had worked out the way they should have, but boy if she'd been left to her own devices, that may not have been the case. She'd been a wreck this morning. She didn't remember ever feeling that out of control in her whole life.

It had been an emotionally draining day, and she'd like nothing better than to decompress, but as maid of honor she still had duties to take care of.

Derek turned on Blackwater Draw Road. Megan twisted around in her seat to see the long line of cars following them. "Looks like a parade."

Flynn started practicing her parade wave. Down the road, through the elbow turn and finally right down the lane to the inn.

The chunky gravel kicked up under the big tires of Derek's truck.

A rush of anxiety nagged her. *Hope you went slowly down this lane, Jackson.* She prayed those rocks hadn't pinged the otherwise flawless paint job.

The DeSoto was parked at the far edge of the parking area in front of the inn.

She wanted to open the door and do one of those action-star rolls out of it while it was still moving, so that she could run over and check for damage. Seeing the DeSoto parked there was like the feeling you got as a kid seeing Santa. Thrilling. Unexpected. And hard to believe that it was now hers.

They got out of the car and Megan followed along with the others inside.

Derek and Katy had planned everything out like pros. A staff of people were greeting the guests and handing out flutes of champagne as they entered. Music was already playing—a surprise for Jackson and Angie—the *Night Crawlers*. The same band that was playing on their very first date at the car show in the next town over.

Noah jogged up beside Megan. "Hey, gal."

"Hi, yourself."

"Can I get you some champagne?" He gestured toward one of the waitresses carrying a tray of crystal flutes.

"No. I might be wearing a dress, but this girl still prefers a cold beer. I hear the bar is out on the patio."

"I'll join you."

She stopped and then started walking again.

"What's wrong? Did I say something wrong?" Noah looked confused.

"No, it's fine. I was kind of hoping you might be my designated driver tonight."

"Drive the car home? To your home?"

She shrugged. "It's silly. Have a good time. I can do it."

"No. I'm in." He clapped his hands together. "For a chance to drive the Adventurer again? I'd drink root beer, and I hate root beer, by the way."

"Great."

"And if you're riding shotgun. I'm a happy man."

"Good, because I need a drink."

"I'll get you that beer. You stay right here."

"Thanks." Megan saw one of her customers, Vivian, walk in. She went over to greet her and chat. While they were talking, Noah handed her an ice-cold bottle of beer in a blue huggie with *Jackson loves Angie* and the wedding date on it. "M'lady."

She raised the beer in the air and took a swallow. "Now, that's good and cold. Thanks, Noah."

"You're welcome." He flashed his perfect smile.

"Viv, this is Noah Black. He's in car restoration out in California. He and Jackson grew up together."

"So nice to meet you, Noah."

"And you. Did you grow up here in Boot Creek too?" he asked, but he could tell from the accent that the likely answer was going to be yes.

"I did. Never have lived anywhere else," she gushed.

"Boot Creek is a very nice town to be in. I've enjoyed my stay," Noah said, but Megan could feel the undercurrent. He was ready to get back to California. He didn't seem the type to sit still for long. She'd miss him.

Derek stepped in. "Can I grab you two for another picture?"

"Excuse us, Viv. It was very nice to meet you." Noah took Megan by the hand, and then followed Derek outside.

They bunched in with the rest of the wedding party, and Noah stood behind her. He settled his hand on the small of her waist.

She hitched a breath at his touch.

As soon as the pictures were taken, he leaned down and whispered into her ear. "Does anyone ever leave Boot Creek?"

"I come and go all the time," she said, knowing that's not what he meant. "And yes, people leave. But some visitors get here and never leave, like Jackson."

"Never is a long time."

"Takes all kinds."

"What kind are you?"

"I'm taking my life wherever it leads me."

"Really?" He walked her over to the love seat next to the fireplace that now held a bucket of iced-down beer instead of firewood. "Because it seems to me you've left some of those paths untaken."

"How so?"

"The art." He fixed his gaze on her.

"There's a lot to that story."

"More than a starving artist? Because from what I've seen, you would not starve for long. You've got real talent."

"It's complicated."

"I'm listening. I want to understand."

This man had a way of opening her secret compartments. The things she held precious for herself. The things even her closest friends didn't talk about. She'd tell him. She knew she would. So, she leaned back and relaxed into the love seat. She hadn't told this story since the year it all happened. "It's not a pretty story."

He tipped his finger under her chin, raising it to his level, then brushed his thumb across her lips. "You are beautiful. Inside and out. I can see that. I already know that. Tell me. I want to know."

She looked around the room. Her mother raised her glass and flashed a smile and an I-so-approve look her way. Flynn stood across the room with a goofy smile. "Not here. Let's go outside. To the dock. It's quiet."

"Let's go."

She took his hand and wove through the crowd. Heaving a sigh as they stepped onto the porch.

"Seems like they multiplied in there," Noah said.

"I was thinking the same thing." She pointed to the old boathouse next to the small dock. "This way." She slipped off her heels and placed them at the edge of the porch. "Won't be needing these." She hiked her dress to keep it from dragging and walked down to the water.

Noah paused at the water's edge. "This is nice."

"Yeah. This is Boot Creek. The actual creek. Isn't it great? The water is so clear you can always see to the bottom. And you can traverse those rocks right out to the middle. I swear it's like you become one with the water out there. It's freeing."

Noah kicked out of his shoes.

"What are you doing?"

"Experiencing Boot Creek." He tugged off his socks and dropped them to the ground. "With you." He grinned and reached for her hand.

Her own giggle sounded young and silly, but she couldn't contain it. She gathered the bottom half of her gown, twisting and knotting it below her hips.

"Ahh, a fashion diva too. That dress is way prettier as a miniskirt," he said with approval. "I like it."

"I'm no diva." She stretched her tanned leg out and pointed her toe. "But my talents are rather endless." She leapt from the bank to the first rock, and then the second. Only pausing to look over her shoulder to see if he was following her.

Noah was right behind her. He had good balance, standing there tall and strong not so unlike the trees along the water's edge on the opposite side of the wide creek.

"Careful," she called over her shoulder. "The rocks toward the center are smoother. They can be a little slippery."

"Right behind you."

She'd run these rocks so many times in her lifetime that she couldn't count, but he was keeping up with her like a local. As she got closer to the middle, the rocks were larger. Boulders really. Like little islands on a miniature ocean.

"This is great." Noah stepped from the large rock behind Megan to join her on the largest, right in the center of the creek.

She dipped her foot into the water, lifting a splash in his direction.

"Slow learner. Remember what happened last time you tried to pick a fight with me?" His grin was sexy and taunting.

"You think I'm afraid? You're on my stompin' grounds, California boy." She kicked water out toward the center of the creek, provoking him.

"Hey, don't start what you can't finish."

"Oh, I'll finish."

He stepped closer, hooking her leg back down to the rock with his foot. "If we didn't have to go back inside, I'd pull you into this water right here and now."

She pressed her lips together, wishing neither one of them had duties back up at the inn. But as maid of honor and best man, they'd surely be missed. She sucked in a staggered breath, rose to her toes and wrapped her arms around his neck.

"Was that a threat? Because it doesn't sound like much of a punishment to me."

He squeezed her waist between his hands, making her feel tiny and safe in his arms as he leaned forward and took her mouth into his. "Do you have any idea what you are doing to me?"

She nipped at his lip. "I have a pretty good idea. I'm feeling it too." She turned, her back to his front, and he wrapped his arms around her, resting his chin on top of her head.

"See the turtles?" She pointed to a downed tree on the other side. A family of stair-step-sized turtles lined one of the branches, taking in the sunshine.

He nodded. "And fish." Pointing to a school of minnows below, he pretended to get ready to toss her in, but caught her just as she squealed. "Kidding."

"Not funny." She twisted free of his hold and made the nine leaps from rock to rock back to the safety of the shore. She stood there with her hands on her hips laughing. And waiting.

Jackson swept two fingers from his eyes to hers over there on the shore. "Got my eye on you, girl." He made the trip back to shore easily, but she'd already made her way to the dock.

By the time he caught up, she was sitting on the dock, her feet dangling in the cold water.

He sat down and took her hand. "Got a story to tell me?"

She closed her eyes, letting the warm sun stream down over her. A deep breath in, and the words came so easy. "I'd been painting like crazy. I didn't have a studio back then. Just a dream and the dining room table in front of the sliding glass windows where I had everything sprawled out. I thought my life was absolutely perfect."

He didn't say a word. Instead he listened intently.

"I was living with my fiancé. A little house over on the other side of town. I think it had been his aunt's. Someone from his family willing to rent to us cheap. Anyway, we were going to be married."

"Serious stuff."

"Yes. It was. We weren't planning a fancy wedding like Angie's. I wasn't spending big bucks on a gown or anything like that. We were in love and just making it official. We'd gotten the marriage license and everything, but we were going to have a very simple ceremony as soon as we'd saved enough money for our honeymoon."

"Sounds like a good plan."

"I've always been a goal setter," she said.

"Me too," he said. "Like you make yourself earn everything?"

"Exactly."

"Sorry, didn't mean to interrupt."

"Anyway, I was making good money on my paintings. Kevin was selling them like nobody's business. He was an awesome salesman. He would gush over my work, and I guess his enthusiasm spilled over because people seemed to be clamoring for them. It was a really exciting time."

"I bet. I can understand his enthusiasm. Your work is great."

She shrugged. "Kevin was my biggest cheerleader. He was so proud to introduce me as his fiancé and as an artist."

She laughed. "Like it was some big deal, even though we were eating ramen noodles and Beanie Weenies half the time. It always made me laugh, because he introduced me like everyone should know who I was, and people seemed to believe him. It was crazy. But nice. Even if I never felt that special."

She swung her foot, her toes just brushing the cool water. It was freeing to actually talk about this with Noah. Different. Safe.

"You married?"

She shook her head. "Oh, no. Never married."

He didn't say a word; instead he pushed his leg against hers.

It felt like minutes had passed. But he didn't rush her, and she was thankful for that. "He died."

Noah straightened.

"An overdose." She felt the tears glisten, but they didn't fall. She forced herself to continue. "Accidental overdose is what they said. He'd been on crystal meth. I didn't even know. How did I not know?" She looked into Noah's eyes. There was no judgment there. "I knew he partied. I didn't, so I didn't really hang around in those situations. I kept painting. Doing what I loved, and it seemed to make him so happy."

Noah stroked her hand, pulling it into his lap.

"He'd always seemed so happy." She lowered her head. "And then he was gone."

She squeezed her eyes, and then his hand.

"You don't have to tell me," he said.

She shrugged. "I barely got through the days. The sorrow I felt cut so deep that I couldn't even see my own life separate from him. My mom threatened to move me home. Angie finally made me get out of bed. I didn't even want to live, much less paint. The days were so long. I slept all the time, praying and hoping the next day would bring something brighter. I couldn't wrap my head around Kevin keeping a secret like that from me. He had a problem. I would have helped him. I could have."

"It's not your fault."

"You're not the first one to say that." She regretted the tone of her comment. "I know it wasn't my fault. Now. But it doesn't hurt any less. He's never coming back, and my whole life had been planned with him."

"But yours isn't over."

"I know. And things change. It's been good to see Derek be able to start over."

"What happened with Derek?"

"His wife died. Cancer."

"That's rough."

"Especially when you're one of the leading cancer doctors in the country. It was like the disease was fighting back, making a personal attack on him. He was a mess. I totally got it."

"Not much different."

She withdrew her hand. "It got worse. Turned out Kevin had been lying to me. I wish I'd never found that out. It just made it worse. Like it wasn't bad enough to have lost him."

"Addiction is hard for people. It's the drug. The addiction that drives those people to lie and hurt the ones they love. I'm sure he loved you." He pressed her hand into his.

"The best he could, I suppose. When Angie and I were going through all of his things we stumbled on to notebooks where he'd been tracking all of the sales from my paintings."

She pulled her feet up onto the dock, hugging her knees. "I'd been making a pretty good living on those paintings. I just didn't know it. He was pocketing most of the money. For his habit. He even tracked those payments to his drug dealers, and he still owed people when he died according to the notebooks they'd found among his things."

"Wow."

"He'd been using my art to pay for his habit. I paid for him to over-dose in a way. I will never stop wondering if he really loved me . . . or only loved me for the way I enabled him. His energy. His confidence, motivation, it was all drug driven. After that I lost the inclination to paint."

"Sometimes we find new reasons to appreciate the same things in a different way." He pointed out across the creek. "Like this. I haven't been in a place like this since my childhood. Didn't think I'd ever care to. But here with you. It's different. Maybe you'll find that one day. You shouldn't waste your talent. It's a gift. It should be shared."

"My candles exercise my creative side."

"But you have so much more to give. Something pure and special and something only you can do."

It sounded so simple coming from him. But he hadn't lived it. She dropped her knees, sitting Indian style on the dock. "That's my story. I'm a hot mess." She winked, trying to lighten the mood, thankful that this man made her feel safe enough to talk about the past. Maybe even face some of those fears again. "But then who isn't, right?"

He laced his fingers between hers. The strength of his hand seemed to vibrate a new awareness through her.

"You're not. But I'm sensing a theme here."

"Here? On the water?"

"No. With you." He ducked, catching her straight on. Eye to eye. "You don't drive the car because of all the wonderful memories you don't want to lose. You don't paint anymore because of the yesterdays tied to that."

So?

"You don't see the connection?" His question wasn't judging; it sounded more like a concern.

"No."

"Megan, you're living your life through yesterday's lens. You can't live your fullest life like that. It'll suffocate you." He wrapped his other hand around her bare foot. "Like cement boots in the middle of this creek. Girl, you need to embrace the good side of those memories. Laugh. Love. Create. You have something very special. Don't chain it down."

She lifted her shoulders. "I don't want to lose Daddy's memory. And I sure don't want to live with the guilt of losing Kevin."

"God makes those decisions, girl. You're special. Hot as hell. I might even label you a goddess the way you looked today . . . but you are not God."

She couldn't help but laugh at that. A right-to-the-belly kind of laugh. "Thank you, Noah. That's probably very wise advice."

"I had a good mentor. My granddad."

"He must've been pretty wonderful."

"Oh, yeah. I try to make him proud every day of my life."

She turned away, looking out at the water rippling across those rocks. The family of turtles still sunning on that branch. You could count on them. Always there, like someone had just painted them right into the landscape.

He's a beautiful soul. Daddy, I hope I'll make you proud every day too. She turned back to Noah. "You are so easy to talk to. You are an excellent listener."

"You're easy to listen to. And for the record, I don't think you're a hot mess. I think you're pretty special and unique, and I really like that about you."

Silence hung between them. He said, "Should we get back in and do our best-man and maid-of-honor duties?"

"Yeah, we'd better."

He stood and helped her up, untying her skirt with quick and nimble fingers. "A little wrinkled, but at least it's not wet or muddy."

She swept at the wrinkles. "It'll have to do."

They walked back up to the house without conversation. They'd already said what needed to be said, and the quiet was comfortable.

A raucous laughter came from the far side of the inn.

"What the—" Megan stopped in her tracks. Anger rose in her so quickly that she couldn't even form words, pointing instead. She marched toward a group of young men circling the DeSoto.

Noah keyed in on the scene and ran past her. "I've got this," he said. He ran like an athlete, fast and light.

Her heart pounded. Those guys circling the car had already hung stuff from the back of the car. And one of them was holding a can of something. *Dear God, don't let them have damaged it.*

Daddy would've sat right out here with it. Exactly what she should've done. Her stomach knotted.

Noah hollered as he got closer. "Guys. Whoa! None of that."

"Dude, it's a wedding. It's what you do," a snarky guy in black jeans and a tuxedo T-shirt said. "Chill, I'm Angie's second cousin. These guys are my friends. She used to babysit us."

"*You* chill." Noah's voice was steady and authoritative.

She stopped and watched from a distance. He'd be way more effective than her screaming at the top of her lungs, which is exactly what she'd been about to do. A Southern hissy fit with all the trimmings.

She couldn't hear the rest of the conversation, although it appeared to get heated before it finally started simmering down. She saw Noah hand one of them something, and then he disarmed them, taking what looked like shoe polish and shaving cream from them. The guys dispersed and Noah walked around the car, checking it over. He examined the "Just Married" sign that had been tied to the back, and then walked back over.

"Thank you," she said.

"Glad you saw them." He lifted the paraphernalia in the air. "They didn't mean any harm."

She put her hand over heart and shook her head. "They never do. But still . . ."

"Damage averted. I paid one of them fifty bucks to watch over it to be sure no one else messed with it."

"Who else would do a thing like that?"

Noah took her hand and started heading back toward the inn. "Probably no one. But it will give us both peace of mind."

"True."

Noah slowed down as she navigated the gravel in her high heels. "She'll need a good gentle cleaning after today's romp, though. I could come over and help you detail it."

"That would be nice. Thanks."

"I was thinking." Noah stopped and shoved his hands into his pockets. "Think you might like to come to a car show with me? I'm headed to one week after next. They have two days of memorabilia auctioned before they start running the cars across the block. I think you'd have fun."

She hesitated, but only for a moment. "I might be able to squeeze that into my schedule. I could check on flights."

"My assistant, Sonya, will take care of it. She's my right hand at the shop. I'll have her work on it. Out of RDU, right?"

"Yeah." She was a little stunned. Had she just agreed to meet him somewhere? What was she getting herself into? Her heart tingled. Joy. It was joy in her heart. She had nothing tying her down. There was no reason not to. "I'm excited."

"Me too. I don't want to quit spending time with you. I have to button up a couple of projects back in California, and then we'll be shipping the cars out ahead of us. It's a pretty neat event. Bring your pearls. There are some VIP events."

"You're a VIP, I presume."

"I am in those circles." His eyes narrowed. "What is going through that pretty little head of yours?

She blurted out, "Isn't that a lot of money for you to spend to fly me out there?"

"The way I see it, if it costs me a few hundred bucks to fly a girl like you out to spend time with me who will enjoy it as much as I do it, it's worth it. Besides, a dating service like *It's Just Lunch* costs five times that in my area. You're a bargain." He winked. "And I already know I like you."

Megan spotted her mother across the way, giving her one of those go-get-him-girl looks and fanning herself. There was no doubt that Noah was fast becoming a VIP in her circle too.

Chapter Sixteen

Megan walked back into the inn, all smiles despite the almost-catastrophe with the car.

Jackson met them just inside the door. "I need Noah. Do you mind if I snag him?"

"Not at all," Megan said.

Jackson swept Noah off into the crowded room.

"Hey beautiful daughter, did I just see you come back in with that handsome best man?" Bootsie looked like she was already planning the wedding.

"We were out checking on the car. Don't go leaping to any conclusions, Mom."

"Oh, Megan. That car is just a car. Pay attention to what's around you. Can't you see he's smitten with you? And he's so good looking. And successful to hear folks talk."

Megan hated it when her mom got that judgmental look on her face.

"Mom. Don't." Only Megan didn't have much fight in her about it, because she was pretty smitten with him too, as much as she hated to admit it and make Mom right. "You really think he's into me?"

"Honey, only a blind woman couldn't see that."

Megan felt the lift of confidence inside her.

"You like him too, don't you!" Bootsie practically danced in her shoes. "I knew it. And he was going to get you roses the other day, but when I told him daisies were your favorite, he didn't hesitate. That's a man who wants to please a woman."

Oh, he'd please her all right. If the other night was just the beginning, she couldn't wait to see just what kind of firework levels of pleasure were on the horizon with him. "He invited me to go away with him."

Bootsie threw her arms around her. "Megan. That's great." She stopped and shook Megan by the shoulders. "Dear goodness, do tell me you said yes!"

"I said yes." Megan could barely control her excitement. Not only to spend a little more time with Noah, but the car show was something she'd never done before. She hadn't even asked where it was. Hopefully somewhere she'd never been before.

"Oh, don't turn around." Mom's eyes flashed wide. "Here he comes now. *Shhh.* Talk about something else. The air-conditioning. Tell me about the air-conditioning at your place. That's good." Bootsie plastered a pleasant smile on her face and nodded like they'd been talking casually all along.

Megan sputtered and then said, "So I need to get two whole new units to cool the whole place properly. It's a ton of money."

Bootsie winked at Meg. "It'll be worth it. Never does pay to cut corners. Better to wait and do it right than scrimp and regret it."

"I know. I—"

Noah placed his hand on the small of Megan's back. Excitement rippled up her spine. "Oh, hi. You're back," she said turning into his arms.

"Didn't go far. Good to see you, Bootsie."

"You too, dear. You look so handsome all shined up."

"Thank you," he said glancing down at his shoes. "Heard you talking about the air-conditioning. I was thinking about that after you mentioned it to me the other day," he said to Megan. "That's a big place you've got. I wouldn't be surprised if you needed three zones even."

"I have a couple estimates." Megan sipped her drink. It was just a little white lie. She'd gotten caught up in the charade with her mom, who looked particularly pleased with the situation.

"You know there is a quick-and-fast answer to that problem. I mean, if you need one."

"How so?"

"The DeSoto. It's worth a lot more than just the fifteen or twenty grand it would cost to get a top-notch system. I'm sure even the best air-conditioning system probably won't cost you that much."

"*Just* fifteen or twenty thousand?" She'd thought it would be ten. She hoped he was exaggerating or flat-out wrong.

"It's a lot of money, no doubt about it. But an investment you'll get your return on."

"True." Megan glanced in her mom's direction.

Noah pushed his coat back, tucking his hand into his pocket. "You could buy air-conditioning systems for the whole block with what your DeSoto Adventurer is worth."

"Yeah. Right." Even her mother laughed at that one.

"No. I'm serious. Have you done any research on that car? Do you have any idea what it's worth?"

"No. I mean, I've had a couple ridiculously high offers."

"Really? How much?"

"Twenty-eight thousand dollars," Megan said proudly.

Bootsie straightened. "And you didn't sell that gas-guzzling beast of a car. Twenty-eight *thousand* dollars." Bootsie swept her hand across Megan's forehead. "You sick?"

"I wouldn't have taken that deal either," Noah said.

"Thank you," Megan said.

"Because it's worth much, much more than that." Noah slugged his drink back.

"How much more?" Bootsie asked.

"Mom! Stop."

"I'm just curious," Bootsie pouted.

"It's okay, Bootsie. I'd match that offer of twenty-eight thousand that she got, plus give Megan another one hundred thousand dollars for that car right now."

Megan choked on her swallow of beer. Leaning over, coughing from the bubbly liquid going down the wrong path.

Her mom slapped her on the back three times. "You okay?"

Megan nodded. Everyone was starting to look in her direction. She raised a hand and tried to smile, motioning that she was fine.

Bootsie spun back around. "One hundred thousand dollars? Like a tenth of a million?"

Noah laughed. "Yeah. I guess that would be the math."

"Now you're just flexing your money," Bootsie said with a nudge to Noah's ribs. "I don't mind that in a man at all."

"No. No, ma'am. The car is worth every bit of that."

Bootsie's lips pursed. "Well, I shouldn't be surprised. If there was one thing Farley Howard was, it was lucky in investments. As long as you don't count that worthless woman he married after me. That could solve a lot of problems for you, Megan. I guess your daddy did do right by you leaving you that car."

Megan was almost afraid to speak, else she'd start coughing again. "You never liked that car anyway," she managed to choke out. "And I don't have any problems. I like to run a cash life. No credit. No debt. It's the way I like to live."

"Nothing wrong with that," Noah said.

Bootsie shook a finger at Megan. "Well, I'm up to my eyeballs in credit debt and far as I know you can't take money with you, so you may as well live it up. And I may not have been a fan of that car, but girl you treat it like it's life support to your father. He's gone, Megan. He isn't coming back. For goodness sake, be smart and take the man's money."

"Mother!"

"I know when I'm not wanted." Bootsie marched off.

"Yeah, take my money."

He was being playful, and that was cute, but she wasn't going to take his money. This car was worth more to her than any money, or even a new air-conditioning system. "I told you I'm not selling it. To anyone."

"I'll take really good care of her," he said.

"Not even you. And who said my car is a she? I've always rather thought of this car as big and manly. Like Max." She lifted her chin. Yes, she liked the name Max for that car just fine.

"Max Howard?"

"No," She pursed her lips. "Just Max. Extra special. You know like Prince or Elvis. Or big as he is, more like Shaq."

"I'll take good care of Max. I'll even make sure Max has his own room and thermostat. Only the best for Max, and you can visit anytime." He stepped closer to her. "You could visit me at the same time. It could be a good thing." His stare was bold, as if he was daring her to deny it.

She laughed, but it didn't tame what his gaze was doing to her. He might as well be caressing her with his hands, rather than his eyes. Putting a little distance between them, she turned away. "Not interested. Thanks anyway."

"Really?" Noah stroked his hand over the sexy scruff on his chin. "Name your price."

She felt awkward. Like he was pushing her. "There isn't one."

He shook his head. "Everyone has a price."

"Not me." Megan glanced over at Ford.

"You'll have the money to do what you need to do, and I'll fly you out for visitation," he said.

"You can come here and visit," she said playfully.

He looked confused for a moment, and then he nodded. "You know what. You're right. I *can* do that."

"Want to grab some food? I'm suddenly starved," Megan said.

Noah lifted his chin to someone across the room. "I'll catch up with you shortly."

"Oh, well—" She was going to say she'd wait, but he'd already made his exit.

~

Megan felt revived after getting some food into her stomach. She hadn't even thought about the fact she hadn't eaten a thing all day until her stomach started growling like a lioness in heat.

She walked over to where Jackson and Angie were, for the first time sitting at a table alone. "When do you two want to do the garter, flower toss, and cake?"

"We're just now catching our breath for the first time," Angie said. "What a day! Thank you for helping make all of this happen. All of you have made this such a special day for me."

"For us," Jackson interjected. He lifted Angie's fingers to his lips and kissed them.

"We don't have to leave to go to the airport for a while. So no hurry. I'd rather let people eat and mingle. No one seems to be in a rush."

"I think everyone is having a great time," Megan agreed.

"Might as well enjoy ourselves. No hurry, right?" Jackson shrugged.

"Of course not. This is your day. I wanted to be sure we were keeping everything on schedule and things were going the way you wanted."

Angie's face lit up. "My favorite song."

"Let's dance, my beautiful bride." Jackson stood and held his hand out for her.

Angie beamed, waving a pretty good-bye to Megan, as Jackson, her prince, whisked her off to the dance floor.

Noah walked over to Megan. "Come on," he said, taking her hand.

"I—"

"You always have an argument. Come on. It's just a dance. Not a competition. Just have fun with it, and let me lead."

She let him pull her close. "This is a pretty song." He led her with strength and confidence, moving her like she didn't need to even hold her own weight.

"Friend of Jackson's family from Nashville wrote it. Guy named Tim McDonald. Heckuva pianist." He lowered his cheek just above her own. His breath warm against her face. "Let me love you," he sang the chorus, and his voice caused her senses to wash back like the tide. *It's just a song.*

Megan watched Jackson and Angie dance nearby; the joy between them shone like the brightest star. Easy and pure happiness. Angie had abandoned her shoes at some point. She looked tiny next to Jackson without them on, and her skirt swept the floor as he swayed her to the music with as much grace and skill as one of those sexy professional dancers.

Noah turned her and then lifted his hand, turning her chin toward his. "You're beautiful tonight."

She blinked, her lips parting but her instinct was to make a wise comment. That wasn't what she was feeling, though. No, nothing close to that. And she thought he might kiss her, but he didn't, instead pulling her closer to him. Her heart beat against Noah's as the piano repeated a beautiful succession of notes reminiscent of a music box.

"I need to download that song," she said.

"And we'll dance again. In the kitchen while the coffee brews."

"Yes." She pulled her lips together against the smile that reached her heart. *Yes, please.*

They walked off the dance floor and Megan was pulled into a conversation with old friends from high school. They'd clearly had too much to drink, and were talking about glory days like they were yesterday.

Noah excused himself, and by the time Megan pulled away from the group, he was nowhere in sight.

Bootsie flagged her from across the way. Pointing to her watch and then to the cake. It was probably getting close to time to start those festivities.

Megan scanned the room for Noah so she could give him an update on the timing of the rest of their duties.

Walking toward the front door to see if he'd stepped out to see how their car guard was doing at his security job, she noticed him standing next to Ford down the hall containing the east-wing guest rooms. They had their heads together talking about something. *Probably an escape route.* Surely they'd had about enough of the festivities by now. She doubted weddings were any man's favorite event, except for the groom. And he was highly incentivized to look and act happy.

As she got closer, the sound of her name in their conversation made her stop. She made a quick backwards step into one of the suites and listened.

"Megan is hot," Ford said. "There are a lot of nice looking women in this town."

Megan rolled her eyes. Men gossiped as much as women. Harmless. She recognized Noah's laugh. "You've just been in Alaska too long. Welcome back to civilization. Don't let it go to your head."

"I think you've met your match with Megan."

"What's that supposed to mean?"

"It means, I think you're going to lose that thousand-dollar bet you made with Jackson."

Megan's ears pricked. What did he mean?

"She isn't going to sell you that car."

Megan sucked in a breath. Her fingers pulled into tight fists.

"It's not over yet." Noah sounded confident. And yet they'd just had this conversation earlier. Could he have been playing her this whole time? She brushed her fingers across her brow. Suddenly she felt hot. Hotter than if she'd been standing on Main Street in a parka on Fourth of July.

Ford's voice carried down the hall. "I was talking to Derek. He said she'd never sell that car."

"You told him about the bet? Man, we don't even know him. Why'd you go and do that?"

She peeked around the corner. She didn't know them well enough to know who was who talking, but this conversation was bringing a whole new clarity to Noah's generous offer this afternoon.

"Hell, no, I didn't tell Derek about the bet. We were talking about the car. He started telling me about how much it means to her. I think all the charm in the world isn't going to work for you this time, Noah. But on the bright side, Jackson will be treating Angie to an extra thousand dollars' worth of fun on their honeymoon. Good for Jackson. And at least you won't break a heart on this trip."

She stepped farther into the room and leaned against the wall. He'd been playing her the whole time? What a fool she'd been. She'd confided in him.

Hot tears of anger burned her eyes. She tiptoed back into the washroom and ran a bright white washcloth under the sink. She dabbed a cloth over her eyes. Cooling them, and hoping to keep her eyes from reddening. Oh no, he wouldn't get any tears from her. He wasn't worth it. She'd known better. Why had she let herself be seduced to believe he was anything else but bad news?

She heard Ford and Noah talking as they passed by the suite. She stood in the bathroom. Not likely they'd come in. They hadn't seen her.

Her breathing was heavy and she needed air. She needed to get the heck out of there. And fast. Rather than have to explain her exit, she walked down the hall in the opposite direction from where everyone was congregating and took the side door out. The DeSoto was parked right there, but she couldn't take it. Not only did she not want to drive it, but also Jackson and Angie would need it after the cake cutting . . . luring folks to shut down the party. They had it all planned out.

She stood there, shifting back and forth feeling trapped, until she spotted mom's car parked across the way. She lifted her dress and ran across the lot. Ducking beside the car, it didn't look like anyone had seen her. The car wouldn't be locked, but she needed the key to start the thing. She shoved her hand under the wheel well. Like daddy had always taught them, a Hide-A-Key. Momma might not speak all that highly of Daddy anymore, but she still heeded all the advice he'd ever given them.

Megan opened the door and slid into the driver's seat. Her hand shook as she inserted the key into the ignition. Mom could easily catch a ride home with someone else.

She put the car in reverse and backed out, using all the restraint she possessed not to floor the little Toyota to get the heck out of there without spiting gravel and drawing attention to herself.

Puttering out of the parking lot, she waited until she got clear past the inn before pressing the accelerator. Then dust flew up behind her like a rooster tail. She was glad not to have to see anything in her rearview.

Before she knew it, she was parked behind her car in front of her house. She didn't even remember steering through the hairpin curve on Blackwater Draw Road, going over the bridge and up the hill or down Main Street.

She laid her arms over the steering wheel and put her head down. The air-conditioning blew against her face. What was she even supposed to say to Noah now?

How could she have been so stupid?

She'd seen the way he'd drooled over Daddy's car. She knew he was in the car business, and he'd been straight that he'd been looking for a car just like that for a long time. She should have known.

Sitting in the car right in front of her house, she noticed a bright orange slip of paper in the handle of the storm door.

Any reason to not go back and have to face Noah was a good one, although she knew she had to go back. She would never let Angie down. She was important. Noah? He was not.

She got out of the car and walked over to the door. She grabbed the note and started walking back to the car, unrolling it as she did.

A corporate logo filled the top third of the card-stock mailer.

"Reliable Carriers"

Below that someone had written:

Arrived early. I'm parked at the USPS.

Can pick up today if convenient.

Pick up? The delivery guy had probably gotten the cross streets wrong. For a town as small as Boot Creek, it wasn't unusual for that to happen. They even got each other's mail. Funny how that worked.

She ran across the street to spare her feet from the hot asphalt. She would have had to do the same thing with those fancy high heels they'd been wearing; they were almost like going barefoot anyway.

A fancy burgundy and bright orange big rig with fancy black-and-white striping on the cab took up a good portion of the parking lot adjacent to the small post office. The enclosed trailer was as bright as a jack-o'-lantern, but it wasn't until she had knocked on the truck door that she noticed the smaller words painted there beneath the logo.

VEHICLES TAKEN SERIOUSLY®

Her blood pressure rose. Her jaw set. She banged on the door with every ounce of her.

"Whoa. Hang on there. I'm coming." A handsome gray-haired man with a ponytail flung open the door, looking ready to give her a piece of his mind, but calmed into a smile when he saw her standing there. "Good afternoon, young lady. What can I do for you?" He climbed down out of the truck. "Sorry. I was sleeping. Something wrong?"

She flashed the note. She was so darned mad she could barely get her mouth moving. "Got this," she managed to spit out. Standing there, she shook that paper repeatedly in his direction.

He looked a little worried. "Yeah. Right. Think I could go ahead and load the car today? I was hoping to leave a little early. I have to pick up a car in Oklahoma on my way to California. Every hour sitting is dollars wasting."

An enclosed car transport trailer? "Who set this up?"

"I take it by your reaction, it was not you." He reached behind him and pulled out a silver clipboard. "Got that right here. California Dreaming Restoration arranged the haul."

"Noah." *Of course he did. How could she have been such a fool?*

"No. I spoke to a nice woman. Here it is. Her name was Sonya. She set it up on Monday."

"Monday?" Megan thought she might boil over right there and evaporate into the atmosphere. Sonya. Oh yes, he'd mentioned the amazing Sonya. She was probably his girlfriend. Or his wife!

She spat out the words contemptuously. "You can leave whenever you like, because you will be leaving without my car. It is mine. Never has been for sale, and it is not leaving my garage. Ever!"

His mouth twisted up. "I'll need you to sign my paperwork. They'll charge them a penalty for this. I went quite a bit out of my way to get here."

"Have them charge him double. I don't give a damn."

He pulled the paper close to his face and then made a couple marks and handed it to her. "Can I get you to sign my paperwork? I can't leave without a signature. You know, so I get paid."

"Oh, I'll sign your paperwork." She scrawled her name across the paper on the line. Then wrote *unauthorized pickup* across the middle of it. "I'm sorry. I realize this isn't your fault. But someone is up to no good. I have never had any intention of selling that car."

"I'm sorry, ma'am. I'm just doing my job."

"Thank you. I hope they make it up to you. If not, sue his butt. I'll be happy to press charges to help you get your money."

She didn't bother waiting for his response. She marched across the street, oblivious to the heat under her feet, got into the car that was still running in front of her house, and nailed it. She was more than ready to be back at that reception now.

∽

Megan talked to herself the whole ride back to the reception. There was no way she'd let her stupidity or that lying man mess up this day for her best friend.

He wouldn't know real friendship if it hit him in the face.

Oh, I've got a ride for you, Mr. Black.

California Dreaming? Oh, I'll be your worst nightmare.

She strode in with her head held high.

She needed to check with Jackson and Angie, but it seemed as good a time as any to get the final activities rolling and get this party shut down.

She went over to the band and waited politely as they finished playing, then stepped up on stage. The lead singer stepped back from the mic and handed things over to her.

"Hey y'all," Megan said. A shrill squeal of feedback pumped out over the speakers. She winced and held the mic out.

The singer ran over and whispered to her.

"Ahh. There's a trick to it. This is better. How's everybody doing?" Everyone clapped.

"For those of you who I haven't met, I'm Megan Howard and I'm Angie's best friend and maid of honor. I'm excited to give you a quick heads up that we will be doing the garter and flower toss here in a few minutes. Then . . . what all my young friends have been dying for. The cake! So don't stray too far. We'll be doing those things right here in a few minutes."

"Thanks guys," she said to the singer. "Two more songs and then we should be ready." She stepped down to join Angie and Flynn.

"You got it." He lifted the neck of his guitar and strummed a few chords, and the band fell right in along with him with a fast-rocking version of *Sweet Home Alabama*.

"Thanks, Megan," Angie said. "You're the best," she said as she was being pulled away by Jackson to dance.

Megan forced a smile and nodded.

"What is going on with you?" Flynn said.

"What?" Megan shrugged it off.

"Don't play that with me. You look like you're twisted as tight as one of those rubber bands on a balsa wood plane. I'm afraid you're going to zing right across this room if I don't calm you down. What is wrong?" Flynn put her hand on Megan's arm.

"Noah." She tugged her arm away from Flynn. "Noah Black is what is wrong with me." She leaned in. "He's been playing me just to get his hands on Daddy's car this whole time. He doesn't care about me."

"No," Flynn shook her head emphatically. "I don't believe that. I've seen the way he looks at you."

"An act. All a big act." Her voice shook. "Give the man a doggone acting trophy."

"What makes you think that it's all a big act? What on earth happened?"

"I heard the guys talking. They made a bet on it. Jackson was in on it too. They must think I'm such a fool."

"No, Megan." Flynn blinked. "Jackson wouldn't have a part of something like that. Something isn't right."

"You don't have to tell me it isn't right. It's wrong fourteen ways to Sunday if you ask me."

"No. I mean, you must be mistaken. I saw the way you and Noah acted. It was there. That little spark from the first moment. Before you even noticed it."

Megan did not want to hear that mess. "You're a hopeless romantic, Flynn. You see love when bumblebees fly by." She instantly felt bad for being so snippy with Flynn. She'd only been trying to help. But this was no time for rainbows and flipping unicorns.

Katy stepped up next to them. "Megan. Calm down. I heard what you just said to Flynn. What is going on between you two? That's not fair."

"I'm sorry, Flynn. You know I didn't mean it."

"We're fine," Flynn said. "No offense taken, Megan."

"Thanks." Megan brushed her hair back from her face. Her hair was beginning to fall down in all the drama. She probably looked a mess *and* a fool. "This is Angie's day. Just let it go. I'll deal with Mr. California Dreaming later, because if he thinks he's leaving Boot Creek with the title to my car . . . he *is* dreaming!"

～

Once they got through the rest of the festivities, people would begin to leave. The plan was for Jackson and Angie to drive off in Daddy's car, but he'd actually be taking Angie to see the surprise of Billy's bedroom, then come back for a little quiet time with just their close friends. As soon as they left, Megan could slip off to the bathroom near the kitchen. She knew her eyes had to be a mess from the tears that wouldn't seem to stop. Hopefully, people would mistake them for joyous tears for her best friend. She hitched herself up on the vanity and sat there, trying to catch her breath. *It's Angie's big day. I can't ruin it for her.* And she still had a toast to make, and all the other bridal niceties had to happen like the garter, the bouquet, and the slicing of the cake.

I never should have let my guard down.

I was foolish to have thought that the memories Noah and I shared over that old car meant something. He probably didn't even have a grandfather.

She managed to get through all of her duties with no interaction with the enemy. Wherever Noah walked, she crossed in the other direction.

"We ready for them to make the exit?" Derek asked her.

"Yes," Megan said. *The sooner, the better.*

Derek punched the number into his phone. "Coast is clear. Affirmative."

"You sound like a spy."

"Feel like one. Kind of fun," he said. "You look tired. Hard work being the maid of honor, huh?"

"Yeah. It is." She slipped off. Hoping to lay low until she could score a ride home. *Where's Mom when I need her?*

"Are you dodging me?" Noah asked with a smile.

"You noticed." Her words were clipped and tight.

"Hey, hang on a second."

"Look," Megan said turning on him. "Just because you have no intention of ever settling down, you do not have to ruin it for everyone. It's really no wonder you've never been married. You are not the marrying kind. All suave and sexy and . . . and . . . and smooth-talking—"

"You think I'm sexy?" The left side of his mouth pulled into a grin.

"Stop it."

"Come on. You feel it between us. And what has you so mad?"

"I'm not falling for your mess. You're trying to turn things around. I know your type."

"In all of a matter of days, you're an expert on me?"

"I know enough."

He stepped back looking confused. "Are you mad at me?"

"Don't act so surprised."

"I'm not acting." He held his arms out like he had nothing to hide. "I am surprised. I mean we were fine a little while ago, and now you look like you'd like to gut and quarter someone. Or something worse."

"Oh, definitely all of the above." She spun around and walked off, heading straight down the hall to the guest room she'd been in earlier when she overheard the guys talking. She went inside and closed and locked the door behind her.

A steady three-rap knock came to the door.

"Go away."

"What is going on, Megan? Is this about the car? They'll be back in just a little while. Jackson is just taking Angie to see Billy's room. Once everyone clears out, they'll be right back. Everything will be fine. I promise."

"Promise," she practically shrieked, then flung the door open so hard that it slammed against the wall and then stuck there in the plaster. "You're going to pay to fix that."

"Me?"

"Yes, you. And you." She poked him in the chest. "You. You. You. You are the problem. You . . ." She couldn't even get the words to come out right. "Errrrgh," she growled out of frustration and reached for the door.

He pressed the palm of his hand against the door. "Please don't slam it again."

"Don't tell me what to do."

"What has you so spun up?"

"I know about it. Your little bet. Well, big bet." It struck her all at once. "Oh, my gosh!" She snapped her fingers. "That thousand dollars! You said it was worth a thousand dollars to meet me. I thought you meant the price of the plane ticket. You meant the cost of the bet!" She bit down on her lip. She was shaking from her very core. "You are a piece of work."

"The wager." His shoulders sagged a bit. "You've got this all wrong, Megan."

"Oh, do I? Tell that to the driver of the Reliable Carriers truck."

"What?"

"Yeah. He got here early. A day early according to him. Left a note on my door. I spoke with him. He told me all about you and Sonya setting up the transport for *my* car."

"It's not—"

"Just stop." She held her hand up. "Stop it. I don't want to hear your lies."

He ran his hand through his hair.

"Tell me one thing. Were you just going to drive my car from here to that enclosed trailer and steal it?"

"I'm not a thief."

Stole my heart. Didn't even blink about that, did you? "And I bet Sonya is in on all of it. What? Is she your wife? Or just another woman you're manipulating to get what you want?"

The color drained from his face. "I offered you a fair price for the car. I told you to give me your number. I had every intention to purchase it from you."

"It. Wasn't. For. Sale." She accentuated each word. Each syllable. How many times had she told him that that car meant more to her than anything in the world? Not like she was being coy about that. He'd acted as if he was even consoling her. "You call your little girlfriend or wife or whoever she is and tell her the jig is up. They'll be charging you for the driver's inconvenience too."

"Sonya is not . . ." He nodded. "I don't have anyone. Steady or otherwise."

"You expect me to believe that? You are crazy. You and your little Sonya can both go to H-E-double—"

"Whoa. Hang on. Sonya works for me."

"No doubt, dipping your pen in the company ink. Not a smart move. I thought you were at least an honest business man."

"I am." He reached for her.

She took a giant step back.

"I'm sorry. I forgot I'd had Sonya set that up. I'm not used to not getting what I want. It's true. But—"

"But this time—"

He held his hand up. "Please hear me out. When I saw that car, I had Sonya start working on setting up the haul immediately. It's not an easy process. Sometimes it takes a while to get a car on a load. It doesn't matter. That's not the point."

"Your point is?"

"The point is . . . I know I'm not getting that car."

"Darn right you're not. You are a player."

"I'm not a player," he said softly.

"Hot Rod?" *Oh, yeah. Everything was falling right into place.* "I should have seen this coming all along."

"Megan. I wasn't playing you." He shifted and leaned against the doorjamb. "Well, at first I just wanted the DeSoto. It's true. Megan, I'll be the first one to admit that when I saw that car I was mesmerized. Laser focused on securing the deal."

"What? You think you're like the Donald Trump of cars or something?"

"Not far off. But seriously, you can call my shop. Every single person that works for me knows that DeSoto Adventurer convertible is my ultimate desire. It's not just the car . . . like you . . . it's the memories tied to it."

She let out a sigh.

He held her gaze.

"I'm not blind," he said. "And I *have* been listening. I see what is in your heart about that car. I get it. Lord, if anyone gets it. I get it. I had no idea that you were going to be—"

"So stupid," she practically spit the words at him.

"So special," he said slowly.

"Well, you're not getting it."

He shook his head, his eyes narrowing as he placed his hands on her shoulders. "No, you're not getting it. I wanted that car more than anything, but it was different this time. I've *never* let anything get in the way of me getting a car that I wanted. Nothing. No amount of money. No hurdles at all. But you became more important to me than the car."

"Please stop it." She could barely get the words out. Her voice was just above a whisper, and trying to hold the tears back was becoming impossible. "I've had enough of your smooth talk." She turned and walked into the room.

He was at her heels. "Please. These aren't just words. I'm trying to tell you that I'm falling for you. It's crazy. I know it. A few days ago, it was the car that turned my head, had my heart racing. All I wanted to do was touch it, caress it, experience it, feel the stories of it. But, Megan, it's you I feel all those things about now. You."

Noah pulled her into his arms, kissing her full on the mouth.

"No!" She pulled away. "Don't. You're not getting the car. This is it. Over."

"I don't want your car. The offer is off the table."

"Good because, sugar, I wouldn't sell you that car now if I was penniless and living in the dad-burn thing!"

"Okay," he said.

"And that driver deserves to be paid. You wasted his time. The driver of that truck. You hurt me and him and who else?"

"Don't worry about the truck driver. I'll personally make sure he's compensated. I promise."

"And that's supposed to make me feel better?"

"Megan, I believe that you and I will make memories as strong as those we carry for that car and the ones we loved. I want that."

She stood there. Numb.

His voice softened. "I still want you to come to the car show. I still want a chance. You're not like anyone I've ever met before."

She couldn't look him in the eye, couldn't fall under his spell. "I don't think you know what you want. Nothing you said means anything anymore."

"Everything was sincere. I loved working on that mural project with you. Getting to know you. You make me laugh. You get my stupid jokes. You are so easy to be with. I've never met a woman like you."

I never met anyone quite like you either. But I won't make this mistake again. "Leave. Please, just leave."

Chapter Seventeen

Noah walked out to get some air.

He'd screwed up. He didn't blame her for being mad about the bet, though he'd all but accepted defeat on that wager.

He leaned against the porch rail, looking out over the creek. There'd been a moment standing out on that rock that he'd felt something really special. And as crazy and foreign as it seemed, he didn't want to let go.

Derek walked out and sat in one of the rockers. "Long day."

"Yeah." Noah turned around. "I guess right about now Jackson is showing Billy's bedroom to Angie. I hope she likes the surprise."

"I'm sure she will. It was really thoughtful. Looks awesome. Don't think Katy would go for it, though."

"I hear ya." Noah walked over and sat down in the chair next to Derek. "Nice place out here."

"It is. Never thought I'd be coming back home to Boot Creek, but things have worked out."

"Hmm." He wished he could say the same thing. "How long you known Megan?"

"You two hit it off, didn't you? I've known her since school."

"I did something stupid. Hurt her feelings."

"Uh-oh." Derek took a sip of his beer. "I wondered what was up with her. She didn't seem herself during the last half of the reception."

"That would be my fault."

"She'll get over it."

"I don't know. It was foolish. Thoughtless. I made a bet with the guys earlier this week that I'd get her to sell me the DeSoto."

"She'd never sell it." Derek leaned forward. "Is that why Ford was asking me about it?"

"Probably just nosey. But yeah, he knew about it."

"I take it she found out."

"Yeah, and I admitted at first that was all I was interested in. But that was before I got to know her. She doesn't understand. I've been looking for a car like that for years. They are damn near impossible to find in that condition."

"But?"

"But I understood her position. That car means as much to her as it would have to me. I get it. And I like her. She doesn't believe my intentions were real. I shouldn't blame her. It's hard for me to believe she's had this effect on me."

"You sure it's not just the car?"

Noah smiled as he looked back over the creek again, thinking about sitting on that dock with her next to him. "Oh, I'm sure."

"I'm kind of surprised myself. I mean, weren't you the one trying to give Jackson a ride out of town to not get married?"

"Guilty."

"If you can't beat them, join them?"

He laughed. "No, more like, you can't say no when it hits you in the middle of the heart. That girl hit me like a dart gun. She's rendered me practically useless."

"So what you're telling me is that you don't want the car. You want the girl??

"Yes. That's exactly what I'm telling you, and she doesn't believe me. And trust me, no one back at my shop is going to believe it either."

"Hell, I don't believe you. And Megan is Angie's best friend. I've known her darn near as long as I've known Angie. I'm rather protective of those girls." Derek looked serious. "You better convince me or I might deck you."

"*I* hardly believe it. But it's true. Seriously. I know she's the one for me. Which sounds totally idiotic. I've known her what? A week?"

"Love is some seriously weird and unexplainable stuff." Derek shook his head. "I knew Katy was the one the first day I saw her."

"So it happens."

"Oh yeah, it happens." Derek rocked back. "I'll marry her as soon as she's ready. We both have a lot of baggage. You can't plan these things. It just happens. A force of nature. But we'll be together the rest of our lives. I know that."

"What am I going to do?"

"If Megan's mad, then buddy, you've got your work cut out for you. She's a spitfire . . . you're not going to schmooze her over very easily." Derek slapped him on the back. "I don't envy your position."

"All the things I like about her are what's going to make this nearly impossible."

"Exactly." Derek got up and walked inside. Leaving Noah out there alone.

But there has to be a way.

He got out of the rocker and stood up. He always did think better standing up.

~

Megan stood there next to her mom, putting on the mother of all performances that things were fine. "Aren't you ready to leave yet?"

"No, honey. Are we in a hurry? I thought we might wait until Jackson and Angie got back. I wanted to have a quick little personal chat with her before their honeymoon. I have something for her."

"What? Condoms?" She regretted the smart-mouth response as soon as it left her mouth.

"Megan!" Mom's mouth dropped open, making her look like that scream painting.

"I'm sorry. You just made it sound like you were going to have *the talk* with her or something."

She *tsked*. "I have some money for them to do a little something special on their honeymoon. You know that I think of her like a daughter."

"I do." Megan reached up and hugged her mom. "I know, Mom. Thank you. You're still the coolest mom in Boot Creek. And if I didn't say it earlier, the flowers were absolutely beautiful."

"Thank you, honey. Now, tell me what's going on with you and Noah. Did you take the deal on the car?"

Megan smirked.

Bootsie's face softened. "Okay, stupid question. Of course you took the deal. I mean, one hundred thousand dollars. Lord, that's a lot of nickels."

"I didn't."

"What? Why not?" Her mother looked shocked and then a chuckle escaped her lips. "Oh, I get it. Because y'all are going to be a couple. I saw the way you two look at each other. You two will make some beautiful babies together. I've always wanted to be a grandmother. Maybe I should save this money for your honeymoon!"

"Whoa. Slow down there, Mom."

"He's so sweet. And charming. I like him so very much." She looked around for him. "Where is he? He is one good-looking hunk of man."

"Stop it."

"What? Don't be embarrassed. Honey, I've been in love. I made you. Remember?"

"I'm not taking the deal on the car. I'm not getting rid of Daddy's car. He loved it. Getting rid of the DeSoto would be like losing Dad all over again."

"Don't be silly, Megan. It's a car. A big, old, ugly gas-guzzling car. Your dad didn't give it to you to saddle you with it. He'd want you to take that money. You know what a wheeler-dealer he was."

Yeah, not as big a one as Noah Black. "Mom, he was just playing me to get the car. He doesn't care about me. It was always about the car."

"Are you sure?"

"Positive. He'd made a bet with the guys. I was mad, so I went home to get some air. By the way, you need gas in your car."

"You stole my car?"

"I borrowed it. I needed to get away, but that is not the point. The point is there was a car-transport truck there ready to move the car."

"What? Now, honey, that doesn't make any sense. He made the offer only a few hours ago."

"Exactly. The truck driver said he'd made those arrangements at the beginning of the week."

"Oh, dear."

"Exactly."

"I'm so sorry, Megan. I thought he was perfect for you. A win-win. I know you're disappointed."

"I am." She knew her mom was too.

"Let's go, honey. I'll give my little present to Derek to handle. He won't mind. You wait right here."

Megan shifted uncomfortably. All she wanted to do was get home, climb in bed, and pull the covers over her head.

Derek was just coming in from the front porch. Bootsie walked across the room and spoke with him. Megan saw her give him the envelope for Angie. That was a really sweet gesture. Mom was thoughtful like that. A little crazy sometimes, but she did always come through.

Megan walked over to meet her mom at the front door.

They walked outside and Bootsie clotheslined her with her arm. "Wait right here." She veered off to the left. Megan stopped and watched her mother walk right over to Noah and wallop him in the gut with her purse.

He folded over from the unexpected attack.

I love you, Mom.

Bootsie marched off toward the car, giving Megan a come-on-now look. They piled into the car and rode in silence all the way to Megan's house.

Megan kissed her Mom on the cheek, then got out of the car. "Thanks for the ride home."

"Want me to come in?" Bootsie asked. "I can stay a while."

She got out of the car. "No, ma'am." She felt fifteen and heartbroken. Back then Momma would've made her favorite cookies and they'd have talked through it until they were laughing about every flaw that poor boy had. Laughing and bidding good riddance to the loser. But it was Daddy who'd always been her hero. He'd have piled her into the DeSoto, cranked up the scratchy AM radio, and taken her on the road. Not just a slow cruise either, whenever she was down, he'd open that car up and let it roll like a race car. And that made her miss him even more right then.

"I'm tired. I'm going to go and crawl into bed." Megan walked to the door and waved good-bye.

"Call me if you need me, baby." Her mother smiled gently, her head half cocked in that way that made you feel the love even from twenty feet away.

"I will." Megan walked up to the house, unlocked the door, and went inside. Unzipping her dress as she walked down the hall, she couldn't get to bed fast enough. All she wanted to do was sleep and put this day behind her.

She turned off the ringer and tossed her phone on the nightstand, then changed into her favorite yoga pants and the XL North Carolina

State University T-shirt Daddy had won her at the state fair years ago. The T-shirt was huge and ratty, worn soft from hundreds of washings. She swept the comforter back and slid under the sheets.

Exhausted and disappointed, she pulled the pillow under her head and closed her eyes. The heaviness in her heart weighed on her. Quiet tears fell. She let them pool, not bothering to sweep them away. She wasn't even sure who or what those tears were for.

For being flat-out exhausted?

For being so stupid?

For putting my heart out there again? I'd promised to never do that again.

For Daddy? I miss you so much, Daddy.

The rumble of the garage-bay door closing woke her. She glanced at the clock. Jackson must have brought the car back and put it up. Of course he did. He wouldn't have let Daddy down any more than she would have. It's why Daddy had offered it in the first place.

She picked up her phone. Almost nine thirty. Derek would be taking Jackson and Angie to the airport hotel so they could catch a few hours of sleep before their crack-of-dawn flight to the honeymoon of a lifetime.

Too tired to even go check on the car, she simply rolled over and closed her eyes again.

The buzz of her cell phone dancing across the nightstand woke her from a hard sleep. She rolled over onto her back and opened her eyes. She lifted the phone to see what time it was and who was bothering her.

Eleven fifteen, and the unfamiliar area code belonged to Noah. Didn't he know it was impolite to call a friend after nine unless it was an emergency? And he'd lost that status anyway. She'd deleted his name from her phone earlier hoping to never see it again. But things were never that easy. She'd already memorized his number. She pressed the IGNORE CALL button. She'd already missed three other calls from him.

She pulled the phone to her chest and rolled over to go back to sleep.

Twice more during the night her phone went off.

Same caller. Only texts this time.

Noah.

Couldn't he take a hint? She'd already said everything she needed to say to him. He'd be gone Tuesday. She could lay low that long. There wasn't anything so pressing that she needed to do that couldn't wait.

~

The next time her phone buzzed, the sun was up.

"Seriously?" She picked up the phone, ready to ignore the call, but it wasn't Noah. It was Katy. "Hello?"

"How you doing, sweetie? I was just talking to Derek. Did you and Noah get things sorted out?"

"No. What's there to sort out? He tried to dupe me. I was stupid and starry-eyed." She was tired and groggy.

"Oh, Megan. You were not. I'm coming over," Katy said.

It wasn't a question.

"I'm not getting out of bed," Megan said.

"That's fine. But do let me in, would ya?"

Megan felt too tired to even sit up, much less get up, and walk all the way to the front door. "There's a key under the flowerpot."

"That's imaginative," Katy said with a laugh.

"Don't lecture me, please."

"I won't. I'll see you in a few."

It seemed like she'd just laid back down for a minute, when suddenly the bedroom light came on.

Katy stood over her. "Rise and shine." She whipped open the drapes, letting the sunshine pour in.

"You cannot be serious," Megan grumbled.

"How are you doing? You look like hell."

"Thanks." Megan put her forearm across her eyes to shield them from the light. "Did my mom call you?"

"No. Derek told me about the thing with Noah."

"How did *he* know?"

"He spoke to Noah at the reception. From what I gather it was right after y'all had the knock-down-drag-out."

"I didn't knock him down. But I should have. Mom got a good whack in as we left, though. I took some joy in that."

Katy sat down on the edge of the bed. "I take it y'all didn't sort things out."

Megan pushed back the sheets and sat up. "There's nothing to sort out. I made a silly mistake. I opened myself right up for it."

"How so?"

"All he was interested in was my car." She gave a choked, desperate laugh. "I thought he cared about me. Like he was *the one* or something. I knew him less than a week. I'm smarter than this."

"I only knew Derek a couple days when I had those feelings. I couldn't believe it either," Katy said. "At least you weren't on the rebound from your husband cheating on you. Good lord, talk about bad timing. And yet it worked out for us."

"You're different." She was swimming—no, more like treading water—through a haze of emotion. "I don't know what I was thinking."

"You probably weren't thinking. You were letting your heart lead the way."

"It's like he knew exactly what to say. Understood how I felt. I wasn't even looking for anyone. You know that. I've been perfectly happy alone. And then he said everything right, and it was like we were supposed to be."

Katy nodded. "I know. I know exactly how you're feeling. I was running from my problems, looking for an escape when I bumped into Derek. The last thing I needed was the complication of someone else in the mix. But you don't get to pick the timing for that stuff. It just happens. And when it does, it's like lightning."

"Lightning? What does that even mean? That it'll kill me, because that's pretty much how I feel right now. Beaten down."

Katy laughed. "You're tougher than that. No, like good lightning. It's sudden. Explosive and undeniable. You can't run or hide from it."

It had been like lightning. Just not the good kind. But rather, the kind that stole my energy and knocked me on my butt.

"Derek said Noah was a mess after you found out about the bet."

"Noah *should* have been embarrassed," Megan said.

"He wasn't embarrassed. He was sorry."

"I think he's pretty sorry. I'd agree with that."

"Derek flat out told him he didn't believe he cared about you either, but Noah convinced him otherwise, and you know how protective Derek is about us. Derek believes him. I think you should at least talk to Noah."

"Why? So he can lie to me again? If not about this, about the next thing? Katy, I know you mean well, but I've traveled this path before. I will not fall into that trap again."

"Maybe he made a mistake. Or his intentions changed as he got to know you."

"That doesn't change anything. I don't want that kind of man in my life." Or any man. What had happened to that plan she'd been following? Things had been going along perfectly fine before he'd happened into her life.

"If you didn't care about him, you wouldn't be lying there in a heap."

Well, there was that.

"Here. This was at the door." Katy tossed a puffy manila envelope to Megan.

She caught it and turned it over. "What is it?"

"I have no idea. I didn't bring it. It was sitting against the front door when I got here. I picked it up from the front stoop when I came in."

Megan frowned, turning the mailer over in her lap. It wasn't postal mail. There was no postage. No address. Only her name in perfectly straight block letters.

She tore the envelope open, reaching inside.

She pulled out something black and held it up in front of her. "It's a California Dreaming Restoration T-shirt." She twisted it around for Katy to see and something fluttered from the folds of the fabric.

Katy picked it up. "A card. And a print out of an electronic ticket for a flight? Not to California, though."

"He invited me to a car show in a couple of weeks." Megan's defenses began to subside as she read the card. Then looked at the ticket. Then to Katy.

Katy's face lit up. "I don't know what that note says, but your face says it all. You're intrigued. Interested. There's something there. It's worth checking out. Go after him."

"You think?" A glow coursed through Megan. "I'll read it out loud. You want to hear?"

"Of course I want to hear."

She swallowed, and began to read the note.

Megan,

I never meant to hurt you. The first time I laid eyes on the DeSoto, I looked to heaven and said, Granddad. I found the one, man. And she's not getting away.

Yes, I meant the car. It's true, but I had no idea that a few days later, that statement would apply to you, not the car. I'm done chasing that memory. I'd much rather make new ones with you.

Please forgive me. At least consider it. Enclosed is a plane ticket to the car show. I hope I'll see you there.

Noah

Katy's head cocked slightly. "He's in love with you."

"You really think so? It's all been so quick."

"There's not a timeline for these kinds of things," Katy said. "Trust me. Derek swooped in without so much as a warning. But it's right. And so perfect. And what if Noah is yours?"

"Then I'm afraid." The swirling in Megan's gut made her feel like someone had just poured concrete in her veins. "So afraid."

"When's the car show?"

"It's next week." Megan bit down on her lip. "I so wanted him to be the one."

"He clearly feels the same way. You should go to Flynn's and talk to him now. Why wait? Go now. Megan, what are you doing just sitting here?"

"You think so?"

"Did you hit your head on something? Yes, I think so."

Her eyes filled with tears. "I thought I knew what I wanted. This is not what I had planned."

"Trust your heart," Katy said.

"You're right." Megan threw the covers back from the bed. "I've got to go." Still in her yoga pants and T-shirt, she grabbed a pair of flip-flops from her closet.

Katy pointed to Megan's hair. "Brush?"

"My teeth! Yes." She dashed toward the bathroom. Good lord. What was she even going to say? She prayed the right words would come.

"Your hair?" Katy called after her.

Megan stopped. "Hat! Dresser," she called back to Katy. "The red one. It matches my shirt." Then raced to the bathroom to brush her teeth.

A moment later Katy was standing in the doorway to the bathroom with the cap in her hand. "How appropriate." Katy tossed the Life Is Good–logoed hat her way.

"Thank you," Megan said with a mouthful of toothpaste. She spit and dabbed at her mouth.

"I'll lock up." Katy swooshed her out of the room. "Go. Go."

Megan started then stopped, turned, and gave Katy a hug. "That's for Derek too. Thank you." She ran down the hall. "Wish me luck!"

She ran out the door and made a dash for her car. Revving the engine, her tires squealed as she made the turn onto the road, making the short ride to Crane Creek B&B in record time. With the excitement coursing through her, she probably could have run the short distance just as quickly.

She forced herself to settle down. Taking the time to catch her breath, she looked in the rearview mirror and swept her fingers under her eyes, then tugged on her ball cap, pushing her hair behind her ears.

This was as good as she was going to look under the circumstances. She drew a deep breath and forbade herself to tremble. She took slow, thoughtfully paced steps to the door, trying to keep her cool. The front door was open, and the smell of fried bacon wafted out into the warm summer air. "Knock, knock," she called out, as she stepped inside. "Flynn?"

Flynn poked her head around the corner from the kitchen. "Hey, gal."

"Noah?"

She flipped a dish towel over her shoulder. "He just left. Want to stay and have breakfast? It's your favorite. My famous Flynn Pecan and Blackberry French Toast."

"He left?"

"Yeah. He had one of those fancy town-car services cars come and pick him up to take him to the airport about fifteen or twenty minutes ago. Said he was going to fly standby."

She turned and left with Flynn hollering after her. "Where are you going?"

Nancy Naigle

"Chasing tomorrow." The screen door slapped against the door frame behind her as she ran down the steps. She was not about to let yesterday stand in her way another day.

Please let it have been fifteen minutes. I can catch him with that head start. She pulled her car out of the driveway and headed for the interstate. She pushed the speed limit. It was the only way she could catch up. Ahead she saw a black Cadillac. She raced to get next to it and looked over.

Please be Noah.

A man and woman sat in the front seat. A family car. Not a car service.

That would have been too lucky. She headed on toward Raleigh-Durham Airport without any luck of spotting another black town car. Circling the departure loop, she carefully scanned the area for any sign of Noah. He was tall. He should be easy to spot.

Where are you?

She pulled up along the curb in front of the American Airlines entrance.

A security guard walked over to the car. "You can't park here, miss." He gave her a move-along wave.

She didn't even know what airline Noah would be on, and by the time she found a parking space in the garage, he'd be through security. With a moan of distress, she languished back in her seat.

A thousand thoughts pushed for her attention.

She could call. Ask him to turn around? But she needed to do this face to face. Needed to know that without a doubt she still had that feeling inside even after what had happened.

I can't do that on the phone.

But what choice did she have? At least she could stop him from leaving. She took out her phone and punched the button. The moment that he'd put his number in her phone replayed in her mind. So much had happened in such a short time.

Her hand shook as she held the phone. The ringing on speaker sounded like it was in slow motion compared to her beating heart. But he didn't answer. It went to voice mail. She ended the call.

She'd missed the opportunity to catch him, and he'd be on a plane back to California.

Accepting that she wasn't going to get to see him today, she put her car back in drive and merged back onto the road to exit the airport.

By the time she'd gotten home, she'd wasted darn near another whole day. And for someone so certain she didn't want to be in a relationship, she couldn't wait to get this one sorted out.

She walked inside and rather than going to her apartment, which was her first inclination . . . to just crawl back under the covers until it was time to fly out to that car show . . . she turned left and headed for the garage bay. She stood at the glass-windowed door. Her hands pressed flat against it as she gazed inside.

What am I feeling? Is it the car, and a bunch of mixed up emotions from the best yesterdays of my life?

The picture Noah had wanted to buy caught her eye.

A warm glow coursed through her. She opened the door and stepped inside. Carefully she made her way around the car, checking it for any damage from its big adventure yesterday. Except for the dust, it looked just like it did when they'd taken it out of the garage. She'd take care of the dust later.

For now, she had other priorities.

She knew what she wanted. What she needed. And she didn't really have to wait at all.

She walked over and picked up the painting.

What she was feeling wasn't just about the car. It was the man. Noah. He did something to her that she couldn't explain. And wasn't that how it was supposed to be?

She tucked the painting under her arm and walked back into her apartment. She slid open the door to her studio, and propped the painting up on the easel.

This painting had been one of Dad's favorites too.

Light filled the space. She used to love being in this room. Today it felt new again.

She slid the metal swivel stool over to the easel and climbed up on it. She sat there, with her feet hooked on the rungs, twisting and contemplating.

With her foot, she dipped her toes into the wide tray of the easel, pushing the tubes of paint, in varying stages of use, from one side to the other. Some full. Some squeezed like a tube of toothpaste to get the last dollop out. Some of them had been sitting there unused for probably the better part of six years.

She leaned forward and picked out three tubes, massaging them in her hand to see if they were even still malleable.

Stepping down from the stool, she squeezed three tiny drops of paint onto a tray, and then selected a tall thin brush from the coffee can on the shelf behind her.

The pink and white can was rusty around the edges, and the pink faded, the white yellowed, but the words *It's a Girl!* still sharp and clear. Her birthdate was scrawled up one side of the can in her dad's handwriting. She could only imagine how he must have been that day passing out cigars. But she knew exactly how she felt when he gave the cigar can to her. Like the most special girl in the world.

He'd always had a way of making her feel that way.

No one else, until Noah, had ever even come close. *Daddy, I think you knew exactly what you were doing leaving me that car. You led Noah right into my life.*

She dipped her brush in the paint and worked in the slight change on the canvas, stepping back to make sure it was exactly right. Then she turned the wrapped canvas frame around and went to work on something special on the backside.

Time slipped away as she painted. Closing her eyes. Remembering the precise moment. The feelings. Committing those memories to color, shapes, shadows, and lines. Only stopping to go to the refrigerator for another bottle of water. Never checking her phone. Or even stopping to eat.

The image was coming together.

She sat on the stool and examined it. So far, so good. She got up and continued until she was too tired to continue.

In her bed, the image she was painting hung in her mind like the moon. It was all she could see, the only thing peacefully lighting her way.

When she woke up she brewed a pot of coffee and went straight back to her studio. Only she didn't feel the hurry she had yesterday. Today a welcoming calm had replaced the frantic panic that had over-taken her recently. She took the old white men's shirt she used to love to wear while she painted and slipped it on over her clothes. Then settled in. Slowly, adding in the layers of light and shadow that would finally pull the image into motion. Making the likeness as vivid as that moment in her mind.

She got up and walked over to her Balanced Buzz office. She checked the orders that had come in over the weekend. As she pulled from inventory, boxed orders, readying them for shipping—the paint-ing continued to fill her thoughts. Colors, emotion, imagery.

She stacked the orders by the front door. She'd drop them off at the post office in the morning. And then she had more important things to do.

With those responsibilities out of the way, she googled Noah's California Dreaming Restoration. The website was snazzy. Shiny. Vivid. Impressive. She clicked through the pictures, enjoying the before-and-after shots of his most recent projects. And there on the *About Noah Black* page was the same story he'd told her. About his grandfather. And that same blurry picture of that kid standing next to the car that looked like Dad's. *Mine.*

She wrote down the address on the pad of paper next to her computer. A quick search of the closest airport confirmed that Burbank was where she needed to go.

She went back to her bedroom and got the card and plane ticket that had been in the envelope. Rereading the card, her heart had the same reaction. Like a somersault with a twist.

No way was she going to wait another week to answer these questions. She picked up her phone and entered the phone number to the airline.

"Yes, I'd like to see about exchanging a plane ticket for a different time and destination."

Chapter Eighteen

Following nearly ten hours from the time she'd left Boot Creek and a three-hour time change making it seem silly that she was so tired, she stood in the line for a taxi at the Burbank airport. On the bright side, she'd been able to stretch her legs on the multiple plane changes.

She propped the wrapped painting on top of her suitcase, scooting them up a foot at a time as the line slowly moved her closer to the next ride.

There seemed to be as many people in line here as there were residents of Boot Creek, and everyone seemed too busy to even say hello or gesture a quick nod.

All around her, folks had their heads down, thumbing through their phones. No words. Just ring tones, chirps, and boings as the sun descended.

When it was finally her turn she handed over her luggage, but carried the huge painting toward the car.

"No, ma'am. That goes back here."

"No, thank you."

"It must. It's too big."

"Look, I'm more comfortable with it in my care. Do you want me to find another driver?"

The man shut the trunk lid, shaking his head all the way around to the front of the car.

"Thank you," she said as she slid in with the painting carefully balanced on the center hump in the floorboard.

He copped an attitude, and she wasn't sure if he was always an aggressive driver, slinging her from side to side as he changed lanes in the stop-and-go traffic, or if this was payback.

Just get me there.

She was too tired to even lecture him.

And although the ride had been anything but a pleasure, she tipped him the standard just for getting her there safely. It had been a much longer ride from the airport than she'd anticipated. At home she planned a minute a mile. Not the case in California.

She'd picked the hotel closest to California Dreaming Restoration. It came with a big price tag, but she hoped it would be worth it. Besides, it would be that much cheaper to catch a ride over to the shop, and it looked like they had a shuttle that might provide that service.

The lobby was bright and plush. She checked in at the counter, feeling like a bit of a celebrity by the way they treated her.

"Welcome, Ms. Howard." The desk clerk pushed her keys across the shiny granite counter. "If there's anything at all we can do to make your stay more comfortable, you let me know. I'm Rena."

"As a matter of fact," Megan said. "Tomorrow morning I need to go here." She pulled out the page she'd printed from the internet. "I think it's just a couple miles away."

She looked at it. "Yes. It's not far at all."

"Would the shuttle be able to take me there, or could you arrange a car for me?"

"We'd be happy to take you there. What time?"

She sucked in a breath. *The earlier the better.* But she didn't want to get there before he arrived. "How about nine fifteen?"

"I've got you down. Your driver will be waiting for you here in the lobby."

"Thank you so much." And as if those butterflies hadn't been breeding in her belly all day, now they practically lifted her off the ground with excitement.

She went to her room and laid out her outfit for tomorrow.

Yesterdays are behind me.

Boots, black jeans, and the black California Dreaming Restoration T-shirt he'd left for her.

Well, not exactly like he'd left it. That sucker was an XL for goodness sake. She'd run it by to Carla for some quick alterations to fit. The logo was a little far left, but at least she wouldn't look like a frump.

She slept well, but an East Coast girl on the West Coast just guarantees being wide-eyed and bushy tailed before the sun wakes up.

There was no fighting it. So she got on up, but that made nine fifteen seem like another day away.

Megan made coffee in her room and was delighted to hear the paper drop at her door at six.

By the time to leave to go surprise Noah, she'd been up so long that she was ready for a nap. Not that she'd be able to sleep.

She checked herself in the mirror three times before she finally went downstairs.

As soon as she stepped into the lobby, a gentleman in a blue suit said, "Ms. Howard."

"Yes."

"I'm your ride."

"Thank you," she said.

He held the door for her, and she slipped into the back seat of a brand-new, shiny, black town car with her painting. He didn't say a word. And he smiled. The way it should be.

The soft leather of the interior still smelled new.

She watched out the window as he pulled out of the lot and made a few turns. It didn't look like what she thought California would look like. He turned off of the main road to a side street where the buildings were more industrial looking.

Another mile and he pulled to a stop in front of a long low building with large bay doors across one whole end of it. The logo on the sign at the street and over the front door of the building matched her shirt.

The coffee she'd drank earlier seemed to percolate in her gut.

Please don't let me be making a huge fool out of myself. Again.

"Shall I wait?"

"No." She tipped him. "May I call when I need to get back?"

He handed her a card. "Yes, ma'am. My direct number is on the card."

"Perfect. Wish me luck."

He laughed. "Yes ma'am."

She carried the painting toward the door, wondering if she was even going to be able to speak when she got inside.

The door was smoked glass with shiny chrome-like lettering on it. Noah's touches filled the space. A couch made from an old car seat, but with highly polished wood legs and arms. Matching leather chairs had been fabricated out of what looked like the bucket seats from some kind of race car. And tires under a huge glass round served as a coffee table.

A guy with short blonde hair and the bluest eyes she'd ever seen walked in. He looked surprised to see her standing there.

"Hi."

He cocked his head. "You're one of us?" He pointed to the logo on her chest.

She practically folded in on herself. "No. Well, it was a gift. From Noah."

"Oh? Yeah, we don't get many visitors without an appointment. Hope you haven't been waiting long."

"No. Not long." She bit down on her lower lip. *This was more awkward than she'd planned.* "Is he here?"

He walked over to an antique Coca-Cola cooler and pulled a soda. "Yeah. You want a soda? Got Coke, orange, grape."

"No thank you."

"Suit yourself. Follow me."

"Thanks."

"You an artist?" He nodded toward the painting.

She started to object, then smiled. "Yes. I am."

A pair of doors painted a shiny candy apple with chrome car door handles on them separated the small front lobby from the enormous shop.

She walked through, wanting to take it all in. To see him in his environment, but before she'd even scanned the room the guy hollered, "Noah. Unexpected company."

It sounded like a warning. Like he'd just shouted "Incoming," to his troops so they could run for cover.

A flush rose from her neck to her cheeks, and her knees shook. She was quite literally quaking in her boots.

Beyond a line of cars in various stages of renovation, Noah emerged, wiping his hands on a pinkish-red shop rag. His mouth had dropped open as if he were going to say something, but instead he broke into a smile and headed toward her.

A smile trembled over her lips as she clung to that painting like a life ring.

He walked up to her with a grin of amusement. "You are one surprise after another."

"I hope it's a good surprise."

"Good? No. It's great. Come." He grabbed her hand and led her across the building.

She ran to keep up, her boots clomping like one of those river dancers.

He pulled her into his office. A sleek room with more chrome and shiny stuff.

"I can't believe you're here." He ran his hands down her arms. "That shirt never looked so good."

She laughed. "I had Carla hook me up."

"It's good to see you. I haven't been able to stop thinking about you."

"I know. I mean, me either." She held the picture out. "This is for you."

He took the large package from her and set it on his desk. He popped a knife from his hip and slit the tape with one quick flick of his wrist, then tore the paper, and Bubble Wrap away.

His smile was thank you enough.

"Thank you." He held it up, looking at it like it was a treasure. "Hey, you fixed it."

"I did."

He kissed her on the nose. "I love it. Thank you so much."

"No. There's more."

"More?" He sat on the edge of the desk and pulled her between his legs. "You are all I want. I promise you. With all of my heart."

She leaned in and kissed him. "I wanted to believe that so badly."

"Believe it."

She stepped away, and picked up the painting, turning it over. Then she took his hand and stood next to him. "This is the moment I knew I was in love with you."

He reached out and swept his fingers over the paint, wrapping his other arm around her next to him.

"You are amazing. It's like being there. I can almost feel the roughness of the rocks, how cold the water was, and the way the sun danced off of it that day. And your hair. It danced off of your hair too."

She laid her face against his chest. "I can't believe this. I was so scared."

"I remember what I was feeling when we were standing there." He shook his head. His eyes glistened. "I can't believe you painted this for me." His face held the softest, sweetest look. "Special. Just for me."

"I did. Just for you. My heart was so full that I couldn't not paint that scene. And this seemed like the best place to put it. On the back of the picture of the car that you love so much. Our moment. Only ours."

"It's perfect. You are perfect. Perfect for me."

"I'm done with looking in my rearview mirror. I'm leaving every yesterday behind. I'm living for today, and tomorrow. Want to join me?"

"More than anything."

The heartrending tenderness of his gaze turned her heart over.

Reclaiming her lips, he crushed her to him, sweeping her into his life in that single moment.

She knew it would last. The dynamics of this relationship were on even ground. Noah was not Kevin, and Kevin no longer held her from living. The freedom that brought her had her heart soaring high.

His tongue explored the recesses of her mouth, teasing, promising of so much more.

Her fingers splayed into his hair, her thumbs caressing the stubble along his strong jaw.

"When do you go back?" he asked.

"I don't know. I got a one way ticket, in case you sent me packing and I'd have to buy a return right here."

He leaned his forehead against hers. "That is not going to happen, my love."

"I wasn't sure, but I wasn't going to risk it." Her heart was full, and she didn't worry where this path was going to take her, because home would be wherever they made it. Although Boot Creek had been known to pull more than one or two people back, even after just one visit.

"We'll figure it out. And about abandoning those yesterdays," he said, "I may have spoken out of turn. Those yesterdays led us to each other. I'm pretty thankful for them. Especially if you're going to let me love you."

She slid her arms along his waist, leaning back to look into his eyes. "You're right. Yesterdays are special, no matter how bad they seemed at the time." She twined her arms around him. "But let's just keep our eye on today."

He dropped a kiss on her nose. "And tomorrow." Without hesitation he smiled and lowered his mouth to hers. "I want you in my arms today, tomorrow, and every yesterday from here on out."

Acknowledgments

As with all books, it takes many people wearing many hats to make a story go from idea to publication. I have the best team of professionals behind me at Montlake Romance. Thank you for believing in me and being there through each story idea to help me reach my goals and live this dream.

Thank you to Ron Cava of the First Baptist Church in Henderson, North Carolina for the history and lovely descriptions of their beautiful church—the perfect backdrop for a Boot Creek wedding.

They say behind every song, there's an untold story. When I heard singer-songwriter, Tim McDonald's song, *Let Me Love You*, I knew it was what was playing when Noah and Megan danced in this story. A round of applause for you, Tim. You told my three-hundred-page story in three minutes. Thank you for letting me use your special song as the backdrop for the book and video trailer. Hugs and best wishes in every facet of your life.

Every Yesterday was extra special to me because of the topic—cars. I love pretty cars and have always had a great appreciation for them. I had so much fun doing the research for this book. Thank you to my dear friend, David White, for chatting with me about the process of finding and restoring his favorite cars.

I did some legwork for this book. During my visit to Kissimmee in January, 2015, I got to check off an item on my bucket list by attending the annual Mecum auction, talking with other enthusiasts, and even buying a car. Accidently on purpose. Who can resist a shiny red 1998 Mercedes Benz SLK convertible? Seriously? Thanks to Dale at Reliable Carriers for getting my impulse buy home, and for some insider 411 on the business.

Thanks to the gang at Barrett-Jackson who supplied quick and detailed responses to my questions about the '58 DeSoto Adventurer Convertible. They even had one go across their auction block in Scottsdale two days before I turned this book in. Very cool to see that beauty!

Thank you to Edward X. Petrus from Pennsylvania for his in-depth knowledge of these cars, and to Bodie Stroud, of History Channel's American Restoration and owner of Bodie Stroud Industries, who shared his enthusiasm and love of all things automotive. You are the real deal, my friend! Bodie, your enthusiasm was absolutely contagious and I hope half of what you shared shines through in this book so everyone understands it. Who knew that your wife of twenty years had been driving a Karmann Ghia when y'all met? Just like Megan in this story? Now that was truly a coincidence. When you told me that story and your tender memories of that day, I knew I had the right guy talking to me. Happy twentieth anniversary to you and your bride, Bodie. *Readers, I happen to know that Bodie's bride is getting an extra special car-guy present from him one day soon. It's so romantic that I might just have to use that in a book someday!*

Thank you to my dear friends and family for their support. Y'all know who you are and there are too many to list, but I will thank Anna DeStefano for an awesome week in Isle of Palms, South Carolina during deadline month, and to Tracy March who cheered me on every single day until this book was complete.

After a heads-down week to get this book done while in the Bahamas, I treated myself to a day at the spa. Thanks to my new friends at Renu Spa in Freeport, especially Cookie, for the smiles and much needed pampering.

Pam Murray, thank you for being with me through all of the high and low points of not only my writer journey, but my life, and never saying I'm crazy—out loud or in public. You're the best friend ever. Thanks for the giggles, laughs, tears, and hugs.

About the Author

Photo © 2013 Clements Mayes Photography

USA Today bestselling author Nancy Naigle whips up small-town love stories with a dash of suspense and a whole lot of heart. She began her popular contemporary romance series Adams Grove while juggling a successful career in finance and life on a seventy-six-acre farm. She went on to produce works in collaboration with other authors, including the Granny series. Now happily retired from a career in finance, she devotes her time to writing, antiquing, and enjoying the occasional spa day with friends. A Virginia girl at heart, Nancy now calls North Carolina home.

Made in the USA
Monee, IL
04 March 2022

92063931R00173